CEO'S SECRET BABY

IONA ROSE

Publisher: SomeBooks
ISBN: 978-1-913990-03-9

AUTHOR'S NOTE

Hey there!

Thank you for choosing my book. I sure hope that you love it. I'd hate to part ways once you're done though. So how about we stay in touch?

My newsletter is a great way to discover more about me and my books. Where you'll find frequent exclusive giveaways, sneak previews of new releases and be first to see new cover reveals.

And as a HUGE thank you for joining, you'll receive a FREE book on me!

With love,

Iona

Get Your FREE Book Here

AUTHOR'S NOTE

CHAPTER 1

LEAH

"*L*eah..." Anne groaned. "Shut that thing off!"

I came to from my light doze. The crowing from my phone's alarm finally pierced my subconscious. My eyelids lazily fluttered open.

"Leah!" She groaned again.

It took me a few more seconds to process what her complaint was about. I reached for the phone on the stool by my side and cut the ringing.

"We'll burn, Leah," Anne complained. "Set it for another half hour."

I turned from my front, and rested on my back. I ignored her for a moment as I tried to recollect myself. My eyes opened fully then, squinting a little at the daylight's sharp reception beyond the shade of our wicker parasol.

There were now hordes of people in the ocean and around the sandy beach, much more than had been present when we'd arrived about two hours earlier.

I picked up my phone, and reset the alarm.

Slender, but hostile hands reached out to repeatedly tap my arm. "Change the sound from that damn crowing cock. It's driving me crazy."

I turned my gaze to my pestering friend.

Laid out by my side in an orange gingham bikini, Anne's blonde hair looked matted wildly on top of her head, akin to a bird's nest. Her expression looked drowsy as her face contorted irritably.

"You're becoming a nightmare," I growled as I lifted my hands above my head. The stretch was almost magical, the creaks and soreness I hadn't even been aware of smoothened out of my overly rested bones.

She sighed and went back to sleep.

I turned to the beach bed by my right, to see that the third member of our party was missing. "Where's Tracy?" I drawled.

I didn't get a response so my gaze roved across the expansive stretch of sand and people, hoping to spot her one-piece Coca-Cola swimsuit somewhere amongst it all.

I had no luck, so I gave up and was about to shut my eyes when I heard her high-pitched call. I looked over at the shout.

Tracy was waving excitedly from the distance with one hand, while the other supported a basket of snacks as she headed over to us. Behind her was Mehmet, the genie from the beach's snack bar we had acquainted ourselves with since our arrival two days earlier.

He was approaching with a tray of colorful fruit garnished cocktails.

This sight instantly made me sit up.

"Anne, I brought you a Mai Tai," Tracy announced as she arrived. "Leah, the Hurricane's for you."

"Thank you," I cheered as I reached out with both hands for the red gradient drink. "Thank you, Mehmet." I smiled at the gaunt, bearded server.

"You're welcome ma'am," he said, his eyes lowered to the ground, his response was somewhat shy.

I couldn't blame him. We were all half-naked.

I took a good long sip of the fruity rum punch, and it made me feel like I'd been resurrected from the dead. A moan escaped my throat, as I thanked the gods for a good life.

Tracy settled into her bed as Mehmet placed the remaining cocktail on the stool by her side. "Anne, I'm taking yours," she said.

Our *presumably* sleeping friend got up instantly. With a sharp look at Tracy, she rounded our beds and picked up her drink. Then she grabbed some cookie packets from the basket, and returned to her corner.

It was amusing enough.

We all soon settled in, watching the vastness and flurry of activities beyond as we consumed our light refreshments.

"I want to lounge there tomorrow," Tracy said.

I turned to see her longing gaze on the beds and parasols on the pier extended over the sea.

"Keep dreaming," Anne said. "In order to get a spot there you have to be up at the crack of dawn to make the reservation."

"I'll do it," Tracy said brightly and picked up her phone. "I'll set the alarm for 6 am."

Anne shared a look with me.

I couldn't help snorting with laughter into my drink. "We came here to get away from alarms, Tracy," I said. "Not continue to set them."

She was adamant. "Well, I want to lounge on the pier, so I'm going to get up to reserve it."

"Good luck with that," Anne said. "By the time we get back from Pirates today, who knows if we'll even be able to walk."

Tracy and I both turned to her.

"What do you mean?" I asked.

"We're going back there?" Tracy complained.

"There's a foam party tonight," Anne replied. "The hot bartender told me."

"Foam party?" Tracy spat, her tone laced with disgust.

I remained indifferent because no matter how crazy things got I planned to stay on the sidelines.

"Yup! Foam party," Anne repeated unapologetically.

"What are we, nineteen? Foam parties are ridiculous!" Tracy huffed.

"No, they're not!" Anne countered. "They're a helluva lot of fun, and did you miss the part about 'the hot bartender'? I have a grinding appointment with him tonight."

4

"His mouth was in yours half the night yesterday, and you still don't know his name?" Tracy countered.

Anne set her empty glass down and leaned back on her bed, her arms behind her head, eyes shut with a massive smile across her face. "I don't need to. What's important is that the entire floor is going to be steamy... and *wet*... and he's going to be there..." She gave us a glance, bright with perversion. "Preferably behind me. I'm wearing white and no bra."

I smiled. "I've never been to a foam party before," I said to Anne. "Heard about them though. Are they really that bad?"

Tracy's eyebrows shot up. "Really? Not even in college?"

I shook my head.

"Well, you're not missing anything. They're disgusting. The entire floor is covered with soap suds that may or may not blind you before the end of the night. Everyone is wet and stepping on you and pushing each other out of the way. And the falling? Ugh, that's the worst part. You'll most likely be sliding and slipping into vomit and pee. People even have sex in there so you can add a floor full of cum to that mix."

"Oh my God. Tracy!" Anne scolded. "Leah, don't listen to her. It's gonna be fun."

"Hate to burst your bubble," Tracy countered, as she couldn't hold back her smile at the pun. "You're going to wish you came with me to the Fire of Anatolia dance show." Tracy nodded.

I smiled with her. "Dance show?"

Tracy sat up excitedly, eager to sell her agenda. "Yes, and it's going to be fabulous."

"Isn't that held at the Aspendos Arena?" Anne asked.

"Yeah, it is."

"Leah, that's a two hour drive."

"Oh hell no," I refused. "I got carsick on the way here from the airport. I'm not riding in anything until we're leaving."

Tracy settled back on her bed with a defeated sigh.

Anne chuckled in victory. "Don't worry, Leah," she said, "the actual foam dispensing will only begin at about 2 am."

"Oh, I'm not worried," I said. "I plan to watch from a very safe and dry place."

Tracy's gaze turned fiery. "I will kill you." She turned to Anne. "And you."

Anne tapped my hand. "Great choice, Leah. Great choice.

JUST BEFORE MIDNIGHT, we arrived at the Havana club in the center of the city.

We were dressed accordingly-me in a leather miniskirt, a black tube top and knee-high alligator sandals.

Tracy wore baggy jeans and a fitted graphic tee with the words, *don't talk to me,* printed across the front. She was long over what had been our routine since our arrival of partying until sunrise and then heading back to the hotel to deal with the resulting hangovers and exhaustion for the better part of the following day.

Anne however, was the star of the night. She wore a smile she hadn't been able to wipe off all evening at the prospect of her night. She had come as intended, braless and in a white cotton dress.

"You're already nipping," Tracy pointed at her chest as we headed down the dimly lit stairs towards the club's main entrance.

"I'm also already wet," Anne said unashamedly.

"Wow!" Tracy responded.

"Exactly," Anne said. "I'm choosing to have fun. You can hang out in the corner with your flats and sip water." The club's stamp was pressed to the inside of her wrist then she shimmied to the rhythm of the deafening electronic music as she made her way into the club.

I put my hand around Tracy's reluctant frame and led us both along.

"Why does she have so much say over our itinerary?" She grumbled.

"Because she arranged the trip," I said.

"If I don't get a say in what we do tomorrow, I'm going home." Tracy pouted.

"Let's just give her a few more days," I said. "She'll tire of the clubs soon and we'll be able to get to all the other fun stuff."

After this, we couldn't speak without having to lean in and scream into each other's ears, so we saved our energy and headed straight to the bar.

Two glasses of dirty martinis were already waiting for us, and Anne's beloved bartender's tongue already down her throat as she leaned across the counter.

"Makmad!' Someone yelled at him.

He pulled away from his frolicking enough to notice myself and Tracy as we took our seats. "Ladies," he greeted.

We gave him a nod before turning condemning looks to our lust stricken friend.

It was then I first spotted him.

Somehow, it was as though I felt his eyes on me and was compelled into turning my gaze specifically towards him.

He was quite the distance away at the curve of the circular bar and just as I picked up my glass, he did the same to his tumbler of golden liquor.

He was speaking to the man by his side, his gaze fixated on him and the vibrant hues from the lights around the club dancing in his seemingly translucent eyes.

He looked handsome, more handsome than any man I'd seen in a long time, and I found myself unable to look away. His structured face was clean shaven, a particularly rare sight for people on vacation on this side of the world. I'd spotted the occasional stubble, but a clean shave seemed quite rare.

He appeared to be confident, but it took absolutely nothing away from the raw, masculine aggression I could almost feel from where he sat. A chiseled jawline and silky hair brushed away from his face in perfect waves. His lips… they were just the perfect curve to compliment his features. His eyes looked so intense that they could literally make me combust if they were to ever settle on me.

And then they did.

He turned as though fully aware of my staring and rested his gaze on me.

I immediately turned away, my hand almost missing my glass as I dove for it as cover. I lifted the rim to my lips, ignoring the thudding of my heart against my chest and faced Tracy. "Texting Jared?" I asked, glancing at the phone in her hands and the worried look on her face.

"Yeah," she said. "He was sick today. He couldn't even go to work."

I sucked in my breath. "That sucks."

"Yeah," she said.

Then I noticed Anne was missing.

"She went to the bathroom," Tracy told me.

Nodding, I turned around to watch all the fun people were having on the dance floor beyond. I tried to push away the thought that perhaps the man had noticed me just like I had him, but I didn't expect this to be likely, given the plethora of women who paraded near us in even shorter skirts and dangerous stilettos.

I chatted and laughed lightly with Tracy, but my mind was no longer with her. It was across the room, with the hot looking stranger I so desperately wanted to come up to me to introduce himself.

I set my empty glass down to my left and didn't bother ordering a refill. I hoped to God that he would take the hint and come over with an offering to buy me another.

The minutes ticked away... and nothing happened.

My hopes fell, as I fought with myself about turning towards his direction to catch another look, but my head refused to move, especially since I'd already gotten caught staring. So I continued speaking to Tracy, "What's the best way to get a man to come say hello to you?"

Tracy rested her gaze on me. "What man?"

"No one," I shifted on the stool. "I'm just asking."

"I have no idea," she answered and returned her attention to her phone.

"Didn't you meet Jared at that French coffee shop?"

"He came up to me on his own. I had nothing to do with it."

"Ah, so I'm screwed."

She paid attention then. "Where is he?" she asked and started to look around.

My heart almost gave out. "I will punch you," I threatened.

She laughed. "Seriously, where is he?"

I turned in my stool to face the bar. "Nine o'clock."

She faced it too. "Yours or mine?"

"Mine," I groaned. "Towards the end of the curve, he's talking to someone."

She looked, discretely enough I hoped.

"There's no one there," she said.

My brows furrowed. "Are you sure?"

She nodded.

I shot my gaze over to where he had been sitting.

Tracy was right.

He was *gone.*

CHAPTER 2

*T*he hours that followed were completely uneventful.

Loosened up after a few drinks, myself and Tracy eventually went down to the dance floor. But we remained in a safe corner, moving in comical spurts with each other and then pausing when we got tired to watch the rest of the crowd.

They all seemed to grind and twist their bodies against each other to the rhythm of the deafening music.

Anne was in the midst of them somewhere, as we had long set her free to experience the night in the very wild way she wanted to.

Soon enough, Tracy was itching to return home and so was I, but a corner of my heart still held out the hope that perhaps I would see the hot guy again. So I stalled, refusing to take her suggestions of leaving to heart. "When the foam machines begin, we'll leave," I said, so we pressed on.

Soon enough, the machines started.

After an announcement that no one could make out amidst the deafening blare of music, the lights went out for a moment, plunging the entire club into a frightening darkness. Then the sound of running machines sounded across the room. The lights came back on and from the ceiling, soap foams were blasted down.

The crowd went wild!

"Time to go," Tracy said and held my hand as we tried to get off the dance floor, but people thrashed around in wild excitement. Everything and everyone seemed to have chosen to stand in our path, so getting around the railing to the exit steps got harder and harder.

My stomach roiled with the concern that we would eventually be trapped in the midst, unable to get away before the bubbles made everyone wet. My heart also went out to my sandals. They were low heeled and comfortable, but had cost me quite a ridiculous amount, so having them ruined was not part of the agenda tonight.

A cloud of foam began to drift towards us but thankfully a group of half-drunken people attacked it. The middle of the club was fast becoming completely covered in foam and we were running out of time.

"Get out of my way!" Tracy yelled as she pulled me along.

I went amusedly along with her.

We eventually made it to the steps before things could get out of hand, and I released a deep sigh of relief.

Tracy let go of my hand, and I held onto the railing, but then suddenly I slid on something wet and I started to go down.

A hand suddenly locked around my arm, holding me upright and I was able to regain my footing. "Thank you so much," I said, and lifted my gaze to see who'd saved me.

It was *him.*

Every external noise seemed to fade into the background, and for the longest time I couldn't speak until I heard Tracy call out my name. "I'll be right there," I called back to her, and tucked my curly hair behind my ears as I glanced at him. "Thank you."

"You're welcome," he said and retreated till I was on solid ground. I turned to walk away, my knees wobbly.

He called out to me, "Can I buy you a drink?"

My legs almost gave away again as I turned and nodded much too eagerly and had to catch myself.

He smiled in response, perhaps finding me endearing. I hoped.

"But I have to speak to my friend for just a moment," I said. "I'll come join you."

"Sure," he said and went on his way.

I returned, dazed, to Tracy.

She had ordered herself another drink and was waiting. "Who was that?"

"The guy that disappeared earlier," I said.

For a moment, her face remained blank. Then it hit her. "Ahh... Oh."

"If you turn to look at him, I will smack you," I said with gritted teeth.

She laughed, but still peeped at him. "That's the second time tonight you've threatened to deck me because of him."

"I'm sorry," I muttered. "I'm just so nervous. I don't know why."

"Oh, I know why." She nodded. "He's fucking gorgeous. Those broad shoulders and long legs are enough to mess with a girl's head."

I couldn't help my amusement. "Well, I'm going over. He's buying me a drink. I'm sorry for leaving you alone."

"It's fine. I'll keep an eye on you..." She looked out towards the still enlivened crowd... "and try to see if it's still possible to spot Anne. You know this scene makes me wonder if any of us really grow up, because all I see right now are a bunch of five year olds. They're fucking going crazy over bubbles. I don't get it."

"You're an old soul Tracy," I told her.

"What? You don't get it either."

"I do, I just don't want to get wet."

"Well with him now in the picture I'm sure you already are."

I smacked her arm.

"Ow!"

"How does my face look?"

"Stunning," she said.

"Lipstick on my teeth?" I asked, and grinned just enough to flash her my pearly whites.

"You're all good," she assured me.

I let out a deep breath. "See you later."

"Have fun," she called after me.

I walked away and headed towards him. With every step I took, it felt like I was heading towards a significant moment.

A moment that could quite possibly change everything and it made me not want to proceed, but then I reached him.

He got off his stool. "Hi," he said.

I couldn't get myself to respond, so I just focused on settling as gracefully as I could on the stool, which was quite the task given how easily it swiveled around.

He on the other hand, set his foot on the ground as he took his seat.

I realized then just how tall he was. I calculated that the top of my head would barely reach his shoulders.

He called the bartender over and turned to me, a smile on his face. "What do you want to drink?"

I decided to be confident. I wasn't one who felt irrefutably convinced of their own charm, but since he *had* noticed me, there was undoubtedly something here I could work with. Somehow, being in his presence made me feel sexier and more desirable than I ever had. The tip of my tongue softly rimmed the inside of my upper lip as I took a second to think, and then the words slid out of my mouth like butter, "Sex on the beach, would be great."

He didn't blink.

His gaze lingered boldly on my lips, painted a stark red, and then he lifted his eyes to mine.

At first sight I had thought his eyes were grey, but as it turned out, they were green. An aqua shade of green and *mesmerizing.*

"Sir..." the bartender called.

He peeled his gaze away from mine to place our orders. "Just a Macallan for me, and Sex on the Beach for the lady."

I relished the husky tone of his voice. It sounded so smooth and quiet, but the underlying authority was unmistakable.

He resettled his gaze on me. "My name is Carter Edwards." He held out his hand.

I paused, realizing we hadn't even introduced ourselves. I accepted the offered hand and replied, "I'm Leah... Leah Peters."

"You're American, I suppose," he said.

My gaze lingered on the joining of our hands as I slowly pulled mine away, almost convinced they were beginning to sear from the contact with him. "I am." I thought about mentioning that I was from Indianapolis, but I didn't think it was needed. Tonight was about two strangers meeting in a different part of the world, choosing to be in each other's company for a little while.

Perhaps it would be just tonight, so the less we knew of each other, the better off we would be, but exactly what was I expecting to happen between us tonight? I had never had a one night stand. I never believed I could pull one off, but right now as I stared at the insanely gorgeous man before me —it was all I wanted. We could spend the remaining hours of the night together, and then before the sun rose, we would be out of each other's life, just as quickly as we had come into them.

I loved the sound of that.

"I'm from Minnesota," he said.

"Oh, I'm from Indiana," I replied, choosing to just follow his lead and take each moment as it came.

Our drinks were delivered then and he lifted his tumbler to his lips for a sip.

I noticed when our legs touched, his jean clad knees brushed against the exposed skin of mine. It sent tiny prickles of excitement coursing through my body.

"So what brings you all the way to Turkey?" he asked.

"Just a quick vacation," I replied. "With friends."

"And how long are you here for?"

"About two weeks."

"Hm. And you've been here…"

"Two days," I replied. "What about you?"

"I'm here on business. It's my first time here, so I have been struck by how beautiful this city is. I might just extend my stay for a proper vacation. Now that I'm here I think I need one."

I smiled. "Don't we all?" I lifted my glass, the liquid wetting my lips as my gaze lowered to the sliver of rich, olive, skin beneath his white dress shirt. I couldn't seem to look away. The way the material molded to his torso was nothing short of art. It wasn't tight, but fitted enough to show the ripped build of his frame underneath. I looked towards the dance pit of adult kids and now wanted to be in the midst of them, *with him.*

Quite a lot of people had taken layers of their clothing off. What a great excuse it would be for him to do the same. But somehow, I couldn't picture him being there. He seemed too... respectable for playing in bubbles. This fact made me feel happy and sad at the same time.

"So what do you do in Indiana?" he asked.

I just wanted him to kiss me already. The information exchange just seemed too slow for me, especially since I'd just gotten out of a non-relationship with a guy I'd met online. We'd talked off and on for about three weeks before deciding to meet. I'd later come to find out after a few more dates that compulsive lying to cover his wilting confidence at being thirty-five and unemployed was a trait he'd forgotten to share.

So my enthusiasm for a love that would *go the distance* was currently nonexistent, especially given the breathtaking man sitting next to me. My body was currently brimming and humming for him, and I wanted to give it what it wanted-his mouth on mine-on *me.* "I work in marketing," I answered.

"Oh," he said. "I'm involved in marketing too. We're actually out here handling the new campaign for the Splash brand."

"Oh, I'm aware of them but aren't they majorly in Dubai? They're opening a branch here?"

"They are. We're in charge of the marketing and advertising for their year-end launch. What agency in Indiana do you work for?"

"Steer Point. You've probably never heard of it, we're really small. We're involved in digital marketing around the metropolitan area."

"Interesting," he said. "I've never been to Indiana, but maybe one of these days I'll stop by for a visit since I now know someone there."

"You'll be welcomed," I said, unable to control my smile. Damn, he was so magnetic.

He leaned in.

I paused, especially when his eyes bored into mine and I didn't dare breathe. Something about his gaze was so arresting and I couldn't quite place a finger on it.

"You're incredibly beautiful, Leah," he said.

"Thank you," I breathed the words out. "You're um—you're beautiful too."

He leaned back and laughed. "Nothing compared to you, but message received."

"I mean it, you're beautiful too—oh God. I didn't mean like pretty... I meant you're handsome."

A massive smile showed on his yummy lips as he placed his hand over mine on the counter, and once again leaned towards me. "Well, I'm glad to know you think so. I hope you don't have a boyfriend, Leah. Because, I don't think I can go any longer without kissing you."

I stopped breathing.

His gaze remained on my lips, focused solely on my mouth.

Simply frozen, my mind going blank. I know that I responded along the lines that I definitely did not have a boyfriend. But otherwise, I couldn't seem to focus.

His left hand slid around the side of my neck.

Instantly, I dripped between my thighs.

He gently drew me closer to him.

My startled gaze roved over his unbelievably beautiful face as his forehead met mine. My eyelids fluttered shut as I inhaled the exotic scent of his skin… a heady mix of lemon and some kind of woodsy scent, and I knew I would never forget it. The warmth of his breath tickled my face, and then our noses met, stroking lightly.

His mouth captured my lips and for a moment—my heart stopped.

It all came at once… something warm started in my belly and seemed to spread out to my limbs. It seeped into the crevices of my body, and rendered me completely limp. I struggled to hold on to his waist for some semblance of balance.

His tongue slipped into my mouth, bold and velvety as it tasted me with long, leisurely licks. His hold around my neck tightened, and so did my grip at his waist. He *tasted* like heaven. The flavor of the scotch he'd consumed right before, an elegant mix with his unique taste, clean and heady with the promise of primal fucking, drew me closer and closer to the edge.

I never wanted him to stop and kissed him back like my very survival depended on it.

My breasts felt heavy and tender from the dizzying arousal, my sex throbbed and pulsated with excitement. If he could do this to my mouth, I wondered in awe at just what he could do to other parts of my body. The possibilities made me almost choke with a gasp.

He broke off the kiss and it was punctuated with a low smacking sound. He pulled away, his hand released my neck.

Incoherent, I almost fell off the stool. His hands grabbed my arms to save me. I came back to my senses enough to process what had just happened. I was almost shocked at now hearing the chaos we were surrounded by. Like the sound had just been turned on after the mute button had been on. In the last few minutes with him, the entire world had faded away, just the two of us existed.

What the hell just happened?

I avoided his eyes as I tried to get myself together. I busied myself with adjusting my clothes and brushing off nonexistent lint.

"Are you okay?" he asked.

I lifted my gaze to meet the genuine concern in his, a welcome surprise from the amusement I had been expecting. "I am," I replied. "Thank you for the uh… kiss. It was *nice.*"

He smiled.

I felt like smacking my palm across my head. In situations like this, the less said was always better, but I couldn't seem to stop babbling.

"Let's go somewhere a bit more private," he said, and lifted his gaze towards the rooms on the second floor. "Would one of those do?"

Yes, it was a worn out line, but I *so* did not care. "Sure," I replied, as I tried not to grab him up and drag him out of his seat. I needed to not act so darned eager, but wow... if that kiss was any example—I was in for the hottest sex on the face of this earth.

But I couldn't completely disappear on Tracy.

"I need to umm... speak to my friend for just a moment. I'm sorry, I'll be right back." I hurried towards her.

"Why are you here?" she complained. "I was enjoying the show! Get back and continue."

"We're leaving," I told her. "To a private room. To talk and um..."

"...etcetera?" She asked with a huge grin.

I tightened my lips to hold back my laughter, glad that I had my back to him. "Should I go with him?"

"Do you want to?" She asked.

"I do," I answered. "I *really* do."

"Then have fun. You're on vacation, but keep your phone on you, so you can call me if anything goes wrong."

"What about you?" My tone turned apologetic.

"I'm going home. I'm tired of watching people fall on top of each other and I think those two in that corner over there have been fucking for the last ten minutes. Just don't be that shameless. Do what you want to *some-*

where private, and come back to the room with a good story."

I felt a bit surprised by her easy blessing. "You're actually encouraging me to go through with this?"

"Leah," she said. "Both Anne and I have had one night stands that we're not proud of, but we've both had some that came close to blowing our minds. Remember neck tattoo guy?"

I giggled at the reminder of the restaurant bathroom rendezvous, that to this day, she swore was the best sex she'd ever had. I raised my brows at her.

"Exactly." She nodded. "So go on and enjoy yourself, but please be safe." She took a peek at him. "Plus, this guy looks like something that was dropped like manna from the sky. I'm not going to keep you from such a gift."

I gave her a quick hug, turned around and was on my way.

THE PRIVATE ROOM was on the second floor of the club. And just like the others in its row, the side that faced the dance floor was made of glass and through it the entire mayhem of the club was visible.

We however, felt secluded enough. It had a table, along with an accompanying circular sofa, and an ice bucket of champagne already waiting in the middle. I took my seat and watched as he worked on the bottle.

When the cork popped off, he filled my flute, and then leaned back to take a sip out of his as he watched me, a smile on his face. "Would you like something to eat?" he asked.

"They have this Japanese shrimp tempura that I haven't been able to get out of my mind since last night."

"I would," I replied but his words made me wonder. He had been here the previous night too? With whom, and doing what? Was I just the next girl that made the list? I shook my head to drive away these useless thoughts. Tonight, I was not allowed to think about the past or the future. Only the present and for once, I would completely enjoy this gift.

After he placed the order, I moved a bit closer to him.

He put his arm around me, his gaze boring deeply into mine. "So do you like your job?"

"I do," I replied and didn't know if I needed to bother mentioning more. My short responses seemed vague, but I had no clue about how much to divulge or not divulge in this situation.

"It never gets tough?" he asked. "Do you deal directly with clients?"

"Sometimes. Thankfully, I'm a Junior Copywriter."

"Did you always want to work in marketing?"

"No," I replied. "I wanted to be an accountant. My teenage logic was the banks were where the money was, so I wanted to be around it even if none of it was mine."

He laughed.

The rhythm of his laugh was such a joy to listen to.

"So why did you change your mind?"

I saw genuine interest in his eyes, and decided to carry on, honestly, "I found out at the end of freshman year that I really didn't care for numbers. I think it happened during the Algebra concepts course exam. I'd locked myself in the bathroom, balling my eyes out because I just knew I was going to fail. Nothing was sticking, and it wasn't because I hadn't been studying it all semester. Nothing would stick."

"You sound like many of my clients."

"I've encountered some of those myself. Anyway, my friend eventually pulled me out of the bathroom and explained what she could to me. I got a C and in my sophomore year, I jumped ship to marketing."

He gave me another understanding smile as he moved his hand from my shoulder to wrap around my waist as he lifted his flute to his lips.

I welcomed the increased intimacy and reveled in the electric warmth of his touch.

Just then, a knock sounded on our door and it opened to allow the delivery of our tempura. The server placed our meal on the table, which indeed looked quite appetizing. Some roasted green peas, and shredded calamari were also included.

I picked up one of the fried shrimp for a taste, then moaned at the flavor.

"It's good, right?" He asked.

"Delicious," I replied and settled even further into him. I felt comfortable with him, it seemed like we were just an old couple, enjoying each other's company on a couch. I chose to relish it. "What about you?" I asked. "Do you love your job?"

Pausing, he placed the flute down. "Love is a strong word," he said. "I do enjoy it though because it challenges me. For instance, a few months ago we were tackling a campaign for a Dodge drag car at the New York Auto Show. In that project, everything that could go wrong went wrong. So we ended up having to do a load-in for the whole drag strip on the Hudson's Pier 94, with lighting and pyrotechnics and hero cars all in thirteen hours."

"Oh wow!" I turned to face him fully.

"I know," he said. "Some higher ups on Dodge's side caused the delays with bureaucracy and their ardent need to be dicks. When I got home after that, I didn't move for two days."

"Wow, I mean I'm used to working under pressure but that is just insane."

"It was," he said, but then his teeth troubled his bottom lip for a moment.

I stared, as once again all else fell away beyond my now established need to have this man.

He pulled me even closer to him.

Goosebumps erupted along my arms, betraying my current vulnerability to him.

Catching the soft flesh of my ear between his teeth, he nibbled gently on the sensitive flesh, while my fingers dug into the leather sofa for some stability. His lips trailed down my jawline, just close enough for his heated breath to sear my skin, accompanied with the occasional kiss that sent jolts of delicious pleasure through me.

The sexual tension between us was like nothing I had ever experienced before. The man seemed unreal. I almost felt no shame in admitting with the unmistakable promise in his eyes, he was about to take me to a place I'd never been and wouldn't want to come away from.

What I felt for this man right now was a blazing lust. I wanted him ramming into me in more ways than I was aware of. I could feel my arousal roll down my thighs, as my sex clenched repeatedly with frantic anticipation of his cock, sheathed perfectly within my walls and milking us both of dizzying pleasure.

Suddenly, he kissed me hard and my brain once again, shut down.

Kissing Carter caused a shock to my entire system, making me believe in magic; the kind that created an almost ethereal harmony between two people. His taste in my mouth made me burn from the inside out. So for the first time ever in my life, I wanted to be totally consumed without restraints... without inhibitions.

I didn't even register when I moved but in one moment, our lips were joined, and in the next, we were staring into each others eyes. I rose from my seat, bunched my skirt up over my thighs, and sat astride him.

I noted the heaving of our chests, rising and falling in a united rhythm that heightened our awareness and excitement for each other. My completely soaked sex rested on the rock hard bulge pushing against the fly of his jeans.

As I began to writhe my hips slowly against him, his eyes glazed over. And then they fluttered shut, his head falling slightly backwards as a low moan flowed from the back of his throat. This was my chance to explore him, so I leaned forward, my arms on either side of his head as I placed a kiss on the heated skin that covered his racing pulse.

He jerked slightly at the contact, his arms coming around my waist in encouragement.

I trailed the sculpt of his jaw with kisses, teasing his lower lip with my teeth and then letting my tongue out to playfully tickle the tip of his straight nose.

The tease greatly amused him, his eyes sparkling with excitement as he watched me while his hands slid downward to cup my ass. Abruptly, he straightened, as if he couldn't take any more and whispered into my ear, "What I want to do right now, is bend you over that table... jerk your legs apart and fuck you till you come, preferably screaming my name."

My heart instantly reacted at his declared intention, as it sped up. I paused for a moment to catch my breath, my hands raking through the thickness of his silky hair as I tried my best to commit every second of this moment to memory. "I like that idea."

He leaned back against the couch then, every trace of amusement gone from his eyes as he studied me. "We can't... right now," he said. "I didn't come prepared."

I brushed my hand down along his flawless face... his unpreparedness made me feel just a little bit happy. He hadn't just generally been on the hunt with me being just one prey amongst many others he could have caught for the night. Instead, I was a welcome coincidence.... a gift thrown in his path... like he was to me.

My gaze moved over to the glass wall with its clear view of the madness below. "It would have been something too, for you to fuck me against that glass. We can see them, but they can't see us... but I also came unprepared. What a shame."

Something changed in his eyes. His gaze, overtaken by a longing so dark that it sent shivers down my spine. With one swift sweep of his hand, he cleared everything off the table—it all went crashing down to the ground.

With a brief glance, I could see the shattered glass flutes, the overturned bottle and blocks of ice scattered in every direction. And what was left of our appetizer.

He lifted me off his lap as he stood, deposited me on the table and jerked my legs apart.

With a hard tug the lace of my thong was ripped apart and pulled away to expose my sex.

Open and vulnerable, my pussy was bare to him and I had never felt so turned on. "Carter..." I breathed his name out.

Unexpectedly, he sat back down, hooked my legs across his shoulders, and covered my sex with his mouth.

I almost flew off the table, but his grip on my thighs seemed like a vice, locking me down to keep me from moving. "Jesus," I gasped as his tongue shot out and he gave my soaked cleft a long hard lick from the base to my mound. "Ohhh." I held onto his head.

"You're so fucking wet," he rasped, pulling me even closer to him.

His handling was rough, but it made me feel like he wanted me as badly as I wanted him. My back arched while my body writhed as he shoved his tongue inside of me and then circled the engorged bud between my soaked lips with the pad of his thumb.

I was amazed. Truly and most definitely overtaken by the tumult of pleasure crashing over my body like a tsunami. I'd been eaten out before but it had never felt this good. This man had barely even started and it felt like I was already about to tip over the edge. "Carter," I moaned aloud as the rhythm of his thumb sped up, in gentle but precise strokes while his mouth lapped up the juices that spilled out from my opening.

His hand let go of my thigh and went to my waist to hold me in place as he kissed my sex over and over again, like a starving man, his teeth lightly grazing my tortured clit. His tongue tortured me, licking and stroking, hard and fast between my folds.

My hands pounded against the table. The resulting sting just the perfect amount of relief I needed, just so I could bear more. I moved my fingers into his hair, fisting bundles of the mass as my body jerked and twisted against him. "God, you're good." I gasped. He slid a finger inside of me then another finger joined the assault and my hips bucked in response, shamelessly urging his thrusts.

"Leah you're so tight," he said, his voice hoarse. "Look at how greedy your pussy is for me."

I managed a smile as he pulled me even further towards the edge of the table, pushed his fingers back into me with a pumping rhythm that hastened my race to an orgasm. His motion seemed leisurely at first, and then became frantic.

I couldn't contain it. My core tightened, the sweet tension completely overwhelming me until I exploded into his hand.

I came with a drawn out, torturous cry, my knees knocking against the sides of his head as my body jerked and spasmed at the force of the orgasm. "Fuck," I shouted, my eyes fluttering open to gaze upon the man that had just shifted the world from under my feet.

My legs were still levitated in the air as he pulled away, unbridled triumph in his eyes.

He rose to his feet, then his gaze glued to mine. He held the back of my head in position and leaned forward to end his performance with a slow sensual kiss that had me reeling.

I loved the way I tasted on his tongue and wanted more than anything to repay the service he had just meted out to me.

"You're fucking delicious," he stated hoarsely.

"My hotel is fifteen minutes away," I said. "We can pick up some condoms on the way."

"Mine is five minutes away." He gave me a wink. "I have a few in my luggage."

I was so sold. With a squeal, I got up from the table, but when I landed on my feet, my knees instantly buckled. Oh wow, I was far from a full recovery.

He caught me, amused. "I've got you." He placed a soft kiss on my forehead.

I wondered if he realized the sweet kiss only worsened my state. I held onto him until I felt stable enough, then turned quietly to grab my purse. As I'd stared into his eyes, it'd felt like the wind had been knocked out of me… I wasn't positive yet if this was a good thing or not.

He bent down to retrieve my fallen thong. "I'll hold onto this," he said.

I bit my lip in amusement, hoping I could do the same later, keeping some souvenir from the best sex-capade, I might ever have in my lifetime.

With that sexy smile, Carter slipped the black lace into his pocket. He held onto my hand and led me out of the club.

CHAPTER 3

LEAH

*F*ifteen minutes later, I turned to watch him as he locked the door to his room and reached to undo the buttons of his shirt.

I didn't even spare any time to take in the surroundings as we'd barely made it to the room without attacking each other. With my seized underwear he had gotten full access to my sex and had refused to let go of it on our way here. He'd constantly palmed me at the most unexpected moments, his finger slipping within the folds to continually stroke me every chance he got.

My breasts had been assaulted while in the back of the taxi, my erect buds caught between his teeth through the material and sucked on as his hands had plumped the heavy mounds, bringing me way too close to the brink. I couldn't wait to spend the night with him. I couldn't recall ever feeling so wild, unrestrained and excited.

He stalked me like a predator after its prey as he shoved his shirt aside.

I retreated at the tease, ready to become thoroughly exposed with this complete stranger, while I reached to my side to pull down the zipper of my tube top. My breasts spilled out as I pulled the material away, my hands molding as much of the masses as I could handle.

The flare of appreciation in his eyes spurred me on, my teeth nibbling on my bottom lip.

"You're so fucking sexy, Leah. You have no idea what you're doing to me right now."

A smile broke out across my lips as I stopped retreating and waited for him to close the distance between us.

He had already undone his belt and button, so with my gaze on his, I unzipped his fly and got down to my knees. Gripping the edges of his jeans along with the dark briefs he wore underneath, I pulled on the material.

He gave me a little hand to slide them down his hips.

His cock sprang free, and a small gasp escaped my throat. Thick and lengthened with such arousal as bulging veins lined its sides. I ran my hands gently down the velvety smooth, but rock hard shaft, fair and pretty, ready for my attention. This part of him too, was beautiful.

The intensity of his gaze made me nervous... it felt as though they mocked me with the notion that I wouldn't be able to properly reciprocate... to unravel him as he had done to me in the club. But I was determined.

I flicked my tongue across the damp head, tasting his pearls of pre-cum and relishing the warm, slightly salty flavor. Then I covered the entire head with my mouth, hollowing my cheeks to give it a hard suck. I was rewarded with a grunt of approval, and the sight of his eyes, now clenched shut in enjoyment.

Encouraged, I carried on, weighing the heavy member in my hands and gently fisted him. Tilting my head, I showered wet hard kisses along the wicked length and then braced myself as I returned to the tip and took as much of him as I could into my mouth. I pulled back, my mouth tightening around him, tugging on him.

His hands found their way into my hair. "Damn, Leah..." he groaned as his hips churned, "*Fuck...*"

I was on top of the world. With my hands at the base of his beautiful cock, I increased my pace, my head bobbing as I milked him shamelessly. I kissed his balls, licked up and down his shaft, and pumped him as hard as I could.

His hips bucked above me from the delicious agony, his grip on my hair almost painful as he went mindless.

I lifted my gaze to meet his.

He looked completely flushed, his mouth parted in wonder at the torrent of pleasure coursing through him. "Leah," he gasped. "I'm going to come—holy fuck."

My excitement knew no bounds, my suctions hardening even further, my fisting now almost brutal. He exploded down my throat, with such a sudden force I almost choked.

His roar seemed to shake the room, his head thrown back with his release. He was breathless, his chest heaving as he fought to catch his breath. "Fuck," he called out again.

Pride swelled in my chest as I struggled to swallow all of him, my fist milked him of every last bit of delicious cum.

With a loud, lengthy groan, he opened his eyes, bright with amazement for me and pulled me to my feet. The hard, deep kiss that followed, explicitly conveyed his gratitude and sent my head spinning.

My body went limp when he pulled away.

His eyes were searing mine while full of adoration. "That was the best head I've ever received."

My cheeks heated in response as I splayed my hand across his chest to feel his raging heartbeat. "My pleasure."

Carter laughed and with his hands underneath my thighs, he lifted me into his arms. "I hope you're ready, because I'm going to fuck you until you pass out."

I tried to reign in my smile of excitement, but it widened out of control. "So in how many ways are you going to fuck me?" I asked.

"We're both going to lose count, but first, we're going to start on the bed." He moved with me and in seconds, I was deposited onto the soft warm mattress with a squeal. He came after me, reaching into his luggage by his side to retrieve his packet of condoms. "Want to put it on me?" he asked.

I nodded eagerly. "Definitely."

He flipped onto his back, his hands going behind his head.

I climbed up on top of him, my legs astride him and sat on his thighs.

His cock was rejuvenated and seemed now to have swelled even more in size, greedy and full of anticipation.

My sex pulsated in response, unbelievably damp and ready to take in all of him. In no time I had the rubber fitted on him. With a naughty smile, I chose the first way that I wanted to have him. Then I paused as I gave his beautiful torso the worship it deserved for being such a work of art. I kissed him, nibbling on his jaw before proceeding downwards to tease his nipples with playful flicks of my tongue.

"That tickles," he jerked in response and our mutual amusement bubbled in the air.

"You have the most perfect body," I told him as I tasted as much of his skin as I could, trailing my lips down along his muscled torso while relishing his hard, structured build. His skin was flawless. The heavy scent of both of our arousals swirled in the air around us, turning me on even more than I could have believed possible.

He scoffed. "You're one to talk. When it's my turn, you're going to see what I'm going to do with those breasts and ass of yours." He reached out to take as much as he could of one breast into his mouth, and smacked his palm hard against my ass.

The jolt of the sting almost set me off right there, but I took a few seconds to calm myself. His fingers dug into the soft flesh of my ass as he sucked greedily on my nipple while my arms cradled his head in approval.

With a gasp, he pulled my hands away and fell back onto the bed, his eyes dancing with thorough enjoyment. "It's time for you to fuck me," he teased.

I smacked my lips with total anticipation as if he were a tasty dessert beneath me. "Are you ready?" I asked.

He licked his lips in response. "I could swear that I was born just for this exact moment."

I laughed and moved to position myself across his hips, "You're so silly." I grabbed his cock and slightly stroked it along my wet folds, coating him with my slickness.

"Uh, fuck I love that," he groaned.

I wanted to grind upon him a little bit more, but I couldn't wait a second longer. I needed him inside of me. The night still loomed ahead. We could eventually revisit the teasing again before the sun rose. I rolled my hips to settle his cock perfectly at my entrance.

His expression turned serious as he watched me.

I shut my eyes. Maybe he was right... we both were born for this moment. I wanted to remember this. Every single second, the way his cock felt when it slid into me, inch by inch.

Things were tighter than I'd expected.

At my slight wince, he sat upright, his hand softly cradling my face. "Are you all right?" He whispered.

I opened my eyes to see the genuine concern in his gaze as he searched mine, checking for any sign whatsoever of discomfort.

His consideration touched me and in response, I threw my hands around him resting my face in the crook of his neck as his cock stretched me. I slowly impaled myself onto him, slight whimpers sounding from my throat as my body struggled to accommodate his length and thickness.

IONA ROSE

He rested his hands gently on my hips, guiding me slowly all the while showering kisses across my face, on my forehead, on my cheeks, nibbling on the tip of my nose and on my bottom lip to distract me.

It made every inch slide easier and finally, he was lodged solidly inside me. I slammed myself down on him the rest of the way, and felt him hit the end of me. "Ahhh," I moaned out, throwing my head back as the fullness I craved was flawlessly sated.

"Are you okay?" he asked gently.

I forced my eyes open to meet his beautiful green ones. I nodded, a wild smile breaking out across my lips. "I'm more than okay." I dug my knees into the bed, balancing my hands against his hard torso as I pulled up away from him, just until his tip sat at my entrance. My sex kept trembling fiercely, sheathed around him like a second skin. I slid back onto him, his cock now completely coated with my slickness. The fit of him seated inside me this time around felt like a dream. I rose up once again.

When I slammed down on him, his back arched off the bed. "Holy fuck, Leah," he panted. His breathing coming in short hard spurts. "I'm going to lose my fucking mind."

I felt the exact same way, the friction at my motion much too sweet to process.

As if he were helpless, Carter fell back onto the bed.

Now, I began to ride him furiously. Back and forth, I rolled my hips wildly against him and then held unto his torso so I could pump my hips up and down on his raging cock.

My throat swelled shut, my nose stinging from impending tears of pure feeling. The way he felt inside of me was unreal. I'd never imagined sex could feel this good. My heart roared in my ears, my breath hissing out between my clenched teeth as I fucked him with all I had in me.

My inner walls began to contract around his cock greedily, our bodies shuddering at the building pressure of our impending release.

Unexpectedly, he moved and flipped me over.

I was tossed onto the bed.

He repositioned his cock at my entrance and slammed into me, whatever restraints he had earlier were now completely nonexistent. "Leah," he gasped out in near desperation.

I loved the hoarse, desperate call of my name on his lips.

He thrust deep into me as I pumped my hips upward to meet every single hard frantic drive. I grabbed his ass, my nails digging deep into the taut flesh. I drew blood but at that moment, neither of us gave a fuck.

"Carter," I panted out breathlessly. My eyes watered as he fucked me to within an inch of my life, the frame of the bed jerking and creaking in protest.

His tempo became relentless and overpowering as I thrashed my head from side to side, threaded screams flowing from the back of my throat.

His thumb went to my clit, to massage the engorged bud.

This became my breaking point. "*Carter,*" I screamed, as I unraveled completely, my hips bucking and my cries bouncing off the walls of the room. My release so earth shattering that I scraped my nails against the sweat soaked skin of his back, scrambling for my sanity.

Carter then reached his own peak as he slammed his hand against the headboard above me and roared out his release, the entire bed frame shuddering at the impact. He collapsed on top of me, his whole body rigid as his climax rushed through him.

I wrapped my hands around him, aware of his white-knuckled grip on the pillow at the side of my head as he hid his face along my neck, fighting to catch his breath.

His whole body was burning hot, dampened with sweat, as strands of our hair seemed to be sticking to the sides of our faces.

I curved my hands over his ass, loving the weight of his spent body on me as I basked in the ceaseless wave of my own orgasm.

Eventually, he rolled off me and we both laid there, staring at the ceiling for the longest time.

Finally he spoke, "What the fuck just happened?"

CHAPTER 4

CARTER

*H*er amusement started with a small smile, and then it widened, until she could no longer contain it. She then bubbled with laughter.

Such a soft but hearty sound that made my chest swell until it became almost painful to breathe. I turned towards her, my head propped up with my hand. "Why are you laughing?" I asked, unable to keep the smile off my face.

She turned to me, laying on her side and also propping her head up with a hand. "Why are *you* smiling?" She returned the question.

For a moment, I lost myself in her hazel eyes, ablaze with excitement and joy. There was a peace in them, that seemed to calm the constant anxiety and restlessness inside of me. Lying here, I thought of nothing else, except this woman beside me. Of the way she had just fucked me out of my mind… of just how beautiful she was and most especially, of how alluring her body was.

Back in the club, the lights had been dim, but right now, I could see the light freckles across her nose, the thickness of her lashes, and the small lines underneath her eyes.

She was flesh and blood, human and woman—and I was completely overtaken. My hand reached out on its own accord to trouble a strand of her wild, curly, auburn hair. "I'm smiling because you are."

"Well, I laughed because that was the best goddamn sex I've ever had, and I'm still trying to process it, just like you are."

My smile widened. "It's my pleasure to be at your service."

She shifted a bit closer to me and my gaze went to her exposed, beautiful, breasts.

"Can we do it again?" she asked.

This time, I was the one who laughed. "That sounds like the most fantastic idea ever. But first, I need to eat something. You completely wiped me out." I somehow found the strength to rise from the bed. "C'mon, I'm pretty sure I make the best peanut butter and jelly sandwiches in the world."

I went over to the hotel bathroom to find us both some robes.

"I don't think its great taste has much to do with you though," she teased.

I gave her a sour look as I went around the bed to hand over the robe.

Taking it, she shyly rose to her feet.

"Instead of regular bread, I make it as French toast, and its drip free. I have a great method for locking in the jelly. Little upgrades you might say, it has made many drop to their knees."

She laughed as she slid her arms into the soft cotton fabric.

I stared and for a moment, I thought to lift her into my arms but decided against it. I was becoming way too excited.

When we got to the kitchen area, I pulled the door to the small refrigerator open.

She ducked underneath my arm to see what it contained. "Wow, you literally only have bread, peanut butter and jelly."

"And two bottles of water," I added as I grabbed the loaf and jars then shut the door.

"Two bottles of water," she agreed.

Her dry tone amused me. "I've been having back to back meetings for the last week. These were needed for the days when I forgot to eat or just didn't have the time."

"When will you be returning to the US?" She asked as she brought a plate over for me.

"My flight is supposed to be in three days," I replied as I began to spread peanut butter on the first slice of bread.

"Supposed to be?" She asked.

I held her gaze as I responded, "Yeah, supposed to be. Who knows what could happen?" The message was clear, and I wondered why I was conveying it. Did I truly want to see her again, after tonight? Perhaps this was just what it was intended to be... a chance meeting between two strangers, for just one passionate night together.

But as I went silent, I truly didn't know if one night was enough.

Something about her tempted and entranced me and I couldn't put my finger on it... she literally drew me in like a moth to a flame. She burned, *brightly*... and all I wanted was to bask in her heat. I'd felt this irresistible pull from the moment I spotted her earlier at the bar and it hadn't subsided since.

A night I suspected, would not nearly be enough.

"You're the only one here right?" She asked. "Why did you get such a big suite?"

"It was all they had ready at the time and Desa's office is just about ten minutes away from here. I wanted to be as close as possible to cut down on any commuting hassles." Soon, I was done with the spread, sliced the joined pieces in half and pushed one over to her.

"You didn't make it like French toast," she accused as she gazed up at me from beneath her lashes.

"I'm out of milk and eggs." I shrugged. "Maybe, next time."

"Thank you," she said, and lifted the sandwich to her mouth.

She took a bite, then smiled in amusement.

"Carter, no offense but you definitely had no effect whatso-ever on this sandwich. It is as standard as they come."

I laughed, more at myself this time than at her comment. I was definitely not thinking about the sandwich as I watched her.

When she finished, she headed over to the refrigerator to get the water. "Should we share a bottle, so you'll have one left?"

"Sure," I said.

She brought it over to me.

"You first." I nodded at her.

Leah smiled as she lifted it to her lips.

I watched her as she slightly bent her head backwards and drank, her larynx bobbing as she swallowed, and just like that—I was turned on all over again.

She pulled her head back after her drink, and a small trickle rolled down along the corner of her lips.

Before she could stop it, however, I caught her hand and pulled her to me. My lips kissed the liquid away from her neck and up the trail back to her mouth.

"Carter..." she breathed, just as affected as I was.

I slipped my tongue into her mouth.

The bottle fell from her grasp, hitting the floor with a small thud.

In moments, her ass was cupped in my hands, and her hands buried in my hair.

I loved the way she kissed me... as though she was on the brink of losing all control.

Despite this seeming unbridled response to me, I could sense her holding back at every point. Doubting herself... exercising caution. I had no idea why, but it gave me the sense

47

that she wasn't quite adept at this one night stand thing, and this made me glad.

I didn't even know when I loosened her robe, but in a flash, it was hanging on the crook of the arm that tugged mercilessly on my hair. My hands moved past her voluptuous behind to stroke her swollen clit, before I slipped a finger inside of her.

Her knees buckled. *"Fuck,* Carter," she breathed the words out with a gasp

I chuckled in response. After a couple of finger thrusts, I rose to my feet. I turned her around, my robe giving way to hang open while I pulled hers from her body.

It settled into a puddle on the floor and she pressed herself against my hardened cock.

I grabbed her breasts as I traced searing kisses down her neck, and loved the way she writhed against me as I plumped them in my hands.

They were full and heavy with small, but erect, pink nipples. Hers had to be the most beautiful breasts I'd ever come across. My left hand banded around her slender waist, while the other found its way down to grabbed her soaked sex.

Her heels lifted from the floor.

She was dripping wet, my fingers slipping into the center of her folds to find her clit. I resumed my assault, stroking the engorged bud, hard and fast until she became wild against me, her hands around my wrist in half hearted attempts to halt my tease.

I refused to budge until she came, in a throaty cry… with a dirty curse. "Holy effing Christ!" She trembled, her chest heaving violently as her orgasm spilled onto my hand. After she had recovered enough, she turned to face me, a heart stopping smile on her face.

When I lifted my hand to my lips and cleaned her juices from my fingers with my tongue, her eyes widened in surprise. "I love the way you taste," I told her and pulled the robe from my body.

"That's fucking hot, Carter," she said.

I was in total agreement, as everything about this night was more than hot.

She retreated but her back soon connected with the counter.

With a grip on her waist, I hoisted her up and sat her on the marble. "You ready?" I asked as I pulled on a condom.

Almost immediately, her hands were on my cock fisting the rock hard length with unbridled excitement.

I could now see she had loosened up just a bit more, and was fully ready to thoroughly enjoy her night. She guided me into her and at the clench of her sex around my dick, I stopped breathing for a moment... and then it resumed in a rush... my eyes fluttering shut. She kissed me, her lips sucking greedily on mine her tongue teasing mine in languid, playful strokes.

I began to move inside of her and the rock of her hips in response made me feel like a car skidding out of control. I rested my head against hers, as I rammed into her, my fingers digging into her thighs while hers raked trails up and down my back.

"Oh, God…" Her voice shook to the rhythm of my thrusts, and when I lifted her off the counter to place her against the wall behind us, she rested her head on my shoulders in near collapse.

Her back slammed continuously against the wall as I fucked her, reinvigorated and insatiable.

Somehow, this time was even better than our last, the initial shyness and reservations, now completely gone.

We fucked like we were old lovers, thoroughly aware and in tune with the workings of each other's bodies. We came together and I'd never felt so deeply connected to another person in my life. In that moment of earth shattering release, we had become one… inseparable and completely whole.

I emptied myself into her, and collapsed against her, just as she did to me.

The wall held us both up, until a few minutes later when I found the strength to move. I pulled out of her, and we both watched as her cunt released me, the separation coming with a spill of her release to roll down along her inner thighs.

It was one of the most erotic and intimate things I had ever experienced.

She laughed softly under her breath.

So did I, just as I released my grip of her thighs.

She slid limply down my body, but still held unto me for stability, her arms around my neck.

"Ready to get some sleep?" I asked.

She nodded, her eyelids heavy as she looked at me with the softest, and most beautiful smile on her face. "I can't seem to walk."

I picked her up and soon we were huddled together underneath the luxurious comforter. I spooned her, every inch of her skin plastered to mine as my heart seemed to settle into place.

"I wish I had the strength for a shower," she said.

"No need," I replied, my breath tickling her ear. "I want to bask in your scent."

Her rumbling laughter sent joy prickling through my body.

"You are one fucking sexy, and near perfect man, Carter," she said.

"And you are one sexy and completely beautiful woman, Leah."

"Hey," she complained. "You'll make me feel guilty for not saying you were entirely perfect."

"I definitely am not."

"Well, neither am I."

"I'm not aware of that yet," I said. "If the verdict changes sometime in the future, I'll let you know."

With that... she went silent.

I knew why.

The future.

It loomed before us. The night had come to an end. With its conclusion came the realization, that perhaps it would be our end too.

I thought I'd remain awake, pondering over it all, but in no time, I was fast asleep with a dream of a woman in my arms.

Tomorrow and its mystery would most definitely come, but something calmed my heart, assuring me that things would play out the exact way they were supposed to between us... no need to worry.

"Goodnight," she whispered.

I was almost certain, I mumbled a response back to her.

CHAPTER 5

LEAH

*T*he next morning, I woke up to the rays of the late morning sun, filtering in through the white curtains that covered the stretch of sliding balcony doors. For too long, I watched the billow of the sheer fabric, as the events of the previous night rolled through my mind.

Carter wasn't by my side, but in the distance, I could hear water running, and I knew he was taking a shower. I didn't want to get up but at the same time, I knew I'd already over-stayed. It was just meant to be one night, but with the way he'd spoken just before we'd fallen asleep, I wanted to believe he felt the pull as much as I did, to go beyond just the few hours the rule of casual intimacy stipulated.

The water suddenly shut off, and my thinking immediately ceased. The last thing I wanted was for him to find me still luxuriating in bed. I found my clothes and was dressed in no time. I thought maybe I should just leave, as this should have been the preferred ending, clean and void of frills but I couldn't get myself to move.

What if there was even the slightest bit of a chance for more…. was I going to allow my pride to rule instead?

Suddenly, a hard knock sounded on the door, and it nearly startled my soul out of me.

After regaining my composure, I headed over to the door.

A white gloved waiter stood in front of it.

My gaze lowered to the trolley of food he had with him, so I immediately stepped aside so he could come in.

"Good morning madam," he greeted.

"Good morning," I replied and shut the door.

He placed the trolley by the corner and then began to unload the dishes onto the small dining table by the balcony. "Would you like to have breakfast outside or inside madam?" He asked.

I did not have an answer really. "Just leave it on the table," I said.

He gave me a smile. When he was done, he bowed slightly before turning to head back out of the room.

I took in the served platters, a tad bit surprised at the varied options of what seemed like every breakfast food that existed; fruit, croissants, muffins, juice, coffee, eggs, bacon, sausage, bread…

This had most definitely not been ordered for one person.

I was touched by Carter's consideration, but it all served to confuse me even more.

Where was the indifference to my welfare that he was supposed to have when a one night ended?

"Good morning."

With the sound of his voice, I jumped.

I spun around.

He stood by the door to the bathroom just as he was wrapping a white towel around his hips.

My eyes caught the glimpse of his groin just before he covered it all, and the sight of his semi-hard cock was a very welcome one for the morning.

"Leah?" He called.

I tore my gaze away from the bulge against the towel to swallow the lump in my throat. "Hey," I replied. "I was um… just about to leave."

His gaze met mine and it accused me of being dismissive. My stomach churned at the twinge of remorse, but I had lived long enough to know how to put myself on self-preservation mode, especially when the situation concerned 'unfamiliar' men.

He eyed me. "Have breakfast before you go. You can start without me."

"No need—" I started to say, but he had already closed the door behind him. I sighed.

Wasn't it always best when things like this ended quickly? Me staying around for breakfast like he had asked… wouldn't that complicate things?

I groaned under my breath at the discomfort in the pit of my stomach, and ran my gaze around the room to find my sandals. They had been flung away in the midst of our wild night, and I hadn't laid eyes on them since.

I immediately went in search and found one underneath the massive mahogany bed. The other was by the dresser in the corner, so I retrieved it, and put them on.

He appeared then, dressed in just a pair of dark grey slacks, and a naked torso.

In the light of the day, I could see him more properly than I had the previous night and I was just completely blown away.

His hair looked damp from the shower, uneven and dangling in wavy clumps from his head. His torso was glistening and hairless, carved into slabs of muscles. His arms were muscled as well.

I almost couldn't believe that I'd slept in those arms. Once again, I began to melt and wanted more than ever to be in them again.

"Do you want to eat outside?" he asked.

I took a moment to think about it. I nodded, and headed over to the table, avoiding his gaze. My heart kept thundering in my chest, on the sole account of the person before me and I could hear it… loud and clear. *How could he have such an effect on me?*

He joined me and together, we filled our plates with what we wanted. I chose some toast, scrambled eggs, and bacon, while he selected pancakes, drizzled syrup over them and prepared a bowl of berries.

"Excuse me while I go..." I smiled and pointed to the restroom.

Carter nodded.

I went into the heated and still somewhat steamy bathroom. His toiletries were arranged neatly on the marble counter-top; a small, transparent bag of travel sized essentials, and a bottle of Creed-spice & wood cologne. I paused to open it and lifted it to my nose. Yes, this was his scent, all right. That hint of cedarwood and lemon. There were probably more spices in there I could definitely not identify but all in all, I absolutely loved it. I capped it and set it back where I'd found it.

I wiped the steam away from the mirror to take a proper look at myself.

I was a hot, crumbling mess. My eyeliner was smeared all over my eyes, my lipstick completely gone, and my lips slightly swollen.

If I hadn't been hell bent on escaping, I never would have allowed him to see me like this. It was a wonder that he hadn't immediately kicked me out. I didn't want to wash my face with basic soap so I just found some wet wipes to revert me back to a blank state.

Curly wisps of hair floated around my face and since they softened my appearance, I left them as they were.

I cleaned up as much as I could, completely aware that my underwear was missing and would most probably stay that way. This thought did make me smile for a few seconds though. I then returned to the balcony to join him.

He was on a call, which ended the moment I sat down.

Soon we were both settled in and I turned to gaze at the view beyond. It was of the Taurus mountains and of the beautiful town of Alanya; its castle, and colorful buildings sprawled before the endless blue waters of the Mediterranean Sea. Vehicles, incoming boats, and people were moving around, the view picturesque as everyone went about their business for the day.

"This is beautiful," I said.

Carter nodded in agreement. He passed over the basket of muffins and croissants that he had brought over, and I retrieved a piece of each.

"Thank you.' I said, and we began eating quietly.

I kept my gaze on the town that looked so alive. In the distance, I could see people kayaking, and it made me want to ask him about his hobbies but I wanted to keep it simple. In a few minutes we would most probably be gone from each other's lives... permanently.

I completely avoided his eyes, even though I could feel them on me, searing my skin but I didn't know how to face him.

Then he spoke, "Were you really going to leave?" he asked. "Without a word?" His arresting green eyes, completely unreadable, focused on me.

My hands trembled as they lifted a napkin to my lips, and tried to mask my nerves with a smile as I spat out the first lie that came to mind, "I um... had a thing that my friends and I had planned to do today. Early." My head and voice lowered as I stabbed a piece of scrambled egg. "I didn't want to miss it."

He didn't respond to the blatant lie, and it made the meal all the more excruciating to sit through.

Eventually, I couldn't take it anymore. Never had inhaling and exhaling just to keep myself alive been more of an ordeal. I patted my lips with the napkin and drained my glass of juice. "Thank you," I said to him," for breakfast."

Silent, he watched me as he chewed slowly.

I couldn't help but notice the change in him. Now, in the light of day, he was contained and fully in control, the flirty, bubbly man I had spent the night with completely replaced. He intimidated me to my very bones. I pushed my chair backwards.

Just before I could rise he said, "Have dinner with me tonight."

My brain scrambled to a halt. All I could do was stare at him, absolutely nothing coming to mind to say in response.

"Will you have the time?" He asked.

I settled back into the chair and took a deep breath. "Carter… I don't—this isn't usually how this goes right?"

He leaned back into his chair and folded his toned arms across his chest. "What do you mean?"

"You know what I mean," I replied, well aware that he wanted me to spell it out. I did. "We had fun last night. Aren't we meant to part ways today? Take it solely as the delightful experience that it was?"

His response was simple., "I'm not ready to part ways with you just yet. Are you? Ready to part ways with me?"

My lips parted to speak, but then they trembled with indecision and shut closed again. I honestly didn't know how to respond to that, so I ignored the question. "I'll have dinner with you."

He slid his phone on the table over to me. I picked it up and inputted my number.

"I'll call you," he said. "Is 7 pm all right?"

"It is," I replied.

He rose to his feet.

I did the same, and went into the room to search for my purse. I slung it over my shoulder.

He walked me to the door to pull it open for me. Before I could leave however, he said, "There's a car waiting downstairs to drive you back to your hotel."

"Oh no, that's all right. I'll just get a cab."

"I insist," he said. "He's a personal driver assigned to me for the duration of my stay here. See you tonight."

I thought he would give me a kiss, but he didn't, so I stepped out of the room and went on my way. I didn't look back until I heard the door close behind me.

At the entrance to the hotel, I looked around to see if I could spot the driver, and almost immediately, a black town car pulled up.

The driver got out, a heavyset Turkish man with a thick mustache, dressed in a dark suit. "Miss Peters?" he called.

"Yes, I'm Leah Peters."

He hurried over to the back door to pull it open for me. "I've been asked to take you back to your hotel. Where is that?"

"The Sunprime, C-lounge. Thank you." I got into the sleek vehicle, and was returned safely back.

I WALKED into our room to meet Anne mid-sprint.

I quickly moved out of her way as she dashed for the bathroom, and was about to ask what was going on when I heard the spew from her guts.

I sucked in my breath. "Yikes," I said and turned to Tracy.

Sitting upright in bed, she was flipping through a Kristin Hannah novel. "You don't know the half of it. That's been going on all morning. And it's almost noon, where the hell have you been? We missed out on our space on the pier, and we're meant to go out this afternoon."

I ignored her and walked into the bathroom to meet Anne, still bent over the toilet bowl.

I bent down, brushing away the tendrils of hair that had escaped from her bun. "Sweetie," I called.

She lifted her head to stare up at me. She looked like she was in abject misery, her eyes bloodshot, and her gaze hazy from all the pain and discomfort of the hangover. "I'm dying," she lamented.

I threw my purse aside, and grabbed under her arms to lift her up. "No, you're not. You're going to be fine."

"I haven't been this hungover since college. *Fuck*."

"You'll be fine," I consoled, and led her to the sink so she could rinse her mouth. Afterwards, I led her back to our bed, and tucked her in.

"Take some Aspirin," Tracy called out. "Or better yet, let's go get some soup. They should have one spicy enough with some vegetables that will be able to soothe you."

"I'm not going near food," she growled.

I took my seat on the fluffy bed.

"She's refusing to take anything at all," Tracy complained. "No medicine and not even some food to settle her stomach. I don't know what to do."

"It'll pass soon," I said. "She'll be fine in a few more hours."

Anne groaned aloud.

"I really wanted to go to the castle and the Red Tower today," Tracy whined. "We could even check out the old shipyard too. Can we go, Leah?"

"We can't leave Anne here alone."

"She'll come with us... the fresh air will be good for her. By the time we return, she'll be back to normal. Right, Anne?" She turned to ask.

"Fuck the fresh air. I need gatorade."

"It's settled then." Tracy jumped up from the bed. "Leah, get dressed. There's an awesome farmer's market in town and it's called the Cuma Bazaar. It's only held on Friday, so we have to be there *today*. We'll get some snacks and Gatorade, then head over to the castle."

"I'm coming straight back to the hotel," Anne said.

Tracy lifted her arms in the air, close to losing her mind. "Come the fuck on," she roared, and turned to me. "Leah!"

I was conflicted once again on both of their sides but at the same time on none of their sides. My dinner date with Carter was heavy on my mind, but I also didn't want to give Tracy more reasons to be dissatisfied with this vacation. "What time can we be back, Tracy?" I asked.

She immediately perked up. "Maybe 5:30? 6?"

There was no way I could go with her, and still make it back in time to get ready for dinner with Carter. So I scrunched up my face and turned an apologetic gaze to her. "I'm so sorry, but I can't come with you today. Maybe next week. We'll still be here, and I promise I'll come along with you to wherever you want for the rest of the trip."

"I don't get it, why can't you come with me today? Are you hungover too?"

Anne turned on the bed to face us, "That's true," she said. "Where did you go off to last night?"

I glanced over at her narrowed gaze.

With a sigh, Tracy collapsed back to the bed, momentarily suspending her annoyance so she could listen to what I had to say. "What happened last night, Leah? I tried to reach you all morning."

"My battery died," I replied.

Her response was a frown. She soon shook it away. "So, what happened? Where did he take you?" Her eyes narrowed at me. "And what did he do to you?"

"She met someone last night?" Anne asked.

Tracy nodded so hard that I prayed her head would fall off.

"Oh, wow," Anne said. "At the bar?"

"Yeah, and he is fucking hot. They left the dance floor, and he took her to a private room on the second floor. That was the last I saw of her."

"What happened after that?" Anne asked, her eyes sparkling with excitement while momentarily forgetting her hangover.

"I thought you were hung over?" I eyed her.

She swatted the comment away. "Don't try to change the subject, tell us what happened."

In desperate need of a shower, I turned and walked towards the closet, where my clothes hung. "Nothing much," I said, and began to sort through it to find what I could wear to the market with Tracy if I did decide to go, and later on to dinner with Carter. "We went back to his hotel room and I spent the night with him."

"Oh, my God!" Anne exclaimed.

I turned to her in surprise.

Tracy couldn't stop snickering.

I had never been so confused. "I don't understand why is this such a big deal? Anne, you were with that bartender too, weren't you?"

"Yes, but that's me. I don't hold sex as sacredly as you do."

"I do not!"

"You've only slept with two guys in your entire life, and they were both long term boyfriends. You won't even kiss random strangers when we go out, back home."

"No one should *kiss* random strangers."

"But yet, you fucked one last night," Anne pointed out. "You see why this is a big deal? What the hell happened to you? Tracy, was he that hot?"

Tracy nodded. "I haven't seen a guy so fine in years."

"*Fuck*," Anne cursed. "Why didn't I get to meet him?"

Tracy had her snipe ready, "Because you jumped on the first dick you saw and didn't hold out for something better?"

Anne snorted in response. "What dick? My whole night yesterday was just a fucking disaster. And I fell twice on that disgusting floor. Look at my elbows." She lifted them to our view, and they were reddened and bruised.

"Ugh," Tracy said.

"That looks bad," I said. "Does it still hurt a lot?"

"I wished this was the only pain, my fucking head is about split into two from this darn headache."

Tracy shook her head. "Don't change the subject. Leah, tell us what you two did, *in detail*. It must be *something* to hear about if you're just coming home now."

"Let's finish with Anne first," I said. "Anne, what happened with the bartender guy?"

Her sigh was heavy. "Well, we went to the bathroom to fuck, and then he went down on me. But when it was time for me to return the favor, he pulled down his pants and I found that he was fucking uncircumcised."

Both Tracy and I immediately burst out laughing, well aware of Anne's very dark past with uncircumcised men.

"The last time I went down that road was with Chris... you guys remember right? That poker player we met in Vegas. I threw up. Literally spilled my guts out. I am never going down that road again."

"You threw up because his was... um unkempt," I reminded her. "Not because he was uncircumcised."

"Well from experience, uncircumcised cocks tend to have all that crap hidden in them that sometimes even a shower can't get to. I'll never have that in my mouth again."

"It's called smegma," Tracy supplied, thoroughly amused.

"Ugh." Anne shuddered. "I hate that word."

"So you walked out on him?" I asked.

"He walked out on me!" she screeched. "I was even ready to fuck him. We've been flirting for a few days and I needed a fucking release but then *he* got angry! He called me a bitch and walked out. Can you imagine? We're never going back to that bar again."

"Thank god," Tracy said.

I couldn't stop laughing.

"Anyway, back to you, Leah. What the fuck happened with you and this guy?" She groaned. "And I still can't believe you had a one night stand!"

Now I was ready to speak. My guard was down and I felt safe again. "Well, we slept together, and it was the best sex I've ever had."

"We need details." Tracy groaned and threw a pillow at me.

I dodged it, amused. "What details do you need? We did it on the bed, in the kitchen, he fucked me against the wall..."

"Oh. My. God," Tracy said.

Anne's mouth hung open. "How big is his dick?" Anne asked.

I cocked my head at her. "Why are you asking that?"

"Why the fuck wouldn't she ask you that?" Tracy asked, her eyes nearly popping out of her sockets. "I want to know too."

"Oh, so now you guys are getting along?"

"Answer the damn question!" Anne threw another pillow at me.

This time around, I was smacked right on the head. "Stop!" I yelled.

"Answer us!"

"It was fucking big okay? Smooth and pink and thick. What else do you want to know?"

"Oh, my God," Tracy screamed.

"You lucky bitch," Anne swore.

I refused to shut up now. "There's more." I said and they both perked up.

"Aren't one night stands supposed to end with both parties just going their way?" I asked. "You're not even supposed to be in the same bed by the next morning, right?"

"What's your point?" Tracy asked.

"Well, he wanted me to have breakfast with him... and then he also asked me to have dinner with him tonight."

The room went silent.

I waited for both of them to speak, but they just kept looking at me, speechless. "Is that a bad thing? I shouldn't go?"

"Um, do you want this to be just a one night thing?" Tracy asked.

"Well... I... uh. I don't think it can be more. He lives in Minnesota."

"She's not talking about a relationship," Anne said. "Do you want to fuck him again?"

"Of course, I do."

"Then I rest my case," she said and fell back onto her pillows. "You won this vacation. Have all the fun you possibly can."

I turned to Tracy and met her face filled with concern. "What is it?" I asked.

"Well, you're not the type to sleep with someone and not get emotionally attached. Hell, you don't even let anyone touch you until you're emotionally attached. Can you pull this off? A casual vacation fling that will calmly end next week, without you getting hurt?"

I turned around to face the closet, the question ringing in my head. I hadn't even thought of that. "He's not going to be here that long," I said. "He's here on business, so maybe a few days, tops."

"Alright then." Tracy nodded. "Be safe and have fun."

Anne got up from the bed. "You've just inspired me, Leah. This vacation cannot be a bust for me, at least not yet. I'm going to come with you guys to the market. Maybe I'll meet someone that's hot there that's worthy of my fucking time. If one more night passes without me getting laid, I'm going to fuck one of you in your sleep." She disappeared into the bathroom.

I turned to Tracy with horror running through me. "I'm sleeping on your bed today."

She shook her head in amusement as she returned to her novel. "No, you ain't."

"C'mon?"

"Have you forgotten that you might not even be here tonight?" she reminded me.

Once again, my unexpected plans rose up as reality. Butterflies fluttered in my stomach. "Oh, my God," I grumbled halfheartedly. "Honestly, I'm not even sure if I should go."

"What do you mean?" she asked. "Don't you like him?"

"Of course I do, it's just... what you guys said. I don't want to get emotionally attached."

"Stop worrying about that," she said. "Just enjoy your time with him. If it leads somewhere then fine and if it doesn't, then that's okay too. You'll have the memories of wild sex with some cute guy you met in Turkey to hold on to."

"What if I get hurt?" I asked quietly.

"You won't die from it. You'll heal and be back to normal in no time. Don't overthink this."

I sighed and headed back to the closet to search for something to wear. A few minutes later and I was in a near panic. "I don't have anything to wear!"

Just then, Anne came out of the bathroom, a towel wrapped around her body, and another wrapped around her damp hair.

I turned to them. "I don't have anything to fucking wear."

"You brought a dress didn't you?"

"I did, but it's light and flowy. It's for walking around and hanging out on the beach, not going on a date with someone I actually like." I held it up for them to see. "It has corgis on it, and it goes past my ankles."

They were both laughing.

"Stop! I'm not kidding. I need help."

"What do you want to wear?" Tracy asked. "Did he tell you what kind of dinner it would be? Is it formal or casual?"

I stopped then. "I have no idea."

"Ask him," Anne said as she went through her luggage by the corner of her bed. "Send him a text."

"I don't have his number," I said. "I only put mine in his phone. He asked for it."

"That means you'll go caformal then." Tracy nodded.

"What the hell is that?" Anne asked.

"Casual-formal." She beamed with pride. "I just made it up."

I shared a look with Anne as she shook her head.

"Seriously..." Tracy came over to me. She began to browse through my hung outfits. "You need something like... a dress shirt, but tucked into shorts. A blazer dress but with sneakers."

"Well, I have none of those. I packed light and all I brought along were sun dresses."

"Well, you could wear one of those with a pair of heels?"

"Don't wear heels," Anne advised. "That's trying too hard. You're both fuck buddies, not life partners. Plus, he's already seen you naked. Just put on a pair of jeans and a skimpy top, and you're good to go, wherever he takes you."

"I have a black halter dress you could borrow," Tracy offered. "We're the same size and it fits like a glove. If you don't want to pair it with heels then you can just use your black sneakers. Put your hair up and accessorize with some golden hoops. You'll look effortlessly stunning."

The suggestion sounded great to me.

CHAPTER 6

LEAH

*T*wo hours later, we headed over to the Bazaar in the town center.

It was held on streets along the southern coast, beginning from the harbor under the historical castle.

The three of us took our time, strolling through stalls of clothes and exotic fabric, jewelry, intricate lamps, ceramics, carpets, tea, spices and fruit.

Personally, I was overwhelmed by the staggering abundance and vibrancy of items displayed for sale. The people there came from all over the country and world to participate.

"Tracy, we've done something you wanted today," Anne said. "I hope you won't be up in arms tomorrow, complaining that we never do anything you want."

Tracy sent a threatening glance towards her. "You're already looking for a reason to get out of the tour to the canyon tomorrow? It's not going to happen. We're going, and if you don't want to come along, you can stay behind. Leah will come with me."

Anne shook her head as she finished up her Simit-Turkish bagel, encrusted with sesame seeds. She then went over to steal a quick sip out of the pomegranate juice that Tracy had in her other hand.

"Hey!" Tracy cried out.

Anne scurried away before she could be hit. She stood next to me, now completely cured of her hangover and in a bright mood.

My gaze remained solely on the fruit stalls we were approaching. "I want to pick up some apricots," I said and headed over to a cart filled with the polished orange fruits.

The stall owner, an elderly man greeted me with a smile and immediately offered one to me. I wanted to reject it but he insisted, so I accepted the fruit and took Anne's bottle of water from her. I signaled to him that I would be heading over to the corner to wash it, and he nodded in complete agreement.

The moment I was done, I returned and bit into one of the juiciest apricots I'd ever had. It had been allowed to thoroughly ripen and thus was very sweet. I took another quick bite, not even minding when the juices began to run down the corner of my mouth. "This is so good you guys." I turned to my friends as I wiped the moisture off my chin, but their attention was no longer with me. "Anne, try this," I urged.

She took the fruit from me solely because it was in her face.

I was pretty sure she hadn't heard a single word I'd said. "What are you guys looking at?"

"Look at that man over there," Tracy said.

"What man?" I followed the direction of their gazes and found a company of about four people. Three men and a woman. One of the men was dressed in Turkish traditional clothing with a red hat on his head, while the others were dressed more formally. The woman was in a suit, and so was the man by her side. Then the man my friends had been completely smitten by.

The group stood at a textile stall. The man listened to them as they spoke about the fabric, his hands in the trouser pockets of his grey pants. He wore a matching grey waist coat and underneath it, a crisp white shirt open at the collar. He towered over his companions, in both height and presence.

I didn't need him to turn around for me to know who this was.

"What a fucking specimen!" Anne swore. "Now that's who I want to pin me against a wall."

"I love, Jared," Tracy muttered, "but I'll take one night with him. Ooh, he's turning around!" She diverted her gaze.

Anne did not.

I watched her in amusement, and was about to turn away myself, when I made the mistake of glancing at him. Our eyes met, and I felt my heart stop.

"He's looking over here," Tracy said excitedly. "Wait a second, doesn't he look like…"

I broke our gaze and turned around. My hands were shaky as I picked out the number of apricots that I wanted, and then smiled at the man, my complete attention on him.

"That's Leah's guy!" Tracy said, and then tapped me on the shoulder.

I refused to respond.

"Leah, isn't that your guy?"

"I don't have a guy."

"What do you mean?" Anne asked her tone heavy with disappointment.

"Leah, he's coming over," Tracy said.

My grip on the bag of fruits loosened. "*Fuck,*" I cursed under my breath. "I'm so sorry," I said to the man as he bent down to help me retrieve the fruits. I did the same, trying my best to catch the ones around us before they could get too far away.

The girls also bent down to help me but then one rolled out into the street.

I spotted it, just as Carter bent down to pick it up. He rose to his feet, his gaze on the fruit and then on me. He began to walk over.

I held onto the back of Tracy's blouse. "I think I'm going to pass out."

"Breathe," she said, and had a smile ready for him when he finally reached us.

"Hello ladies," Carter greeted politely.

Anne's hand immediately shot out. "Hello yourself," she said as she lightly brushed her shiny blonde hair over her shoulders.

My eyes widened slightly at her performance, and even Tracy cocked her head.

Carter smiled at her, his smile almost blinding as he took the hand she offered. "I'm Carter Edwards," he said.

"I'm Anne Curtis. This is Tracy Steans and I'm sure you're already quite familiar with Leah Peters."

"Anne!" Tracy smacked her arm.

Not caring, Anne winked at him and flashed her prettiest smile, famous for trapping men in her wiles.

Carter, however, removed his gaze from her and settled it on me, hiding in the back.

"Excuse us," Tracy said.

When she turned, I was forced to let go of her blouse.

"Let's go, Delilah." Tracy turned to Anne and almost had to pull her away.

Soon it was just him and me.

I steeled myself enough to hold his gaze. "I'm sorry about that," I said.

He gave a slight shake of his head. "Not a problem."

"Just a second please," I said and turned around. "Sir?" I paid the shop owner for the fruit and when I turned back to Carter, I found his gaze on the apricot he had picked up.

"Can I have this one?" He asked.

I nodded. "Sure."

He backed away then, so I could walk out of the tiny row of the stall.

I turned to search for my friends and found them in the corner, watching us. "You didn't um... have to come say hello," I said with a nervous laugh. "Again, sorry about Anne." My eyes were on my feet, encased in flip flops. Oh, how I wished I had put in just a little more effort into how I looked before I left the hotel. I had thrown on one of the sun dresses that reached my ankles, tied my hair up into a messy bun, strung a rattan purse across my shoulder, and had on some chapstick. I had never felt more ordinary.

"How are you?" he asked.

I lifted my gaze to his. "I'm doing all right. Just enjoying the afternoon." I hated how flustered I felt, while he appeared so unaffected. It almost made me feel as though he were looking down at me, most probably wondering in the light of day what the hell he had been thinking last night.

I shook my head to snap out of the silly self degradation. I'd never been so condescending towards myself but Tracy had been completely right. The man standing here with me exuded magnetism, power, and beauty... I couldn't believe I'd been so intimate with him.

"I've been thinking about you," he said.

Now, everything beyond him in that moment ceased to exist. The chatter of the market... the traditional music playing in the distance, the smell of roasting street food and the zooming cars along the main road.

All I could see and hear was Carter... and the words coming out of his mouth. Everything else was an indecipherable hum.

He went on, "I thought I'd be able to wait till I saw you later this evening, but I'm close to losing my mind, and I need to concentrate. As you can see, I'm working."

I couldn't help the amused smile that spread across my face. "What?"

He took a step closer to me.

Now, I was greeted with the whiff of his cologne. I inhaled the delicious scent, and couldn't help taking a step towards him myself, closing the gap between us. We were standing as close together as two people could in a public street without being accused of lewdness... and I could see it in his eyes, just like I was certain he could see in mine, nothing and no one else mattered.

"Kiss me," he said, his eyes sparkling as he watched me. "I need that to hold me over until tonight."

I couldn't even hold back my laughter. "You're silly," I said, my hands shyly covering my mouth. "I thought that was just the booze talking last night."

He leaned towards me to whisper into my ear, "Leah, nothing about last night... had to do with the alcohol."

I staggered, and had to hold onto his arms to keep myself in check. The memories came back to me in vivid flashes, painful pangs of sexual awareness hitting me. I felt myself drip from between my thighs, as I lifted my hands to brush his windblown hair softly away from his face. "You're one sexy man, Carter."

"I'm glad you like what you see," he said.

"But I can't kiss you here. We have an audience."

"Fuck the audience," he stated firmly.

The steel in his voice pounded me into a pulp of smitten nothing. I didn't hold back. I slid my hand around his neck to steady myself, as I lifted up on the tips of my toes. My lips connected with his and drew in the first heady taste of him. I cocked my head to the side and kissed him hard, my tongue slipping into his mouth to give and receive just enough of what we both needed from the other.

Breathless now, I pulled away, because the entire world was our current audience. I couldn't even look at him. I turned around and almost ran for my life... from the sweetest embarrassment, from a flushed face, from a treacherously beating heart and from lips that seemed like they would be permanently curved into a smile.

My friends joined me along the way and we continued walking down the street.

"Wow!" Tracy exclaimed.

"That most definitely does not look like a one night stand connection to me," Anne added.

I didn't respond, but I had absolutely no complaints about what I was hearing. I needed time to process it all, but then my phone buzzed at the arrival of a message. I pulled it out and to my surprise, it was from Carter.

Anne was also peeking at my screen. "See you tonight?" She read aloud.

I turned a frown on her. "Hey!"

She stopped me. "Leah, we need to talk about this. Is this a budding relationship or just a fling, because I want him when you're done with him and I need to know when that would be? Before he leaves most preferably. When is he leaving again?"

I oscillated between shock and amusement, but I couldn't fault her for being so blunt. I turned to look at Tracy, who for once, didn't have anything to criticize her for.

"I understand her," she said. "If I didn't have 'what's his name,' I'd be lining up too."

My mouth fell open. "What's his name?"

"I'm joking," she said.

Without a word to either of them, I started to walk ahead.

Anne called out to me, "We're not joking, Leah. Well, I'm not. You need to throw him back in the ocean, so someone else can have a shot."

My heart lurched into my throat at her tone. I spun around to see if he was still in the vicinity and almost collapsed with relief when I saw he had disappeared. I gave Anne a sharp look and began to head back to the hotel.

THAT EVENING, I strolled into the Harbor restaurant that Carter had chosen, feeling exquisite.

Tracy's dress did indeed fit like a glove, the black silk material clinging to the dip in my waist and the curve of my hips. Held up by the tiniest halter strap, it stopped just below my knees. I'd decided to forego the sneakers as suggested and instead, wore my strappy, blocked heel sandals that were alluringly sexy, yet comfortable.

My shoulder length auburn curls softly framed my face, while Tracy had lent me her pair of vintage, pearl studs for my ear lobes.

I felt infinitely more presentable than I had when I ran into him earlier in the day, so I could barely contain my excitement at the promise the evening held.

The only problem... I was running about five minutes late. I thought to call him to apologize, but I didn't want to dampen our spirits for the evening so I hoped he would be able to brush it away when I arrived.

Set in a gorgeous, dim ambience, the Harbor's ceilings were adorned with weeping willows, its tables lit with candles. Soft jazz music played in the background while in the distance the sounds of the waves crashing against the coastal stones could be heard.

All of this was more than I'd expected from this little getaway trip.

I was shown to our reserved seat on the balcony to see it was empty.

"Something to drink while you wait for your other party miss?" The waiter asked.

I ordered all I was sure I could stomach at that moment. "A glass of water, please."

With a smile, he walked away.

I took my seat.

Our table was positioned at the edge of the restaurant, the only thing separating us from the sea, the pile of heavy rocks along the coast. It had an exquisite view of the town's hilly terrain, the ancient castle and boats sailing into the distance.

However, none of that breathtaking scenery could currently hold my attention.

The arranged meeting time had been 7 pm. It was now 7:15 pm, and he was nowhere to be found. Being a little late would be okay but he hadn't called or texted to update me on it.

I put my phone away, quite disappointed, but fought hard to maintain my enthusiasm for the night. So I settled in, watching the other patrons as they chatted and basked in the ambience of their own candle lit dinners.

I couldn't wait for mine to get started.

Twenty minutes passed by, and my stomach began to tighten with fury. He still hadn't arrived, and no text from him.

This time around, a waitress came by and I could almost see the pitying look on her face as she asked, "Ma'am would you like something else to drink while you wait?"

I felt like I'd been slapped in the face, but I knew she was just doing her job. "A glass of your Late Harvest will do," I said, determined to give Carter the chance to still show up late.

She walked away, and soon returned with the sweet white wine in a tall glass.

I took a very long sip, as I took note of how my throat constricted with the realization that he had somehow managed to make me completely let my guard down. Once again, I was reminded of the fickleness of the male species.

He truly was a specimen, but not the kind I'd come to believe.

My gaze was lost on the sea and its infinite darkness beyond, but the moment I felt the tears sting my nose. I picked up my phone and finally sent him a text. *'Where are you?'* I gave him ten more minutes to respond to me.

At the eight minute mark, I asked for my check.

When the ten minutes had elapsed, I pushed my chair out, the iron legs scraping angrily across the wooden floor.

I rose to my feet and exited the restaurant as gracefully as I could manage.

CHAPTER 7

CARTER

J'd lost track of time.

A call from my CFO at the head office had come in just before I'd been about to leave, and the time had flown by.

I'd rushed to the car then, but still remained too anxious to even step away from the call. After I got into the vehicle... it'd finally ended abruptly when my phone battery got drained. I was left staring at a blank screen. I looked around me and realized we were moving at a snail's pace through the east part of the town.

"It's rush hour sir," Makhmad said. "The road will clear in about thirty minutes."

I leaned into the back seat with a heavy sigh, my nerves shot. I didn't have thirty minutes, especially since there was no way to reach Leah, so she would know I was still on my way.

Plus, the crumbling acquisition back at the office of Media Hive... that fire needed to be put out, otherwise eight months of hard work would be flushed down the drain at the crucial moment of completion.

"*Fuck*," I cursed underneath my breath, turning to watch through the window at the cars that crawled past us.

Eventually, the delay eased up and Makhmad increased his speed.

I spotted her the moment I arrived at the restaurant.

She looked angelic… her hair billowing around her face at the mild evening breeze. She however, looked incredibly annoyed, her arms folded across her chest as she no doubt awaited transportation.

Makhmad parked the car at the entrance but just as I got out, a cab pulled up in front of her.

Her hand reached out to grab the door's handle, and her name rang from my lips. "Leah!" I called out, but the entrance was bursting with too much activity. People and cars alike were coming in and leaving, so getting her attention at such a distance was impossible.

So I ran.

"Leah!" I got to the taxi just before it pulled away, and pounded on the bright yellow sedan.

It screeched to a halt just as I came to her window, and it took me a few seconds to calm my breathing.

"Carter?" She called out, surprise in her gaze.

"I'm sorry. I had to handle an unexpected call and then my battery died… I couldn't get to you."

She watched me through the window for a moment, and I could see the hurt in her eyes. She was not in any way taking this lightly. My tone softened. "Leah, please put the window down?"

I saw the resolve hardened her gaze, and knew she had made her decision. Panic struck *me*... I didn't want to know what she'd decided. "Leah—?"

"I'm going to leave Carter," she said through the open window. "I think we've both gotten what we wanted from each other. There's no need dragging any of this any further and wasting both of our time."

"Leah!" I called out.

She rolled the window up, and the taxi pulled away from the curb.

For the longest time, I just stood there, watching the car as it drove off into the evening, blending in with the many cars on the main street.

I shook my head and returned to my car.

Perhaps she was right, but I hadn't approached her just to get a good fuck for a night. I'd felt a spark between us, and meeting her had set it ablaze.

Maybe it had been just a fluke and it was inconsequential. Perhaps she'd felt nothing... at least not like I had.

The moment I returned to my hotel, I charged my phone and continued with my call.

Mark picked up immediately, "What happened?" he asked. "He said you cut the call on him?"

"My battery ran out of juice and I didn't have a charger with me."

He sighed.

"So what's the conclusion?" I asked.

"He's pissed at everything and doesn't seem to remember that we weren't the reason why his agency is going under. He's asking for an increased offer."

"How much more?"

"Three hundred."

"Dollars?" I asked.

The older man on the other end of the line burst into laughter.

It had been a very tense and stressful period for the both of us, so the brief amusement was very welcome.

"Screw him," I said.

"They do have the Nestle account, and David Fogarty. Are we going to let those both go?"

I thought back to the beautiful girl that had refused to give me a chance, as she most probably had disappeared from my life forever. "Yeah," I replied. "Maybe it's not meant to be. If it is, he'll come back begging, preferably on his knees."

I ended the call and tried to soothe my annoyance away, at all the losses that life seemed to conclude I deserved on this day. I was consoled, however, because I knew I'd given it all my very best. Did Leah feel the same kind of peace? Or perhaps she didn't even care enough to be troubled?

Out of sight. Out of mind.

CHAPTER 8

LEAH

*W*hen I opened my eyes the next morning, I felt a sort of shock.

As though there had been a rift in my world, and my soul couldn't accept it yet. Not an unfamiliar feeling, as had always been the case when I made decisions that had a major influence on my life's path.

Last night, I would have been too proud to admit it, but in the light of a new day, the fact I had hoped and even begun to build Carter up as someone who would be a major influence in my life, was inescapable. This was the true source of this rift.

After the way he'd melted me with that kiss at the market, the dream, that perhaps we could come to mean something to each other had taken root. Then I had mercilessly dug it out, too scorned by previous experiences to tolerate any discrepancies.

Had I been too hasty? Had I not given him enough of a chance? I shook my head to dispel these concerns and got out of bed.

The girls were still asleep, so I went ahead and took a shower. When I was dressed I called out to Tracy to head down with me for breakfast.

Anne never ate early, so I left her to her slumber that had her splayed out like a starfish across the bed.

"Tracy it's almost eleven," I lied. "They'll pack up soon."

She dragged herself out of bed then, slipped on shorts, slid into flip flops, and we were on our way.

I was thankful when she didn't say anything to me, but her discreet gaze seemed to be constantly on. It did become irritating. "Stop it." I said just as the elevator dinged our arrival on the ground floor.

"You didn't tell me what happened last night," she said softly. "I didn't expect you to return, and so early for that matter. You just went right to sleep."

I didn't respond. We walked into the breakfast room and began to go through the servings of bacon, eggs, fruit and pastry. It reminded me of the one I'd had with him just the previous morning and for a moment I almost choked up. Anne had been right. I could get too emotionally detached, especially with the loving way he'd acted.

If I were ever to be with someone casually again, the rule would be set in place that no interactions or considerations whatsoever beyond the bedroom would be acceptable.

When we were finally settled and eating, I told her what happened. "He stood me up." I needed someone else to confirm that I had done the right thing, just so I could freaking move on, but after I was done explaining, she instead barraged me with silence, until I couldn't take it anymore. "Say something."

"Okay. He didn't stand you up Leah. He was late, and he tried to explain why."

I couldn't believe her. "So I was wrong?"

Tracy put her fork down and stared at me. "That doesn't matter. My question is why you cared so much that he was late? Isn't this just supposed to be a fling? Without strings? If there wasn't an emotional attachment, you wouldn't have felt so hurt and disrespected." She picked up her mug of coffee and took a sip.

I repeated my question, "So I was wrong?"

"What is wrong?" she asked. "And what would have been right? Maybe you dodged a bullet or—?"

"Or maybe I missed out on something that could have been great."

"*That...* right there," she said, "is the problem. You were already beginning to hope that it would be something more and at the first telltale signs that he perhaps didn't have the same expectation or dedication, you cut him off. Perhaps it was for the best. Did he ever explicitly express that he wanted more?"

"Not exactly."

"So, maybe this was for the best. Hasty or not you nipped this in the bud when it started to become dangerous. Even if you both were to meet again, now you realize why you acted the way you did. Decide from the beginning if you're going to try to pursue something more with him, and stick to it. But if it is to be as you claim… casual, then act appropriately."

I nodded, as this did seem to sum it all up, we finished our meal and headed back to the room.

Anne was already up and had a cup of coffee, as she too gave me a look of concern. Thankfully, she didn't say a word.

"We have two options for today," Tracy announced. "Standup paddling near the Alanya Castle and Red Tower, or a day trip to Sapadere Canyon."

Anne scowled at her. "I'm the travel agent that booked this trip. Why are you more aware of things to do here than I am?"

"Tracy, how far away is this canyon?" I would never admit it aloud to the girls but I wanted to get away… from my getaway. How truly ironic life could be.

"About forty-five minutes away from the town but it will be a whole day's tour. We will have lunch in the village, hike a bit to see the waterfalls, perhaps even take a swim, and visit the Smurfs Cave. Full day."

Indeed and it sounded like just what I needed. "I'm in."

We both turned to Anne.

She rolled her eyes at us. "The purpose of a vacation is to do nothing. It amazes me how you both simply cannot grasp this concept."

Tracy corrected her, "The purpose of a vacation is to explore, and do nothing. Not just will away the time sleeping. I'm going to call the tour center now, to see if they still have some spots for us. They should be starting at about 10:30. So that gives us thirty minutes to get ready. Which do you guys fancy? Jeep Safari or a calmer van tour?"

"It's pretty hot outside today, perhaps a jeep might be good," I replied.

Anne however, immediately protested, "Oh no, I'm not getting squished in a jeep with strangers."

"There's water fights between other jeeps as we ride along," Tracy added with a shrug.

I laughed at the horrified look on Anne's face.

She got out of bed then.

Attempting to stay cheerful, I headed over to my part of the closet to get ready.

AFTER THE SMALL TOUR, we set off to the Sapadere Village and settled down on picnic benches and tables for a well deserved lunch of chicken, rice and salad.

Thereafter, there were short stops at a mosque, a silk factory and watermill, and when the time arrived to visit the Smurfs Cave I didn't have the energy to even care about seeing its stalagmites and stalactites formations.

Afterward, I sat down with the others who were hungry as we waited for the Jeep and pulled my phone out of my pocket.

I saw a missed call from my mother, Layla, and a text asking how the trip was going, but nothing else... especially from him.

I hadn't even realized that I still nursed the hope that Carter would reach out, and the fact that he hadn't hurt more than I wanted to accept.

Anne came over to sit next to me and the only smile I could work up for her was tight. "Fuck him," she said.

The seconds ticked by and when she didn't say anymore, I realized then that those two words were just what I needed. My smile slowly progressed into a low rumbling laughter and I felt the creases in my soul begin to smoothen out. I crushed her into a hug, just as Tracy and the rest of the group returned.

In no time, we were on our way back to Alanya.

CHAPTER 9

CARTER

I could have sworn that I felt her presence before I saw her.

The restaurant was in the midst of a valley, surrounded by cliffs. And instead of tables, the parties of guests were seated in Turkish-style sitting pergolas located above the water. My party of business associates from Desa were almost halfway through our dinner, and were amongst the few pergolas that were somewhat distanced from the other rows that housed other guests.

My skin suddenly began to prickle with awareness. Now, what had just moments earlier been a relaxing outing, the stream of the river right below us and the gush of a small waterfall down the rocks of the mountain providing the most serene ambience, turned into an ordeal.

She strolled in from the entrance with her friends, moving along the narrow wooden walkway, suspended above the water. Her stride seemed to be graceful and unhurried. One of them laughed out in amusement-the blonde one, and held onto Leah's arm. Her response was a wide but quiet smile, that instantly sent my heart racing.

They were seated in one of the berths at the base just like us, quite a distance away, but I could sense her as clearly as though she were by my side.

Her curly hair was piled on top of her head, her blouse made of a very light flowery material that hung off her shoulders, revealing her glistening porcelain skin. I'd once traced my lips across that skin and now I wished I could somehow... do it once again.

I loved the way her curls softened her face, clean and flushed with life, almost giving her the appearance of a teenager. She looked so soft and delicate... I could almost taste her in my mouth once again.

I turned my gaze away, returning to my meal as I tried my best to rediscover the bearings of the conversation, but my attention had been completely seized by this woman I hadn't been able to get out of my mind over the last few days.

You're leaving tomorrow, I reminded myself. *Forget about her.*

For a little while, I listened to the conversation at our table but as though I was possessed, my gaze would shift across the river to settle on her.

She lifted her cocktail to her lips and spoke with her friends, then quietly looked away to take in the ambience of the environment. The pink and orange hues of the setting sun in the distance and the mountains we were surrounded by.

I knew then that I would be speaking to her.

I wouldn't be able to leave unless I did. I didn't know what I would say, but it couldn't be just a mere coincidence that she appeared here, out of all the places in town, and on my last night in the country.

I needed to look into her hazel eyes once more... to take in the seemingly endless depths and to feel the weight of her slender body against mine.

I needed to taste her lips, just one more time, even if it would be the last.

I drained my drink and bid my time.

LEAH

"This place is breathtaking," I said.

"It's like a water park," Anne nodded.

I smiled in agreement as I stared at a small water slide positioned in a corner and through it, those who weren't eating, slid down into the river and swam to their heart's content.

What fascinated me the most, however, was the several levels of pergolas arranged in rows, high on the side of the cliff.

"I told you guys it would be amazing," Tracy gloated.

"Amazing is a stretch," Anne countered. "It's noisy with all the chatter and rushing water... and those egrets on the—"

"You're the only one that would have a problem with egrets on the water." Tracy cut her off.

"Hey!" I scolded. "What is it with you both not getting along during these trips? You're inseparable at home."

"That's because she likes doing things at home," Tracy snapped.

"That's because it's real life, not a vacation," Anne shot back.

Tracy's tone rose. "You're meant to explore during vacations!"

Anne just baited her for the fun of it. "No, you're not."

"Are you serious right now?"

She wasn't, but Tracy was too worked up to see it.

I leaned back against the cushions our pergola was surrounded with and looked away to survey the scene a bit more as we waited for our food.

They kept at their banter, but my mind zoomed out as I watched the people surrounding us. The other pergolas were filled with families and friends, both the town's locals and quite a healthy number of tourists.

I'd been a bit skeptical when Anne had gotten us the deal for the trip, but now, despite the hiccups thus far, I was glad I came.

Until... I spotted him.

At first, I was certain that my eyes were playing some kind of trick on me. Maybe it was the setting sun and the dimly lit ambience. But I was wrong.

There... on the opposite end of the river, and in a pergola with a handful of people, was the man that had refused to get off my mind.

The day had been good. I'd already managed long hours without thinking about him per se, but the sex haunted me as though it was a crime I had committed.

The flashes and the brutal pangs that came with them—of him ramming into me with complete abandon. They'd left me breathless and parched, starved with the need for him.

Now, he was right here, and staring directly at me.

I'd expected him to have left the town... to have concluded his business and returned to Minnesota by now—yet here he was.

I returned my gaze to my friends, and the distinct sounds of their chatter began to register once more.

"We need to visit Pamukkale before we leave," Tracy said.

"Isn't that six hours away?" Anne asked.

"Yes, but it's worth it. We could make it a two day event, our trip within a trip."

"No, thank you," Anne said as she lifted her gigantic glass of Bay Breeze to her lips.

"It's literally the eighth wonder of the world!" Tracy exclaimed.

"That's not true."

"Leah!" Tracy called to me.

My body jumped at her call, my heart missing a beat.

"This place has travertine terraces and thermal pools," Tracy went on. "It's literally a cotton castle. We cannot leave without going there."

I had no clue what she was talking about and for a long time, I just stared blankly at her. All I could see and think of was the man seated with his party just a few feet away from us. This had to be the most goddamn fucking smallest place on earth.

"Leah?"

"What!" I snapped, so goddamn fucking wound up that I could barely breathe.

Her gaze softened then. "Are you okay?"

No, I wasn't... My chest was heaving. "I need some air. I'll be right back."

CARTER

I got out of the pergola the moment she did.

I knew I was pushing boundaries here, as she had explicitly told me she didn't want anything to do with me anymore, but I needed to meet her one more time, and nothing would stop me.

I followed her closely and watched as she asked for directions from one of the waiters holding a massive tray filled with food.

He pointed towards the cliff.

I could see he was directing her towards the enclosed restaurant there.

She thanked him and made her way towards it.

When I got in, I saw the large space, filled with a handful of guests, preferring to enjoy the scenic views of the valley from the safety of an actual built structure, rather than the exposed pergolas.

I looked around for her, but my cock was already stirring with anticipation. So I stopped for a moment, my hand against the wall as I tried to regulate my breathing.

This is not what this is about, I reminded myself. *You're just going to speak to her.*

But how could I forget the way she had tasted in my mouth, and how her pussy had milked my cock of more pleasure than I'd ever thought was possible. During those moments, the delusion that she was made for me had been much too easy to latch onto. So now, it was a notion I couldn't seem to let go of.

When I arrived at the women's bathroom, I stood waiting outside the door, and in no time, it was swung open.

She walked out, her hand brushing her curls out of her face, and she didn't see me.

"Leah," I called out.

She froze.

My heart kept pounding in my chest as I waited for her to turn around.

It took her a few seconds, but when she finally did look at me, many emotions seemed to flash across her face. "Hey," she said, politely.

I straightened and slipped my hands into the pockets of my slacks. "Can we talk?"

She stared at me, her gaze boring into mine and then she shook her head as if to clear it. "No," she said. "There's no need." With a smile, she turned around to leave.

My hand shot out and caught her slender arm.

"Carter!" Her tone was low, but sharp.

I ignored it. I was going to speak to her today, no matter the consequences. I pulled her with me into the bathroom and locked the door behind us.

"Hey!" She lashed out. "What the fuck do you think you're doing?"

"I'm leaving tomorrow," I said. "So, let's talk about what happened between us."

This seemed to calm her, but her chest still heaved, rising and falling heavily as it tried to catch up with her breathing. "What's there to talk about?" She asked. "We fucked and that was it. Isn't that how it's meant to go?" Her tone had gone cold.

It instantly seemed to make me want to show her otherwise. "Alright. So how about one for the road?"

I could see her steel facade crumble then, her eyes filling with moisture. "No, thank you," she said and marched to the door.

Again, my hand shot out, and held it shut just as hers closed around the handle.

"Carter," she said. "Don't turn this into a scene."

"Kiss me," I urged. "Kiss me and I'll let you go. What we had was casual wasn't it? So this shouldn't be too much of a problem." Without even realizing it, I had surrounded her. Her back was pressed against the door to get as far away from me as she could, while I towered over her, my hand holding the door in place above her head.

"I don't want to," she said, but her tone sounded completely breathless.

I searched her face, stared into the fiery depths of her eyes, and found the lie. If I were to touch her right now, she would completely melt, but my pride wouldn't allow me. She had pushed me away once... So this time around, she had to be the one to come to me.

And if she didn't, then so be it. I had my moment with her... and that would have to be enough. So I stepped away and lifted my hand from the door. "Ok," I said, my gaze on her lips then I raised it to meet her eyes.

LEAH

My hand was white-knuckled against the door's handle.

He'd stepped away but he was still too close, because at any moment now, I was going to lose my head and reach for him. I had to put an end to this, especially now that he was leaving. So I unlocked the door, and nearly ran from the bathroom.

When I returned to the pergola, the first thought in my brain was to leave with the girls, but as I settled back unto the cushions, I began to calm down.

I had done the right thing.

I'd been so close, especially after he'd said he was leaving, to throwing myself once again into his arms. But I managed to resist. I felt safe and strong, so I told the girls what had happened.

Tracy patted my arm in consolation, but Anne however, looked very unhappy with me.

"What are you so afraid of?" she asked.

Caught off-guard by the question, I shrugged. "Let's not talk about this anymore."

She pressed on. "Have you ever been in love, Leah?" She asked.

"Let's move on." I groaned.

"That's exactly what we're doing," she said. "This is not about Carter. Marcus and Gordon... those are the only two guys you've ever dated, and you were with them for about four years in total. They did everything right by the books, didn't they? They were attentive and kind and never showed up late... so why did it end? And why weren't you madly in love with either of them?"

"Anne let it go," Tracy warned.

She refused. "I'm not going to."

"Not everyone can be as emotionally detached as you, Anne," Tracy said.

Anne laughed out loud. She looked at the both of us with incredulity. "Do you think that's the problem here? Emotional detachment? She dated these guys for two years each and the day she broke up with them, she asked me the same question. *'Why don't I feel a thing?'* But let me tell you something… the day I broke up with David, whom I only dated for four months by the way, I thought I was going to die. I still haven't recovered from him and it was three years ago."

"Is that what you want to happen to her?" Tracy asked. "You want her to open her heart to him and then have it broken?"

"*Yes!*" She whisper-exclaimed. "I was hurt by David but if I had the chance to do it all over again, I would, with all of my heart. And I would gladly get hurt all over again, because during that time, I knew what it meant to truly be alive. To give yourself so completely to someone, to have your heart set on fire. To be fucking awake!" She turned to me. "What are you so fucking afraid of? I can see just how much this man affects you. What if there's something here? It doesn't have to be a lifetime, but what if with him, you'll get to experience the most amazing week of your life, or month, or even year? He's already given you the most amazing night, I'm sure. I have never seen you this floored by someone in all the years I've known you. And you've only known him a few days. Leah, be honest with me and yourself… has anyone ever fucked you the way he did?"

I couldn't respond, but her words were eating me up inside in a way I couldn't seem to dispute. "Anne," I stated with gritted teeth. "If you don't stop right now I'm going to leave."

"I'm almost done," she said. "So listen carefully. You should have kissed him in that bathroom, and if nothing else, it would have brought you some closure but yet again, you pushed him away. And now, you're always going to wonder about it." She nodded as if she were confident of her little speech. "What an amazing life of *what ifs* you're racking up thus far," she concluded. "Keep it up."

Just then, our food arrived and it all came to a close... our discussion and our light heartedness for the evening.

CHAPTER 10

*L*ater that night, I went to bed battling demons and by the next morning, I was ready to completely get rid of them.

"Let's go paragliding," I said to the girls at breakfast.

For a moment, they both stared at me like I had gone crazy.

Then Anne agreed with a shrug. "Sure."

Tracy's gaze shot towards her, eyes filled with horror. "Are you out of your mind? I'm not doing that!"

"Oh…" Anne's fork clattered dramatically to the plate. She leaned back against her chair. "So *now* you don't want to explore?"

"I'm not jumping off a mountain for no goddamn reason."

"But yet, you want me to stand on a damn flat board and paddle across the sea. What's the reason for that?"

My sigh was heavy. "You both need to calm down."

"Oh, I'm calm," Anne said. "Tracy, if you don't come paragliding with us, I'm not participating in anything else that you want to for the remainder of this trip."

THREE HOURS LATER, the three of us were riding up the mountain in a Safari jeep.

As we bumped along, towards the point where we would take-off, about a thousand meters above ground level, we all remained extremely quiet, deep into our thoughts and contemplating the adventure before us.

To Tracy, however, it seemed to be more of an ordeal. "I feel nauseous," she said.

"It's the car," Anne mocked her with a smile. "When you're thousands of feet above the air in nothing more than a balloon attached to some cables, you'll feel better. The air too will be fresher."

I smacked her across the knee, while Tracy gave her a deadly stare.

After we arrived, we received the needed instructions and met our pilots.

Then Tracy began to tremble. Her knees were knocking together so badly that I had to settle her down on the ground.

"I can't do this," she muttered over and over again, especially after we saw another patron jump off into the air.

"It's okay," I told her. "You don't have to. Anne and I—"

"Actually, none of us have to," Anne came out of nowhere. "I just wanted to torture Tracy and my goal has been achieved. So let's leave a big tip for these pilots for wasting their time, and go over to Cleopatra Beach. I have a lounge chair and a Mai Tai with my name on it, waiting for me." She took off her helmet.

Tracy jumped to her feet.

I couldn't leave. I needed to get rid of my demons. I didn't know how this paraglide would even help me do that, but for once, I wanted to jump, especially with the belief I felt I would feel completely free afterwards. "You guys can go ahead," I said. "I want to do this. Funny enough we'll be landing at Cleopatra Beach, so save a bed for me, and three Cosmos. I'm going to need it."

They both gazed at me, looking stunned by my decision.

Tracy stared at me with concern. "Leah—"

"It's fine," I said. "And it's safe. I'll have a great time and then I'll come tell you both about it." I turned around and walked away before either of them could change my mind.

In no time, I was strapped in with an instructor strapped to my back, so we could jump off the mountain. My heart kept pounding so hard in my chest I thought I might just pass out.

I shut my eyes the moment my legs lifted off solid ground, and all that came to mind was... Carter.

His almost boyish grin, but with that intensity raging in the depths of his glare.

Why am I doing this? I kept chanting to myself, until my instructor called out to me.

"Open your eyes," he urged. "It's incredibly beautiful right now."

It took me a little while longer to find the courage to, but I eventually did, and my breath was stolen from me in a whoosh.

In the distance, I could see the clear, blue waters of the Mediterranean Sea, then the lush undulating green treetops and fields of the landscape. The only alternative way to such a view would be through an airplane, but nothing could compare to being right in the midst of it. The gentle wind caressed my face, but I hadn't forgotten its inherent ability to plunge me straight to my death

The instructor pulled the strings to control the glider aircraft, so that we soared and sailed with the direction of the wind like a feather floating along in the breeze.

It all seemed too surreal to completely take in, but thankfully the driver gave me twenty minutes to enjoy this state of complete tranquility and freedom. From up here, everything else seemed so small and inconsequential... a perception that being in the midst of it all would never have allowed.

I had been so scared to do this, but then here I was, flying and feeling more at peace than I had in a long time.

Anne had been right... what was I afraid of?

The world was cruel, and so protecting yourself from hurt became necessary, but why did that have to mean never taking jumps that might be potentially fatal... never giving yourself the opportunity to soar, even if it would be just for a little while.

Tears rolled down from my eyes. "Could we land a little bit earlier?" I asked the pilot.

He granted my request.

Anne and Tracy were waiting for me on the beach.

But the moment I landed, I didn't take the time to speak to them. "I'll be right back," I said, and ran to the nearest taxi I could find. My heart was painfully full, with longing and regret. I needed to catch him before he disappeared out of my grasp forever.

He had never mentioned when his flight would be, so I was queasy with the fear that I was too late, that he had already flown out of the country. I tried calling his number multiple times but then it would ring to disconnection and he wouldn't pick up.

When I arrived at his hotel, I ran straight up to his room and pounded on the door. "Carter!" I called out. "Carter..."

No response.

With a sinking feeling in my stomach, my legs gave out and I melted down into a puddle on the floor. I thought of what to do, now beyond panic as the realization I had been too late set in.

I looked at my phone and at the unanswered calls. It wasn't too late. I was still able to reach him. So I peeled myself off the floor to head down to the reception. There, I would be able to confirm if he had checked out yet or not.

I hurried away from the door, but had barely gone a few steps when I heard his door click open. I scrambled to a halt, and then spun around to see him.

He stared at me with groggy sleepy looking eyes. "Leah?" he called, surprised.

Staring at him, my knees nearly gave out. "H-hey," I stuttered.

He didn't say a word, but it was impossible to miss the frown that dug into his forehead at the sight of me.

I placed my hand on the wall of the hallway for some stability, and forced my legs to move towards him. "I umm... I wanted to confirm if you had already left."

"My flight is tonight," he said and folded his strong arms across his chest.

I almost shuddered in relief. "Umm... well, I'm sorry for waking you. I just went paragliding and it was amazing."

He stared at me, his face emotionless, his eyes unblinking.

"H-have you ever been?" I asked. "Paragliding?"

His gaze moved then.

Only when it settled on my hands did I realize I had been wringing them mercilessly.

He returned his gaze to mine and released a heavy sigh. "Come in," he said and went into the room.

I hesitated for a moment and then followed, locking the door behind me.

"I only have a bit of orange juice left," he said as he retrieved a jug from the fridge and poured some into a glass. He came over to me, only dressed in a pair of dark briefs, and handed it over. His hair looked tousled in that unruly but boyish way that it got when he'd spent quite a while in bed, like he had with me. He sat on the edge of the bed, and watched me.

"Thanks for the juice," I said and took a long sip.

"Why are you here, Leah?" he asked.

I hadn't planned on finishing the juice but as the question came out, I kept drinking it to bide my time before I had to give a response. When I was done, I held the glass in my hand and hoped it wouldn't shatter. "I uh..." My voice shook. "I went paragliding."

"So you've said. And no, I've never been."

"It's uh... it's really scary. You jump off the mountain strapped to the balloon an... whatever happens, happens."

He gave me a ghost of a smile. "I'm sure it's safer than that."

"Well yeah... it is. I'm still here. It was amazing."

He watched me with those emerald eyes of his.

I knew it was time to say exactly what I wanted, but I didn't know how to form the words in my mouth. Somehow, I felt as though he could see right through me... like he understood me. "I need a little bit of help—to say what I want to."

He smiled, his gaze lowering briefly to the floor.

Suddenly, I felt a bit foolish.

"You don't advise me to go paragliding?" he asked. "Is that it?"

He was toying with me and although it stung, I knew I completely deserved it.

He rose to his feet. "Leah, I have a flight to get to soon. Please let me know why you're here."

"You know why," I accused him.

"Actually, I don't. You've pushed me away now, *twice.* So how do you expect me to be completely positive that I know why you're here?"

"I'm sorry. I-I took things too seriously. It's my fault."

"So now, you're here because you don't want to take things too seriously anymore?"

I exhaled deeply, fed up with the unmistakable notes of condescension. "Carter, are you still interested in me? Because if you are, I want us to spend some time together."

He glared at me. "I'm out of time."

"You told me that you could extend your time here. Can you still do that, for a few more days?"

"Why?"

He wanted me to spell it out, okay I would. "Because I want you," I told him. "And I don't think that either of us is done with each other."

"So this is a temporary thing then?" he asked.

"Sure," I replied. He could have it the way he wanted.

He moved towards me.

I retreated, until my back hit the wall.

He held my gaze, his eyes dipping occasionally to my lips.

I relished every second of this. The way he looked at me as though he wanted to devour me whole. But I still hadn't gotten his explicit response, so I waited, my stomach still tied up in knots.

"When is your flight out of here?" he asked.

"In about a week," I replied.

"Alright then," he said. "I'll extend my departure until then."

My chest nearly collapsed from the relief.

He started to move away but before he could go, I held onto his arm, my hands barely covering his bicep. God he was sexy, and I couldn't believe I'd been able to buy myself a little more time with him. "I'm sorry about earlier," I apologized. "I'll try my best to make it up to you."

"Miss Peters," he said. "You're going to have your work cut out for you, so don't make promises you can't keep."

"I'm ready," I said. "I can handle it."

He moved until his body was solidly pressed against mine, and I didn't even realize when the glass left my grip and fell to the carpeted floor. The tip of his nose stroked mine playfully, his warm breath tickling my face. "Kiss me," he said.

My heart somersaulted within my chest. I didn't hold back for even a second. I crushed my lips to his, and once again felt like I had entered into another dimension. A dimension where everything rational ceased to exist, and in its place was lust... wild, unrestrained lust that couldn't compare to anything else in the world. Our tongues stroked and dipped in each other's mouths, his hands seemingly everywhere on my body all at once, and then settling under my ass.

He cupped the soft mounds hard, lifting my legs clear off the ground and grinding me against his arousal.

We broke the kiss to come up for air but still I couldn't let go of him. His eyes were closed as he tried to get his breathing under control with me still held tightly in his arms. I loved the effect I seemed to have on him, but I didn't allow myself to think too deeply about it.

I ran my fingers through his hair, bringing some semblance of order to the unruly mass.

"How about an early dinner with me tonight?" He asked.

I didn't have to think twice. I nodded eagerly.

A full heart stopping grin spread across his face. "I need to take a shower first though." He lowered my body until my feet landed on the carpet.

"Can I join you?" I asked.

His pleasure at my very existence seemed to quadruple. "I can't believe that I didn't even have to ask." He lifted me again into his arms.

I squealed in high laughter, then my amusement turned into panic when he took me with him fully clothed into the stall. "No!" I yelled. "My clothes can't get wet. I have nothing else to wear." I saw the moment mischief flashed in his eyes. I immediately headed for the door but his hands banded around me as he lifted me away from it.

I couldn't contain my laughter as I struggled to release myself from him, but I also knew if I wasn't able to get free I was screwed.

"You can wear something of mine," he said. "I want to see you in my shirt and pants."

"Carter, no! We're going to a public place. I can't be looking like—" The shower came on just as he let go of me, and I ran from the stall with a scream.

Only a part of my head had gotten wet, and just a bit of my blouse but still, I glared at him with feigned annoyance.

He laughed, and leaned against the door to watch me as I reached for a towel. "You're going to get wet all over again. Just take your clothes off and come in.'

When I didn't respond, he slipped his briefs down along his hips.

My sulking immediately began to dissipate. I watched him, my mouth watering as the material was pulled away to reveal the dusting of hair across his groin and his intimidating cock.

Without even realizing it, I began to take my clothes off, eager to be with him.

With a smile, he shut the door and the faucet came on.

I pulled it open a few seconds later to see his back was to me with the water cascading down his glistening, flawless skin. I'd never in my life taken a shower with anyone else, even with previous boyfriends, so this was a very foreign but exciting territory to me.

It also seemed like quite an intimate thing to do, but I was ready for anything that would bring me closer to him. He pulled me inside to join him under the cascade and I shut my eyes as the warm water drenched my body along with his.

He trailed kisses down my neck and across my shoulder blades.

I couldn't contain the effect of his mouth on my body. The fiery rush of pleasure pulsing through my veins made me squirm, my knees losing all strength until I had to throw my hands around his shoulder to keep me upright. "Are we going to fuck or get cleaned up?" I asked, not seeing how both could happen at the same time.

He laughed, turned off the shower and showed me how. Retrieving the bottle of body wash from the holder, he lathered some of the liquid on his hands. Starting from my ass, he spread the liquid up my back and then brought his hands down my front to take my breasts in his slippery fingers.

I threw my head back then, oblivious to all else beyond the workings of his fingers as he molded the full mounds in his hands, his fingers stroking and teasing my hardened nipples.

His cock was fully erect against me, so I took advantage of his preoccupation, and slipped it between my legs. Holding the rock hard member in place, I ground my soaking wet sex against him, stroking the swollen bud of my arousal until I became breathless, the pleasure intensifying at a dangerous place.

"Carter," I breathed just as he took my mouth in his and I kissed him with every ounce of passion inside of me. I wanted to do something for him too, like lather shampoo all over his hair but at that point, I could barely remember my own name, so I focused on one thing at a time.

He on the other hand however, was out to torture me. He placed more soap on his hand with the pretense of cleaning me up, then turned the faucet back on but at a low frequency. The water washed lightly over us as his hands slipped between my legs and took the place of his cock. He gently massaged and stroked all of my most intimate places... by the time he was done, my limp body was leaning against his for support.

"Fuck me, Carter... we need a condom quickly," I pleaded unable to take any more... unable to wait any longer.

"One moment," he said as he exited the shower. In seconds, he was back, condom in hand. With a swift move, he lifted me clear off the tiled floor as my legs wrapped around his. I kissed him wildly... completely overwhelmed by his very presence, and by his expertise in bringing out a part of me that had absolutely no control or will against the onslaught of this excruciating pleasure.

He drove his sheathed cock into me. When he filled me, stretching me almost painfully thin, it felt like I had come home. Damn, had I missed this over the past few days... my sex pulsing at its absence and my heart almost sick at the thought of how I would never be this intimately joined with him again.

All that was now gone, at least for the following week, and I swore to myself that I would relish every moment of it.

He began to move inside of me and my head fell back in wonder.

"Fuck," he moaned, his hoarse beautiful voice ringing out in the enclosed space. "You have no idea how much I missed this... how fucking much I missed you."

I understood him, more than words could express. I held on tightly to him as his hips slammed into mine, over and over again, my back hitting the wall every time. But I didn't care.

I didn't have the capacity to care about anything beyond the torrent of ecstasy melting my bones into nothing. I cried out and thrashed against him, my teeth biting down on his shoulder in search of some semblance of control over myself, but in the end he completely owned me. "Fuck!" I screamed when I came, my orgasm wrung out of me with a raging molten rush.

He came almost immediately, then he swung me once again under the cascade of water. "Now we can get cleaned up." He grinned at me.

I couldn't help my smile against him. I felt drained to my soul and he felt equally as tired, because mere minutes later of a quick shampooing and wash, we were both out of the stall. I felt completely depleted, legs of jelly, barely able to stand on my own, so he carried me with him and placed me on the bed. He had barely wiped me dry when I found a towel to wrap my damp hair in.

I crawled underneath the covers and called out drowsily when he took too long to join me.

The moment he slid into bed with me, I rested my head on his chest and tangled the rest of my body with his.

I listened to the sound of his steady heartbeat as exhaustion completely overtook me and led me into the most peaceful rest of my existence.

CHAPTER 11

CARTER

*L*ater that evening, I watched as Leah tried on one of my dress shirts just for fun.

We'd slept long past the early dinner we had planned, and now the sun had long set, plunging the small seaside town into a cozy darkness that we were psyched to explore.

"Should we head back to the Harbor restaurant that we were meant to have dinner in the last time?" I asked. "It has a live band down at the beach, so we can head over when we're done, or just enjoy the ambience from our table."

"Sounds great," she said just as she finished buttoning the white dress shirt and turned around to present the fit to me.

Leah was a voluptuous woman, and I relished that about her but apart from the bulge of her breasts against the material, she was almost drowning in it. She was quite petite, so the length of the shirt went almost midway past her thighs. I burst into laughter from my perch on the edge of the bed where I had been putting on my shoes.

She threw some almonds at me from the plate of mixed nuts she had been munching on. Then she turned to the room's full length mirror to properly assess herself. "This could work," she said as she allowed one of the arms of the shirt to hang down her shoulder, slightly exposing the swell of her breast.

She had come to me in a pair of khaki shorts, so she tucked the front part of the shirt into it, slipped into her pair of strappy low heeled sandals, and turned to me with a beaming smile. "How do I look?" she asked .

I couldn't get past the lump in my throat at seeing her in my clothing. "Great," was all I was eventually able to manage as I rose to my feet. Telling her she had to be the most beautiful woman in the world to me, would no doubt send her running once again, and if I was being totally honest, it would probably also initiate my flight mode.

So far, I had been unbothered by the intensity of my attraction to her, convinced that I was in complete control. Then after I'd woken up for the second time since I had met her in bed with her. Just watching her, as she softly inhaled and exhaled, her beautiful, curly hair tousled around her—I had begun to suspect that maybe I was beginning to slip.

It couldn't happen. I couldn't fall for her because it was nowhere near the plan.

So just like she had propositioned, we would take this week solely as the gift given to us by the universe to enjoy each other until our time came to an end.

It sounded good enough to me.

A little while later, she was leaning against me in the elevator while I nuzzled her neck, inhaling her clean scent. She smelled just like me, having dabbed a bit of my cologne behind her ears, and I absolutely loved it.

All of the sudden, she sucked in her breath between her teeth, as she read the message she just received on her phone.

"What is it?" I asked.

She glanced up to find my gaze. "My friends have nowhere to be tonight, so I told them about the restaurant, and they want to go there too."

"That's perfectly fine. Why are you bothered about it?"

"Uh, you met them the last time right? They're not exactly reserved."

Yeah, they weren't but they had made me laugh. "I very much look forward to meeting them again, especially the blonde one. Somehow, I have a feeling she had a hand in you coming back to me."

Her eyes widened in shock before a wide smile spread across her lips. "Yeah that would be Anne. And you have no idea."

LEAH

I couldn't have been more relieved when we entered the Harbor restaurant.

Perhaps it was because I had barely eaten anything all day.

Carter paid more attention to me than he gave to his meal, which at first made me feel shy but I loved every second of it.

Midway through our meal, I received a message from Tracy and my heart lurched into my throat at the notification of their arrival.

I felt guilty because it seemed very likely that from here on out, my time with them would be very limited. I watched when they came in and were seated across the room from us, so I rose to my feet to briefly go over. "My friends just came in. I'll say a quick hello to them and be back."

"Why don't they join us?" he asked, and I felt a bit surprised by this. "Um, ok. I'll ask them."

"Only if it's okay with you." He nodded "I don't mind."

"Alright," I said, and went over.

Tracy smiled heartily at me as I approached.

Anne wore a look that was a mix between confusion and horror on her face. "What are you wearing?" she asked.

"Isn't it obvious?" Tracy quipped.

A few seconds later, Anne finally understood. "Ah, it's his shirt. Thank God! I thought you bought this."

"What's wrong with it?" I retorted. "It's just a simple white dress shirt."

"Honey, it's bigger than you are, but since it's his, now that's sexy as fuck. I approve. Where is he by the way?"

"My four 'o clock," I said and turned briefly to him so the girls could follow my gaze.

"Again," Anne said. "That is one fine man."

"I bet he's tastier than whatever we're about to eat right now," Tracy said.

I smacked her across the shoulder. "Behave you two."

"So what's happening between you two now?" Anne asked. "Any chance you're going to throw him back in the water for the rest of us before this vacation's over?"

"Not happening." I beamed. "He extended his vacation until the end of the week for me, so he's all mine until then."

"So I guess we won't be seeing much of you anymore?" Tracy asked, her tone slightly sad.

I felt bad about this. "Of course you will," I said. "I won't be with him *all* the time." I *hoped.*

"You're allowed to spend the nights with him but when I ask you to come explore with me during the day, you're not allowed to say no."

I gave her a solemn nod, "I'll do my best."

We all turned to glance at him and found him watching us. He raised his hand for a wave, and the girls returned one to him with smiles on their faces.

"God, he's so hot," Anne drooled. "Are you sure I can't even kiss him? This thing between you both is temporary right?"

"Anne, behave," Tracy scolded as she sighed in defeat.

I had nothing else to say, but then I remembered his request of them joining us at our table. I chose to forgo it, not wanting anything to interrupt our time together tonight, so I didn't bother informing them. Yes, maybe it was selfish of me, but this was about me enjoying him.

I soon returned to our table, the milk pudding I had ordered for desert awaiting me.

"They won't be joining us?" he asked.

"No," I replied. "Tonight, is just the both of us."

"I love the sound of that."

His voice had lowered to that deep sexy tone and my heart skipped several beats.

When we were done, he led me across the street to the beach. There, we indeed met a very small band playing, as well as a huge bonfire on the sand surrounded by people.

Carter led me to the snack bar and soon enough, we both had drinks in our hands.

He waited until I'd downed two full glasses of Cosmopolitans before asking me, "Would you like to dance with me?"

At first I hesitated, but then the alcohol had begun to kick in, especially from the bottle of wine that we had consumed during our dinner.

I gave my hand to him and he took it, leading me over to the back of the little crowd that surrounded the singers. He spun me around before pulling me into his arms, and I basked in the warmth and strength of his body.

His hands were around my waist as we moved our hips slightly to the tune of the music. I looked up to the star filled sky and then lost my gaze in the flames of the bonfire.

There had never been a moment as perfect as this, and it brought tears to my eyes that I couldn't just freeze it, or somehow bottle it up and take it with me wherever I went from now onwards. I turned towards the man, and as I stared into his green eyes, wondered why exactly I couldn't be with him beyond this trip.

He lowered his lips to mine, and gave me a soft, sensual kiss that tasted of him and of sweet, intoxicating wine.

I was heady from the man and the night, and my incredibly full heart.

CHAPTER 12

*I*t was a few days later, and the evening after we'd returned from the two day trip to Pamukkale with her friends, when it began.

She started to withdraw from me.

We had three more nights together, and I could see the reality of our impending separation was slowly beginning to set in. And it shook her.

Suddenly, she didn't fall as easily asleep in my arms anymore, and insisted more and more on going back to her hotel to spend the night with her friends.

I tried my best not to let it happen, because although I didn't want to admit it, I was apprehensive too. Like how would I feel if she didn't come back, especially since I didn't have any official hold on her to ensure that she would.

Tonight, I could see she was reaching her breaking point.

We'd just finished from a shower together. I watched her, as she stood in front of the mirror, brushing out her hair to be pulled into a bun, I could have sworn I saw her hand tremble. She met my gaze through my reflection in the mirror when she noticed me watching her, and sent me a smile. Dressed in her khaki shorts and one of my t-shirts, I knew on this night, I wouldn't be able to stop her.

"I'm going to stay with the girls tonight," she said. "We need to start making the needed preparations to leave, so I need to be there to put my things in order too.

As if on cue, a call came in for me, so I gave her a silent nod, and picked up the phone to speak to my CFO. My eyes followed her around the room as she put her things together.

Finally, she was ready, and softly called my name. *"I'm leaving,"* she mouthed to me.

My heart fell into my stomach. For the few moments after, I couldn't speak or even hear what Mark on the other end of the line was saying to me. My gaze took in her petite frame, committing all of her to memory... that was when I noticed her loosened shoe lace.

I dumped the phone on the bed and headed towards her.

She staggered backwards in surprise when I dropped down to one knee.

I held onto the back of her thighs to stabilize her. "Your shoelaces are untied," I said.

Her smile looked shaky. "Thank you," she replied.

I took my time, untying then re-tying the laces, and when I was done, lifted my gaze to see the tears gathering in her eyes. "Leah?" I whispered.

She blinked, as tears streamed down her face. She turned around to hide herself from me.

Too late to hide it now as a drop of her tears had already landed on my cheek. "Leah?" I rose, my hand held out but before I could grab a hold of her, she had pulled the door open and was out of the room.

I didn't go after her, needing the space myself to think, to work out my own emotions- the turmoil slowly brewing in my stomach. My phone began to ring again, and I felt grateful for the distraction. I picked it up from where I had flung it to on the bed, and saw it was Mark.

"Everything all right?" He asked. "You just abandoned the call."

I sat down on the bed. "I'm sorry," I apologized. "Where were we?"

"Birnley's coming around. He wants another meeting tomorrow."

"Okay. Handle it and let me know how it plays out."

"He wants the meeting with *you*," Mark insisted. "He's concerned about the fate of some of his employees after we buy the company, so he needs you to personally discuss these issues."

His request was out of the question. "I can't be there tomorrow, but I will be in two days."

"He's going to London the day after. His daughter just gave birth. I'm guessing this also has some influence on his sudden change of mind. We need to seal this deal before he backs out of it."

My head pounded at the sudden obligation. "I can't leave here until the 17th, Mark."

He went silent. "What's going on, Carter?" He asked. "The deal with Desa rounded up nearly a week ago, but you suddenly extended your stay. Are you coming back with a new nose or a wife?"

The new nose was a stretch but the new wife... hit too close to home.

I rose to my feet, running my fingers through my hair. "I have a great nose. There's nothing to change."

"I agree," he said. "You're also a good boss, and we need you here to make this a homerun. We need this win, Carter. Too many people have been involved in it and at the loss we had last week, it brought the morale of the entire team down. But now they're back to life. It'll add at least two million in business to the agency."

I understood the gravity and truth in what he was saying, but my heart felt the bigger threat at what it would mean for myself and Leah if things ended earlier than we'd both planned. Especially after I'd just seen how much it hurt her at the reality that we would soon be separated.

For me... I felt almost numb. I knew our separation would be difficult from the beginning, but I wasn't a stranger to goodbyes. I'd been well aware of how time had a magical ability to heal most wounds. So unless I was planning to keep her in my life for the long term, there was really no point in pushing this any further.

Perhaps separating now would be cleaner and easier, rather than in two days when we'd have to part ways at the airport.

"I'll get back to you," I told him, and ended the call.

CHAPTER 13

LEAH

I'd fucked up. I'd truly fucked up, and it was bringing me much too close to panic.

The moment Tracy opened the door for me I hurried in, almost breathless from my run to get to the room. "I fucked up," I told her.

Anne was already asleep on her bed.

Tracy's eyes also looked groggy from her slumber, but a quick rub with her fingers seemed to wake her fully. "What do you mean?"

I dropped my purse to the ground and covered my face with my hands. "I cried Tracy... I cried in front of him."

"Let's sit down..." she said.

I allowed her to lead me towards the bed. I sat down and swiped the tears from my face. "I'm so fucking dumb. Why did I do that? But I didn't mean to. I was just going to leave and then he dropped down to a knee to tie my shoe laces and it just melted me. *God...* I hate myself right now." I turned to look at her.

Her hands were clutching her chest in relief. "I was scared there for a minute... when you said he dropped down to one knee, I thought you were going to say that he proposed or something."

I groaned. "That didn't even cross my mind."

"So what exactly is on your mind?"

I inhaled and exhaled deeply. "I knew this was going to happen... I knew I was going to feel hurt when it all came to an end. I just need to keep myself in check until Saturday. Letting out my fucking emotions like tonight was just embarrassing for everyone."

Tracy's smile was sad, her hand gently running up and down my back to soothe me. "Do you really like him, Leah?" she asked.

It took me a long goddamn time to reply, but it wasn't because I didn't know the answer. Eventually I spoke and I was honest, "I do. I really do." Tears filled my eyes again and it made me angry. "What the fuck is wrong with me?"

"You really like him. That's nothing to be ashamed of."

I exhaled then, exhausted and battered by the tumult of emotions inside of me.

"Leah, why did you both decide to end things after this? If you both really like each other, then why not take things further? Connections like this don't come around very often. Why are you both letting go?"

I settled my gaze on her... this was the same question I'd been asking myself over and over, but I lacked the courage to voice it out loud to anyone, even myself. "We agreed on a week. That's all that we agreed we could have."

"Things change all the time." She shrugged.

"He lives in Minnesota, Tracy. I'm in Indiana. How is it going to work?"

"It's going to work if you both want it to work. How long is the flight from both states? It can't be more than two hours."

"It's an hour and fifteen minutes."

"You've done your research!" She beamed. "An hour and fifteen minutes every other weekend to spend time with someone that's special to you is a lot, but it's not that much if you really care about each other. Plus there are calls and texts... and come to think of it, even people that are married have to spend time apart sometimes." She snapped her fingers. "People in the military have the same dilemma too. You don't see them giving up."

I sighed. "I've thought of all of that, Tracy."

"So what's the problem?"

It felt almost embarrassing to admit, but I had to for my own sanity. "What if he doesn't feel the same way? What if it's just this week that he wanted?"

"Have you asked him?"

My throat closed up again. "How can I ask him that? This was supposed to be just a fling! He has never brought up any intention of wanting to take things further. Am I just going to allow myself to be slapped in the face by rejection?"

She went quiet for too long. "Will it hurt more than losing him forever, if you don't try? With you always having to ask yourself 'what if'?"

I turned to her with a frown. "What is it with you and Anne calling me out on my bullshit these days?"

"Because your pride keeps standing in your way, and it only exists because you really like him, so all you can think about is protecting yourself at all costs."

I sighed. "So, you're saying that I should ask him?"

"Yes…" Anne groaned out of nowhere.

The sound almost made me jump.

"You're awake?" Tracy asked, surprised.

"Well, it's hard to remain asleep with all the talking going on. She threw the duvet from her and sat up, her gaze settling lazily on me. "You're usually much more clear headed Leah, but now it's like we have to lead you by the hand every step of the way."

"She knows what to do," Tracy said. "She's just scared."

"Well…" Anne sighed. "What has fear ever done for anyone? You can't ever get something worth having that doesn't include being afraid. Feel the fear and do it anyway… and as cliche as that sounds, you know it's true."

"But why hasn't he fucking asked?" I complained.

"Maybe he's a moron?" Anne shrugged. "A very good looking moron, I admit." She grinned wickedly. "But we've spent time with the both of you and I've seen how he treats you. He definitely cares for you, maybe even as much as you do for him, but he probably doesn't realize it or want to admit it to himself. So one of you has to be humble enough to lay your pride down, or both of you are going to lose out on each other." She walked away and headed off to the bathroom.

"She's right," Tracy said. "And you still have until Saturday Why are you jumping to conclusions now? We're riding with him to the airport aren't we? Maybe he'll ask you then. It might be too early now."

I rested my forehead in my hand. "I'm just so fucking embarrassed that I cried in front of him."

"You're a girl," she said. "Allow yourself to be one."

"Ugh!" I griped and rose to my feet.

Anne came out of the bathroom. "Everything resolved?" She asked.

I was too wound up to respond. I went into the bathroom and sat on the toilet lid, my phone in my hand and my mind running in contemplation. Eventually I summoned up the strength to craft the text.

'I'm sorry about the tears. I just felt emotional about something going on back at home.'

I sent it before I could change my mind, and felt sick to my stomach. *Why did I just lie to him? Why didn't I just tell him how I felt?*

I sighed, and chose to be kind to myself. *Baby steps, Leah. On the last day, you'll be able to spit it out.*

The phone unexpectedly vibrated, and I looked down to see a response from him.

'*Back home? Is something wrong?*'

'*It'll all be fine*', I texted back. '*Not a big deal.*'

'Ok. But I need to talk to you.'

My heart lurched into my throat. '*Oh sure... I'll be in your room tomorrow morning before we have to head over to the castle.*'

'*It can't wait. Can I wait for you in your hotel's lobby? Or at the beach?*'

'*Let's meet at the beach,*' I replied.

'*Alright then. See you in ten minutes.*'

CHAPTER 14

CARTER

I waited for her, close to the snack bar.

It was just a little past midnight, so the people still at the beach had reduced significantly.

I felt nervous, more nervous than I should have been but I couldn't control the agitation humming through my veins. This had to be done either way, and could no longer be delayed.

"Carter!" she called, the light wind carrying her voice over to me.

I turned around to see her waving, and headed over to her.

She'd changed into a light sundress, with a cardigan thrown over her shoulders. "Hey," she said, her hair billowing in the wind.

I wanted so badly to reach out to brush it away from her face, but I had to keep my distance, especially now. "Hey," I said to her, a calm smile on my face. However, I couldn't hold myself back. I caught her arm and pulled her to me for a quick kiss on her temple, and just like that, my body stirred in response to her.

I knew that thus far, in my thirty-two years, there hadn't been a woman who'd captured my attention as strongly as she had. It truly made me wonder... what if? But I wasn't in the position right now in my life to take on such a responsibility, especially with a woman like Leah. Women like her came around maybe once in a lifetime and it was either you started up with them and went all the way, or you fucked up and had to live with the regret for the rest of your life. There could be no clean escape from a woman as fiery and passionate as she was, but I just didn't feel ready to dance to that kind of tune.

"What is it?" she asked with a smile.

Despite the smile, I could see the nervousness in her eyes. It brought to mind her tears earlier that evening, and it all made me feel a bit sick to my stomach. I decided to just get it over with. "Let's take a walk," I said.

We turned to stroll down the shore, side by side.

I couldn't help myself, so I slipped my hand into hers and held on tight. "Leah," I began, my heart pounding viciously within my chest. "Something has come up back in Minnesota. I'll have to leave earlier than I thought I would."

She didn't stop walking and neither did I, but for a few moments thereafter, there was only the sound of the waves as they crashed upon the rocks on the banks of the sea.

"That was sudden," she said as she turned to face me, her eyes completely unreadable. "When do you leave?"

"Tomorrow morning," I replied.

She immediately broke her gaze away from mine, and pulled her hand away.

I felt the loss like a painful jab.

"Alright," she said. "It was nice knowing you, Carter."

My breathing was labored and my chest tightened with a sudden pain. "It was great knowing you too, Leah. This week has been one of the best of my life."

She nodded and managed to lift her gaze up to mine, a smile on her lips.

I'd watched her break out into wild, unrestrained laughter before and knew this smile wasn't real. It didn't reach her eyes, and it made me so very sad. I pulled her into my arms for a hug and held her there... refusing to let go.

I would never know for how long we remained together in that spot, but I was forced to loosen my hold on her when I felt her begin to stir.

Leah turned away from me without a word, and went on her way.

I stood there in the middle of the beach and watched her as she headed over to the tunnel that connected the beach to her hotel.

She went into it and then she was gone.

I couldn't move.

I wondered again, just why I was letting her go? It had never been in my plan to have something permanent, at least not now, and there was a certain hesitation in me that I couldn't brush away. "It's not the right time," I told myself.

But would it ever be? The question came back to haunt me.

I didn't have a clue.

LEAH

"I should have kissed him."

The three of us were buckled in for the flight home, and up till this moment, I hadn't said a word about the parting, but this regret kept repeating in my mind, and it was close to driving me crazy. I hadn't even shed a single tear, yet these words refused to let go of me.

Tracy placed her hand atop mine.

Anne turned from her aisle seat to gaze softly at me. "Why didn't you?"

"Who fucking knows?" I muttered not wanting to think about him or anything else for that matter that had happened in Alanya from this moment henceforth.

The pilot announced our departure, and we began to taxi down the runaway. I wore my headphones, as I slept the whole way across continents and a seeming lifetime, back to Indianapolis.

The moment I arrived back home, Cheryl greeted me at the door.

My corgi had been dropped off earlier that morning by my neighbor, Camilla, after being fed and pampered over at her house for the time that I had been gone.

Her tail was wagging as she circled me in excitement, and my eyes misted at the sight of her. I placed my bags down, lowered to the floor and allowed her to jump into my arms. "You missed me?" I asked, as she showered my face with sloppy, dog kisses.

I felt life begin to come into my heart again.

"Yes you did." I laughed. "I missed you too, sweetheart."

I held the puppy in my arms and for the first time in two days, believed that I would be okay.

"It was just a week," I said aloud to myself as I petted her. "I'll be over him in no time."

CHAPTER 15

LEAH

One month later

"*L*eah, have you seen the new Vice President?" Jeremy, our team's Junior Illustrator asked.

The last thing I wanted right then was to pull my gaze away from the new project's proposal request I was reading through, especially as the meeting was about to start.

"Leah," he grumbled at my silence.

I turned a full smile ready for him. "I'm sorry," I apologized. "I just got this brief from Henry, and I have to get up to speed before the meeting starts. I don't know why he would send it so late to us."

"Marlow took a few days off," he answered, referring to our team head Henry's secretary. "And a bunch of people also got sick on the executive floor. They've been out of the office for days. Apparently, a flu bug is going around."

I lifted my head and gave him my full attention then. "What bug?"

"Norovirus-the flu. It started in the media and operations team. Mariah and Anthony are both going to be absent today too."

I turned to see that the Content Manager and Project Managers usually favored seats in the conference room were unoccupied. "Maybe it's only going around in their section." I shrugged and returned to my documents. "At least, I hope it is. I can't afford to get sick right now."

"My cubicle is in *their* section," he said dryly.

I turned an apologetic gaze to him.

"Well, you definitely won't be able to escape it." He shrugged. "I overheard Aarif asking Henry for a day off earlier today."

"That's Aarif. He never misses a chance to take a day off, so he might actually not be sick."

"Well, I should probably take a page from his book and call in sick tomorrow," he muttered just as the Chief Marketing Officer Bradley Miller and the acclaimed 'new guy' came in.

I had seen him around the building, in elevators and in passing but hadn't paid any attention whatsoever. "That's him right?" I leaned into Jeremy to whisper.

"Yes, that *is* him," he replied with appreciation in his voice.

I turned to him with a cocked head.

His gaze, however, was lost on the suited and sturdily built man with just a dusting of grey at his temples and along his beard. He looked like Joe Manganiello's twin, and was sinfully attractive. No wonder he had stirred quite the buzz throughout the company during the week.

"You interested?" I asked.

He scoffed in response. "If there wasn't the chance that I'd be sued for sexual harassment I would have made a move on him tonight."

I chuckled soundlessly under my breath. "Why tonight? What's happening?"

He turned to me in surprise. "What's been going on with you? You've been so out of it since you got back from your trip."

I didn't want to think at all about his comment, so I ignored him, but I still had one last question before we could no longer speak. I kept my eyes on the executives as they exchanged greetings and handshakes before settling down into their seats. "I'm guessing he brought this account along with him?"

"Earned him the prestigious position of Marketing VP. He's our boss's boss. Makes me want him even more."

I smacked him with my folder just as the meeting officially began.

CMO Miller rose to introduce our new highly esteemed VP Daniel Coghlan. He narrated his accolades.

VP Daniel then rose to his feet and the meeting began. Our task was to introduce the new energy drink into the market, Vita100, a new undertaking from the enterprise that only previously dealt with energy bars. Bottles of the 3 oz drink was passed around and we all took our first taste.

The VP presented the creative brief and established the scope of works. Henry Simmons was officially appointed as Creative Director for the project.

As a Junior Copywriter, I usually didn't bother much with which projects we were assigned per time, but given the competition we were up against like Red Bull and Monster, this seemed like quite the challenge and just what I needed to completely occupy my mind.

I kept my gaze on the VP as he spoke, surprised when more times than not, and despite the ten other people in the room, his gaze would linger on mine for too long. It made me uncomfortable, and built the doubts about having anything whatsoever to do with this account. Being seemingly noticed already at the start like this, was always a bad sign.

"Since this was a personal brief received, we currently have no other competitors but it doesn't mean that this account is secure," he said. "Deskia and Citizen group are also possible contenders so we need to hit this out of the park when we meet the client next Wednesday. That gives us less than a week to come up with a direction solid enough to convince them to hand this over to us."

He paused for a moment, his eyes roving across the room before surprise-surprise, finally settling on me.

It took a miracle not to roll my eyes.

"Miss Peters?" I presume.

I exhaled heavily. I managed a smile and nodded as respectfully as I could. "Yes sir, I'm Leah Peters.

"You made great contributions to the Cass Beer account in the first quarter of the year I've heard. Any ideas so far on the direction for this one?"

I glanced at my boss Henry.

His gaze was encouraging.

So I quickly browsed through my notes. "Red Bull's campaign in March was simple but effective. They targeted mainly students in college but they were also able to through that, increase their sales towards other age groups because most people could relate to having been students previously. So my thought process right now is to choose a very specific audience to focus on, and not just target this to the general populace. Uh... for now the message to be picked up from exhaustion or fatigue or just general life's discouragement is more heartwarming than the usual ones of bringing out the beast inside you or the fighter inside of you. This drink feels more like an embrace than the kick you need so... yeah. Sometimes, we don't want to fight just yet... we want to be picked up first. Red Bull gives you wings, this gives you a hug and picks you back up."

The room went silent.

I could almost feel the eye rolls as I usually expected in these damn meetings, whether I believed what I was saying made sense or not. My consolation over my four years in this career path so far, was that I paid attention and gave my honest thoughts. This was the best I could do.

"Great insight, Miss Peters," he said. "I'm glad to have you on this team." He took his seat then.

CMO Miller concluded the meeting, "Hope you all will be able to bond with our new VP here over drinks tonight, and get to work in time tomorrow to begin."

Light laughter trickled through the room.

"Have a great day," he said, and along with the other executives, filed out of the room.

Jeremy came to my side. "Great job and grandfather doesn't seem half-bad. Think I should make a move on him?"

I turned to him, confused again.

"Marketing VP," he explained. "He's our boss's boss. Makes him the grandfather."

I shook my head at him. "He's not gay."

"Obviously, but he might be bi. People are all sorts of confused these days, so I better take advantage of it, and take my shot."

"I'll be cheering you on," I told him. "Just don't get sued or fired."

"Well, you just have to keep me from having too many margaritas tonight, and I think I'll be able to keep my head on my shoulders."

THE OUTING WAS JUST as I imagined it would be, especially with a new boss around- stiff and tolerable at best. We headed off to a quite pricey bar downtown named Ball and Biscuit and luckily for me, they had food so my sudden craving for some spicy chicken wings briefly took me away

IONA ROSE

from the group. I headed off to a shadowed section of the bar and began to dig silently into my meal when I felt someone take a seat next to me.

For a second I thought it was *him*.

The aura of authority and the way he approached, was too familiar, while his scent of citrus and to cedar instantly pulled my heart into my throat.

It was however, my new boss.

I still almost choked on the food.

He intervened by ordering me a bottle of water.

"I'm sorry, sir," I apologized.

He gave me a disappointed look.

"Daniel," I corrected myself. When I had calmed down enough to meet his gaze, a guarded but kind face awaited me.

"You're quite the loner, Leah," he said. "You always seem to somehow extricate yourself from group gatherings."

I didn't know what to make of that observation, but deep down, I knew he was right. Ever since I'd returned from my trip, going on lunch break with the others was more of a hassle than just eating mine quietly in the break room. Over the past month especially, I'd now racked up a ready arsenal of excuses to get out of anything social.

I couldn't help it.

I wasn't the most outgoing person before the trip, but now since I'd returned from it with wounds that were taking much longer than I'd anticipated to heal, I needed the time apart.

Today however, I had a ready excuse that seemed to be true. Perhaps it was the gradual transition of the weather from summer into the gentle chill of autumn, but I was beginning to feel aches in my body. I sure hoped it had nothing to do with the flu Jeremy had mentioned earlier. "I'm not sure if that's accurate," I said lightly. "But today, I can't deny that it is the case. I feel a bit nauseous and I think maybe it has something to do with the virus that's going around the building."

"The flu? I've heard about that. Can I buy you another drink before you leave?"

"No sir- Daniel," I quickly corrected myself.

He rose up from his seat then and placed a hand on my shoulder.

It seemed somewhat innocent, but I could tell when someone was expressing some kind of interest in me that bordered on romance. And this did not seem so pure, or maybe he was just friendly?

Either way, I remained *very* still.

"You can leave early," he said. "Hope you get a good rest before tomorrow. There's a lot of work to be done on this proposal and I'll be expecting significant contributions from you."

"I'll do my best, and thank you."

He left me.

I watched as he went over to some members of our team who stood in the corner with drinks in their hands.

I immediately finished what I could of my meal, and was out of the door in no time.

CHAPTER 16

CARTER

"*Y*ou won't believe what just happened."

At the unexpected and somewhat unwelcome intrusion into my office, I looked up from the reports I had been reading.

My Chief Financial Officer, Mark Garrity was beaming, his hands hooked on the straps of his burgundy suspenders that somewhat constrained his slightly protruded belly.

"Surprise me," I said.

He took his seat opposite me. "As of ten minutes ago, David just bagged his first major account for the agency. It's not even been up to a month since we acquired Media Hive and the returns are already pouring in. I told you it was a great deal."

I shook my head and returned to my report.

"Wait, let me guess," he said. "Meredith already informed you."

"I found out twenty minutes ago," I said. "She has eyes and ears in David's department."

"Wow," he said, in a tone filled with disappointment and irritation. "That secretary of yours is quite aggravating."

His gripe made me smile. "What did she do wrong? She's aggravating because she's great at her job?"

"I'm great at my job too, but you don't see me overdoing things and stealing the wind out of everyone's sails."

"She's on top of everything that goes on around here." I shrugged. "I pay her heavily for that."

"Thankfully, she's on everything except you," he said. "Yet."

I cocked my head at the blunt comment from the older man, and met his gaze.

He nodded. "I see the way she looks at you and cares for you. She's like a tigress manning the cave and affairs of her cub. Never get involved with her. In fact, never get involved with any woman, especially now that we're scaling so rapidly. They'll make you soft... throw you off your game. Ruin everything."

"You're still not over Bethany, huh," I said, understanding the bitterness that stemmed from his experiences with his now ex-wife.

"Will I ever be? Can you believe I'm still paying her spousal support? It's been fifteen years. We were married for only seven. Curse her. Greatest mistake I ever made."

I smiled, my thoughts bringing up the memory of a certain pair of hazel eyes. I couldn't stop myself from asking, "If you had to do it all over again, would you still fall in love with her? Get married to her?"

He grunted then and looked away in contemplation. "I don't know," he answered honestly. "She was a mistake but the five years when things were good between us, were the best of my damn life. I don't think that anything will ever come close to topping that. Nevertheless, I'm still fucking bitter that I'm the one paying her bills. I also suspect that she's refused to get remarried because of my incoming checks. I wonder how much of it she'll want to save before she cuts me off from her life and decides to fully move on. And why the hell are we talking about Bethany?"

"You brought the subject up," I said. "You were warning me against women in the near future."

"Heed it. You'll save your money and your sanity."

He definitely wasn't going to like what I intended to ask him next then. "I need you to handle something for me," I said, just as he rose to his feet. "There's this marketing agency in Indianapolis."

"Okay..." he said, waiting for the other shoe to drop.

I picked up the file that I had concluded my analysis on and passed it over to him.

He took it and started to flip through it.

"Pivot Marketing. I want you to look into how we can have them on board."

He took a moment to properly process what I was asking as he read through their reports and assets. "You want to acquire them? Why? They're a small marketing agency and although they do seem to be doing fine, we don't need to have them as part of our portfolio. I thought you were more interested in digital marketing and technological advancement for our next purchase?"

I smiled at him. "I know that we don't need them, but it will be good to have them. And since they're small, we have just the right resources and reach that's well able to entice them enough to become a part of our company. That way, they can move up the ladder."

He took his seat again, shaking his head slightly to clear it "I'm confused. Why are you even thinking about this? We just concluded the deal on Media Hive, and if we want to bring another agency on board then my department has a list of five game changers that we could pursue right now. Why are we talking about a small marketing agency in Indianapolis? And so soon after our purchase. We can't scale too fast or we won't be able to milk these investments properly. We'll crash."

"Let's take this as a more personal investment then," I told him. "Whatever it'll cost, I'll personally finance fifty percent of it, and I'll be in direct control of it for a couple of months. I want to incorporate an advertising department into it to expand its scope of services. It'll do great."

He was even more baffled. "You'll be going to Indiana for a couple of months?"

I nodded. I had never seen him so disappointed, but in times like this, he chose to remember that I was his boss.

"We talked about New York, and London," he said quietly.

"I'm willing to be a little bit more patient."

"So it must be *this agency...* in Indiana."

I nodded. "It must."

He sighed. "This is about a woman isn't it? That's why you stayed behind an extra week in Alanya?"

I didn't respond.

He knew not to push it any further. He rose to his feet. "I'll get it done, *sir.*"

I knew he was in total disagreement with what I was doing. Before we had come together five years earlier to run this agency, he had been my boss for about eight years.

Since working together, we had remained sociable and respectful to each other, but whenever my instructions didn't sit well with him, the clear hierarchy between us resurfaced. It always felt like a slap in the face every time.

On his way out of the office, he stopped, and turned to look back at me. "Carter, aren't you worried that this is a big mistake?"

"I am," I replied. "But like you said, if it's one that I can still remember fondly enough in the years to come, no matter how things turn out, then I'll be grateful for it."

He shook his head dejectedly. "It's funny how you only ever pay attention to the worst things that come out of my mouth. Thanks for helping me to shoot myself in the foot once again."

I couldn't help my amusement as he exited the room, but it soon faded into the low hum of panic that was coursing through me.

I was the one who had just most probably shot myself in the foot, and it was more excruciating because I couldn't even tell right now if I had made a good decision or not.

And by the time I would be able to, it definitely would be too late to turn back.

The wound was going to fester, and it may end up costing me more than I wanted to part with.

I couldn't believe what I was doing, but the decision had nagged and tormented me for the last two weeks.

It was my norm now to be woken up in the middle of the night, my body drenched with sweat, and my mind haunted by the vivid memories of the girl I had told myself that I would so easily be able to forget.

In the month since I'd returned however, she had taken complete and total control of me, and it was driving me crazy.

I needed to be with her again… and the longing drowned out everything else in my life.

I understood exactly what Mark had meant by his warning, but still I couldn't stop myself from jumping, my only wish that my story would have a better ending than his.

That when I arrived over there, I would be welcomed with open arms, and that she wouldn't have already moved on to something or someone else that she was convinced served her better than I ever did, or ever would.

Yes, this was probably the biggest mistake I ever made in my life, but it was one… I hoped, would also be one of my very best.

CHAPTER 17

LEAH

I had just arrived back home when the call came in from Tracy.

I hadn't really seen either her or Anne more than a few of times since the return from our trip, so her call was a very welcome end to the day. I plopped down on my couch, Cheryl on my lap, as I settled in to speak with her.

"How was your day?" she asked.

"Tough," I replied and asked about hers, handling toddlers all day as a kindergarten teacher. Then I thought about my new boss-the grandfather, as Jeremy had named him. I briefly filled her in on this.

"You think he's interested?" she asked.

I shrugged my shoulders. "Who knows? His hand on my shoulder was quite unprofessional."

"Maybe he was just being extra friendly," she said.

I acceded to her conclusion.

Suddenly however, my stomach began to feel queasy, and it was soon followed by the threat of a vomiting episode. I tried my best to ignore it, to just continue on the phone with Tracy but then when it seemed as though my guts were about to spew out through my throat, I flung the phone aside and jumped up.

I ran to the bathroom, arriving just in time before the retching began.

I fell on my knees, and spewed the contents of my dinner into the bowl. By the time I was done, I sat back on the tile floor, completely drained of energy.

I was worried. Did this mean that I had also caught whatever was going around in the office?

I rose to my feet, and after rinsing out my mouth, stared at my reflection in the mirror. My eyes were sunken, and my complexion looked sickly pale. I most definitely could not get sick. We had a proposal request to prepare for in less than a week.

I heard my phone ringing again, and headed back to the living room. I put it to my ear and settled back down on the couch. "Tracy?" I asked but there was a pause on the other end for a moment.

"Oh, you've heard from her."

Anne's voice instantly registered. "Yeah, I just now spoke to her."

"Can you believe it?" she asked. "She's freaking engaged. I never thought that I'd actually see the day."

For a moment, it felt like I'd been hit in the head with a rock. Anne continued to gush on, but I stopped her. "What? Tracy's engaged?"

"Yeah, Jared proposed to her tonight. You just told me that you've spoken to her. "

"Well, I spoke to her but she didn't mention it."

Anne sighed heavily then. "I guess I wasn't meant to mention it either."

I sat up. "What's going on? Why would she hide it from me?"

"She wasn't hiding it, Leah. Anyway, I gotta go now, so call her. Is there any chance of you not mentioning that I was the one who slipped up and told you?"

"What's going on?" I snapped. "Why am I being tiptoed around?"

"Call her," she said, and ended the call.

A few seconds later, I was back on the phone with Tracy.

"Leah, are you okay?" she asked. "You ended the call so abrup—'"

"You're engaged?" I asked, still finding it difficult to believe.

Her pause was just long enough to confirm the intended secrecy.

"I don't understand," I said. "Why would you keep this from me? Am I not the first person you'd want to tell? It's such great fucking news!" I realized now they'd been like this since we'd returned from Turkey.

"Leah, I'm really sorry," she said. "I was going to come over personally tomorrow to—"

"This is because of Carter isn't it?"

"Leah—"

"Congratulations, Tracy," I said in a sour tone, and ended the call. I went to bed, but I was unable to fall asleep. I considered the possibility that I was the one to blame. Ever since our return, I had remained so withdrawn from them, but it hadn't been intentional. I just focused on work, expecting that things would fall back into place, and I would return to normal, but it wasn't the case.

I shut my eyes, the image of his face coming to mind once again.

It haunted me—those green, serene eyes. Ones, I wanted so badly to stare into again.

Every time I laid in bed, I thought of him... of the trail his kisses made on my body... and of the way he'd tasted when I kissed him. He took me to a place I wanted so desperately to revisit again. An enchanted space in my mind, a place which made me feel like I was filled to bursting with life, and excitement. But now, I just felt... impassive. I didn't see colors like I had back in Alanya, and the day in, day out in life just seemed to drag on in a black and white slowness.

I couldn't believe that just one week with him had done this to me. I just couldn't believe it.

Perhaps in life, certain people were sent to us... to awaken our souls, and he had done just that.

I wanted to call Tracy back, to apologize but I decided to do it in the morning.

She, however, beat me to it.

I was putting together a blueberry and yogurt smoothie for myself when the doorbell rang. This was an unusual occurrence, especially so early in the day.

She came in with a bag of seaweed rice rolls for me from my favorite Korean restaurant.

I fell into her arms with gratitude. "I'm sorry," I apologized.

She shook her head, tears filling her eyes. "I'm sorry I didn't call to tell you first. You were the first person that came to mind but I wanted to be careful about—"

"I understand. But you don't have to be careful anymore. I'm over him and everything that happened. I've just been feeling a little sick but I'll be better soon."

"You're sick?" she asked, looking concerned.

"I'm not sure," I said as I returned to the counter to put away the blueberries and yogurt. "I don't feel particularly feverish but I am extremely fatigued and I did throw up last night. That's why my call with you was cut off so abruptly. There's a bug going around in the office so I think I somehow caught it. I hate being sick."

"Why don't you stop by the hospital on your way back from work?"

"It's not that serious," I said. "I'll watch it for today and see how things go."

"Cheryl!" She suddenly called out, and lowered to the floor at the puppy's exit from my bedroom to meet her aunt. Tracy immediately lifted her into her arms, and tried to fight off a tongue bath. Eventually, she let her down and smiled at the corgi. "Cheryl's getting fat," she said as she headed over to the fridge. She grabbed a banana and turned to look at the dog wagging its tail at her.

"Yeah. I think Camilla overfed her when I was away."

"I don't think…" She lifted her gaze to mine. "Don't you think she's pregnant?"

For a moment, I felt a punch to my gut that made me want to reel. My hand immediately went to my mouth as I retched.

"Oh, my God. Leah, are you okay?"

It took a moment for the nausea to subside, so I waited, as the last thing I wanted was a visit to the toilet again before heading to work. I was already running late. The moment the wave of nausea passed, I straightened. "I'm fine," I said. "Damn virus. I have to go."

"Take a few damn days off," she called.

I grabbed my smoothie, and the lunch she had gotten me. "I can't," I said. "Lock the door on your way out and please fill up Cheryl's bowl."

"Can I have some of your chicken nuggets?" ahe called out.

I smiled, my response was loud and threatening. "No!"

I WAS CAUGHT with my head down on my desk.

My phone vibrated with a message just as I felt a small tap on my arm, and I lifted my head to see the Vice President staring down at me.

I almost fell out of the chair. "Oh my God, I'm so sorry," I said immediately, burning with embarrassment.

"It's okay," he said, his gaze filled with concern. "Are you all right?"

"I am..." I began to say but then realized I was missing a chance to salvage my being caught slacking off. "Um... I've just felt a bit nauseous."

"Maybe you've caught the bug like the others," he said. "My secretary had to take the day off today."

"I'll get checked out after work today to be sure that everything is fine."

"Ok. I just came from Henry's office. He said you're working on the copies for Vita?"

"I am, sir." My lips tightened at the error. "Daniel."

He smiled. "Alright then. I'll look forward to seeing what you come up with." He went on his way.

I collapsed back into my seat.

My phone buzzed with the arrival of another text message. It was an apology from our web developer and my cubicle neighbor- Sarah Pool.

'Sorry', she wrote. *'I tried to warn you.'*

I checked and saw that she had indeed called me just before he had arrived at my desk. And she had sent a text, 'Grandfather's heading your way.'

My brows shot up at the name. "Jeremy's already spread this title around?" I raised my head to catch her gaze.

"What title?" she asked. "Grandfather?"

"Yeah."

"Jeremy started it?" She looked confused.

"He did, in the conference room yesterday."

She laughed softly, her eyes on her screen. "Did you hear about the acquisition?"

I frowned as I brought my computer back to life. "What acquisition?"

"Everything's been kept so hush hush but I heard Henry on the phone with I think the CMO. We've been bought out."

At the information, I paused. "What? Why? By whom."

"We'll have to wait to find that out. Doesn't matter too much anyway. As long as I have my job and management doesn't become a pain, I could care less who owns the agency."

I returned to work, and once again felt quite out of balance. I had no idea what I expected to happen but my legs just did not seem to be on the ground. I decided I needed a day off. To take care of my heart and to reset. It was just Wednesday, and Friday seemed like a lifetime away at this point. Especially since there'd be work to do over the weekend in preparation for the client pitch on Wednesday.

I waited till the end of the day to report my intended absence for the next day, and it was approved.

On my way home, Tracy called me. "You didn't check my ring," she said.

For a moment, I didn't understand what she was talking about. And then it made sense. "Oh…" I smiled, as I turned the corner onto my street. "I'm sorry. It didn't even occur to me."

"It's okay," she said.

"Send me a picture."

"No need. I'm coming over tonight with Anne. That's why I'm calling. Take the day off tomorrow to take care of yourself, otherwise you're going to have to go to work drunk in the morning."

I was amused. "I already did."

"Yes!" She exclaimed. "We'll be over at 8."

I ended the call and looked forward to the night in with my girls.

CHAPTER 18

LEAH

our hours later, the wine was flowing, and popcorn was littered across my living room as we re-watched Sex and the City.

The series never failed to amuse and bond us, and was the only show that we could watch together without anyone grumbling out of boredom.

Today however, as I paid more attention to Carrie's woes with Big, I couldn't help but ask. "Is this true? That men choose to commit to the next woman they meet when their light comes on and not necessarily with anyone they deem special?"

"I don't think men are capable of deeming anyone special," Anne said, her voice completely devoid of feeling. "They're like dogs... from one bone to the next. No offense Tracy... I'm sure Jared is the exception."

I smacked her arm from my sprawled position on the couch, while she sat on the floor in front of me.

"I'm not offended," Tracy said. "Jared is an exception."

The room went quiet again, but I wasn't done with my questioning, "Is it that they can't commit to anyone special or we're labeled in their eyes... sorted out into categories. These I fuck... those I marry."

"More like those I fuck, this I marry." Anne griped again.

She continued to amuse me, as always.

"I don't think that's true," Tracy said. "They're human beings just like us."

"I doubt that," Anne quickly chipped in.

Tracy ignored her and went on, "They're human. So sometimes, they're not even expecting when that special person comes into their life. Especially, those that never even considered marriage to be in the cards for them. But then that special person comes and the pain of losing her suddenly becomes more excruciating than whatever torment they've believed marriage to be. I truly think it's more like there is this one woman I absolutely can't let go of, and then they get married because that's the only way to keep her."

Anne had a contemptuous look on her face. "Sometimes you're so sappy, I feel myself sweltering just for being in close proximity to you."

"That's your problem not mine. Leah, don't you agree with me?" Tracy asked.

I was no longer in the room. I thought of Carter as he had said his goodbye to me on the beach, and the blankness that had been in his gaze when he had done so. "Maybe I'm one of those that men just like to fuck," I said.

168

"Well, that makes two of us," Anne said, turning to clink her glass against my forehead. "And it's not a bad place to be."

Tracy ignored her. "That's not true."

I kept silent after that until another episode later when Anne rose up to go to the bathroom. Cheryl followed her. By the time they both returned Anne said, "The more I look at Cheryl." She settled back down on the rug. "The more I think that she does look pregnant. Tracy, you might be right."

"She's a corgi..." I groaned.

"Wow. Fat shaming much," Anne joked. "But still, her stomach looks swollen. Much bigger than usual."

I turned to study the puppy, who was now huddled on her bed in the corner, her eyes heavy with slumber. Their observations suddenly began to make sense to me. I hurried over and pulled her into my arms to inspect properly, and found that they were right. "Oh my God," I whispered. "How could this happen?"

"Doesn't your neighbor have a male dog?" Tracy asked. "They always hang out don't they?"

My mouth fell open.

Anne was doubly amused. "Cheryl you dirty girl. You fucked someone?"

Tracy burst out laughing.

Just then, my stomach suddenly lurched. I ran from the living room and straight into the bathroom to the alarm of everyone.

"Leah!" Anne called out.

I was already spewing my guts into the toilet. After I was done, I settled on the floor, unwilling to even peel myself off the tiles.

Both girls filed into the bathroom.

Anne stood by the door watching me, while Tracy came over to tie my hair on top of my head. "You need to see a doctor, Leah," she fussed. "Thank God, you took the day off tomorrow."

"I'll be fine," I said and lifted my gaze to Anne's, but for some reason I couldn't meet her eyes.

And then she asked, "Are you pregnant, Leah?

At that moment, it felt like my entire world stopped. And then anger suddenly surged inside of me. "Why the fuck would you say that?" I gave her a harsh look as Tracy helped me to rise.

Anne shrugged. "Well, you've thrown up twice in the last hour."

"She told you there's a bug going around in her office," Tracy countered.

"That doesn't mean that it has affected you," she said. "When was your last period?"

I didn't respond.

Tracy led me to the sink to rinse out my mouth, and afterwards we returned to the living room.

"Leah, when did you last have your period?" Anne asked again.

I gave her a hard look. "My boobs are swollen," I said. "It'll be here any day now. It's usually irregular."

"Your boobs also become swollen when you're pregnant."

"Anne, would you drop it?" Tracy snapped as she arranged a blanket over me on the couch.

"Why?" She refused to back down. "The earlier she finds out, then the faster she'll be able to deal with it."

"You're making her anxious."

"She should be anxious! Fine." She said and left the matter alone.

I however, had been rattled to my very core.

CHAPTER 19

CARTER

I strolled into the revolving doors of the building that housed Pivot Marketing, certain that on the outside, I looked calm and in total control.

But on the inside, my nerves were tied in knots and my chest had become severely constricted. All of this had absolutely nothing to do with this company that I had just acquired. The last time I had been this nervous, had been more than five years ago when I had gotten fired from my last job.

Today, I was going to find out if I had made a significant and potentially rewarding jump, or if I had made the biggest fool of myself.

What if she wants absolutely nothing to do with you? The question haunted me over and over again, along with the reminder that just calling her, rather than purchasing the company she worked for would have been just as significant a gesture.

But I didn't want to give her a chance to run away, so I was putting everything on the line to show her that if she did reject me, then there would be no do overs or second chances with us like there was back in Turkey.

I was immediately met in the reception by half a dozen men in suits.

I immediately recognized Bradley Miller, the current CMO of the company, and the orchestrator thus far of the entire purchase on behalf of the company's former owner.

Right from the beginning, he had seemed confused, and unable to understand why I was choosing to invest so much into the company, but when he saw how serious I was, he'd had no qualms handing it over to me to steer.

The team of executives introduced themselves to me then we were riding up to the three floors of the commercial high rise that the agency occupied. From the fourteenth to the eighteenth floors.

I was shown to the CEO's office, which had been prepared for me on the top floor, and our handover meeting began.

The meeting was attended by all the major executives and directors in the agency with the needed introductions and announcements made.

I was already very familiar with the workings of the company, its business history and operational culture on paper, but had never bothered to take the trip down to inspect it on ground before my purchase. This was what my CFO back in Minnesota could not understand.

So when we returned back to my office, the CMO immediately offered to bring all seventy-two employees together, so I could officially be introduced to them.

I had a different request. "I'll send out an official letter to the staff, and visit each of the departments and their heads today. Please tell them to ready the HR files of every employee in their department. Over the course of the coming days, I'll pick an appropriate time to invite them over for a light chat."

He seemed even more surprised by the request, but approved of it. "I'll get on that right now, sir," he said and exited the office.

LEAH

The next morning after both girls left, I took Cheryl to the vet.

A little while later, her doctor, Deepika came to me with the news. "Congratulations," she said.

I stared at my poor dog, completely lacking her usual energy, and laying quietly by the corner. Why had it taken me so long to notice it?

My mind went to the previous night and Anne's comment, and I began to shake.

We walked out of the clinic and on our way home, I stopped by the grocery store for some milk and berries. On my way to the counter, I passed by the pharmacy, and took a deep breath.

Cheryl looked up at me, and I sent her a shaky smile. "We've both been busy haven't we?" I said. "Should I check myself too?"

She looked away from me, so I took that as her response and started to walk away, but I could only take a few steps. I turned back around, picked up the test kit and drove away from the store with a hundred pound gorilla in my bag.

When I returned home, I ignored the bag and spent my time making Cheryl's little bed by the couch more comfortable. I changed the sheets of the cushions and even gave up one of my most comfortable blankets for her.

"Unlike you, I used protection," I said as I settled the blanket around her. "I was careful. Right?" I looked her in the eyes and she stared right back. My breath came in a heady strained rush. I rose to my feet, and returned to the couch with a tub of caramelized ice cream in hand for my day at home.

I continued re-watching Sex and the City, completely aware of where the episodes were heading towards. By the time I was halfway through the tub, the eighth episode of the second season came into play... where Carrie suspected she was pregnant.

Right then, the storm that had been slowly gathering inside of me began to brew. By the end of the episode, I rose to my feet, retrieved the bag and headed off to the bathroom.

"You were safe," I assured myself as I sat on the toilet bowl. "You used condoms and took your birth control pills- *religiously.*"

The words of assurance however didn't carry as much weight as I hoped for.

"Just get this over with," I told myself, and slipped the white stick underneath my urine stream.

I kept my eyes shut as I pulled it away.

The minutes ticked by... and I did all I could to gather the courage to look.

Eventually, I did.

I looked at the stick to see the line that it revealed... and my whole world stopped.

Half an hour later, I hadn't moved a single inch from the bathroom and my legs had long fallen asleep. I rose on the numb limbs, and almost crumbled to the floor in a different kind of pain. I was immobile for too long as I waited for the blood to rush back into my legs, and it filled my eyes with tears.

However, I didn't let them fall. I returned to the living room and called Tracy.

She went quiet too, just as I had and then asked a simple question, "Are you sure?"

"There were two blue lines," was my response.

"How about you go for another test, perhaps it was an error. These things break all the time. Plus, you were safe weren't you? You took your pills."

"I did and we used condoms," I said, but again, there was that twinge in my heart that suggested that maybe... just maybe I had gotten carried away and missed one or two or maybe the condom split. We had so much sex, that I honestly couldn't be sure.

Either way, I accepted her skepticism and held onto the sliver of hope that maybe, I had indeed purchased a broken stick.

I ended the call, grabbed my keys and was out of the house in no time.

By late afternoon, I had more than half of the departments' files and reports in my hand, and it was my intention to go through all of them but first I headed straight to those of the marketing teams.

From what I had found out so far, Leah was in the second marketing team.

A quick perusal later, and I had found her.

Leah Francine Peters.

At the top of the page was her photograph, and in it she was clearly a couple of years younger. The fullness present in her cheeks now were absent then, the challenges of getting her degree in marketing from Bloomington, and then subsequently joining the thorny path to find a job, no doubt taking their toll.

Regardless, she seemed happy. Her gaze looked a bit tired, but nothing about her could accommodate the phrase-*dull*.

I leaned back into my chair, my gaze lost on the woman I had made such a huge jump for. My head could still not find any logic in what I had embarked on, and so my nerves were taut with the fear that she would reject me. That what we had experienced with each other in the previous month was an inconsequential history that needed to be left where we had both promised ourselves we would leave it- in the past.

I couldn't wait anymore.

I needed to find out, if I could bring her onto the same page with me, otherwise I was going to lose it. Nothing else in the moment seemed more important, and until we were resolved... I wouldn't be able to do much else.

I got up from my desk, my armor of information in hand, and headed down the elevator two floors below.

She belonged to Henry Simmon's team, but he wasn't the one whom I'd be visiting first. The elevator dinged my arrival to the creative floor, and I took in the sprawling floor area of cubicles and secluded meeting rooms by the sides. Some of the senior staff I had met with earlier stopped to greet me while the others looked on curiously.

Some recognized me from the introductory message I had sent via the company's email server earlier that morning, on which my photograph had been attached. They rose to their feet in greeting.

Thankfully, I got through the area fast enough, aware of the layout of every part of the company. I quickly found my way to Devon Hane's office of Marketing Team 2. He was the youngest manager in the company at thirty-five, but I could tell as I walked in that the skepticism about me, who owned the company at just thirty-three, was a tune that I'd have sung behind my back until they decided that my skills were deserving of my achievements.

They were currently in the midst of developing a campaign to rebrand a home restoration company, whose account the company had been in charge of for about four years. I listened as he spoke to me about the current state of the account and the direction of their campaign, before eventually taking my leave.

Leah's boss, Henry Simmons was next in line, but as I headed down the corridor to his office, I glanced at her desk just by the copy room... empty.

It brought a frown to my face. Was she not at work today? Was there something wrong or was she just temporarily away from her desk?

Her boss received me into his office, a heavy set man that reminded me immensely of my CFO back in Minnesota-Mark.

His smiling eyes immediately set me at ease in his presence. My first question was simple, "Are all the members of your team present today?"

He paused at the question, no doubt expecting the more generic inquisition about the current account he was handling with the new Vice President. "No, sir," he replied, his eyes lifting to the ceiling to ponder. "Uh... two members are absent today. Our Project Manager Lisa Palm, and our Junior Copywriter, Leah Peters. They're usually very prompt and hardworking employees but there's been a stomach flu going around the office and these two were part of those affected by it. Miss Peters will return, I think tomorrow, and Miss Palm will be back to work on Monday."

"Alright," I said, a bit forlorn. How much longer did I truly have to wait to see her?

By the time I left his office, my resolve was to drop by her house after work that day. I wasn't sure if I'd allow myself to pay her a visit, to at least inform her beforehand of my presence at her workplace, but I wanted to at least see where she lived.

At a quarter past eight that evening, however, I was still in the midst of a two hour long strategy meeting with both the CMO and the new VP. My gaze lingered on the clock as I wondered what the best course of action would be.

I decided then to take it slow. Tomorrow would be good enough and by then, I would be ready to meet her.

My hands wrung with anticipation and nervous excitement. I was cooped up in my office but my mind would make the occasional visit to the woman that had sucked me off like no other ever had, and raked her nails down my back.

I could barely wait for tomorrow to arrive.

CHAPTER 20

LEAH

*T*he sun rose the next morning, and I laid in bed, feeling cheated.

For the first time in my life, I had strayed away from my usual norms. I followed my heart and life had dealt me a severe blow.

No matter how things turned out, except I somehow lost the man through no fault of my own- the consequence of creating a child that I didn't necessarily want or was ready to accept at this point in my life- was inescapable.

I had given myself to someone else so completely for the first time, and I was possibly going to come away from it all with pain and regret. I couldn't believe it.

I didn't want to move, but my alarm clock had long gone off and I knew that any more time wasted would send me to work late. A job that I most definitely now needed since overnight, my life and world now consisted of two instead of one.

I was scared enough to rise to my feet and head off to the bathroom. The moment I stood before the vanity, my toothbrush in my mouth, I stared at my reflection in the mirror. I looked dejected and distraught.

My eyes were swollen and bloodshot from the lack of sleep, and my face soaked from the tears I'd shed throughout the night.

I'd never imagined I would be a single mother. How my life would take such a sudden and drastic turn, and all on account of a man I would most likely never set my eyes on again.

My fingers found their way to my hair and gripped the curly mass in trepidation.

What am I going to do? I cried in my heart.

I knew despite being saddled with a responsibility that I most definitely wasn't ready for... I would have this baby.

Tears filled my eyes again, as I moved my toothbrush slowly across my teeth.

How I hated myself right now for being so unlucky... and how I hated him for being absent.

I wiped the tears from my face, finished brushing my teeth, and got into the shower.

As I drove to work, I promised myself there would be no further thought on this, not until the day ended and I returned home. This might be the only way I would be able to keep my sanity because with each passing moment, it felt like I was on the verge of losing it. I had an upcoming campaign and a team to perform in conjunction with. I couldn't afford to fall apart, especially not now.

The moment I arrived, I headed over to the breakroom in search of a cure for my sleeplessness. I loaded my mug with an unhealthy dose of caffeine and stood in the silence of the room, leaning against a corner with my phone in hand to discourage anyone from speaking to me. I needed this few minutes before the work day began to pull myself together.

It didn't work.

"Leah!"

I pretended not to hear Jeremy's overexcited call, but it was impossible to ignore.

"Leah!"

I turned to face him, a smile on my face as he walked towards me, and was a bit stunned by how unusually dressed up he looked. He wore a burgundy suit, complete with a tie and his usually wild, curly hair, cut short and slicked away from his face.

I was confused. "What's going on?"

He beamed at my observation. "I look good right?"

"Umm, why are you dressed so formally?"

"We have a new boss. In short, this is an entirely new company except we're keeping our name because we'll be part of the parent company's portfolio. Whose name I can't remember."

"What are you talking about?"

"The rumors were true." He tapped my arm. "We've been bought up. Didn't you check your work inbox? Not much has changed though but we do have a new boss. I already mentioned that right? God, I'm so nervous."

I drained my mug and headed over to the sink to rinse it. "Why are you nervous?"

"Oh, you weren't here yesterday. Remember what I said about wanting to jump the grandfather? I've changed my mind. My eyes are now on the godfather."

My headache doubled.

I didn't want to ask but I knew he would explain nonetheless, so I turned around and folded my hand across my chest with a deep sigh. Ready to listen. Perhaps his excitement would take away some of the current gloom from my life.

"The godfather is the new boss and Leah, I am telling you, I have never ever seen a man that handsome and forgive my Burmese, fuck-able, in my entire life.

My stomach turned. This was the exact same talk that had landed me in the trouble that I was currently in. Too bad Jeremy was forever free of any consequences, should he choose to indulge the way that I had. I watched his excitement with envy.

"And guess what?"

I couldn't even find the energy to chime along.

He went on regardless, "He is going to be calling one or some of us to an interview in his office."

I was immediately alarmed. "An interview?"

"Well, not exactly, like a little chit chat you know. To get to know the company a little better through our eyes."

I looked down at the creased pants and jacket I'd thrown on that morning, along with the flat underwhelming shoes. I wore no makeup on my face, my hair tied back carelessly, and my eyes looked bloodshot and swollen.

He noticed too, his nose instantly wrinkling. "You truly got sick yesterday. I thought you just took the day off like we talked about."

"Has it already been predetermined? The people that he's going to interview, or chit chat with whatever?"

"Nope." He shook his head. "He's just going to call anyone randomly."

Fuck, I cursed under my breath. Could life batter me any further? The clear indisputable answer was yes. Yes, it could and would. Its sole purpose seemed to be to completely destroy me and so far, it was forging ahead.

"Do you want to quickly head back home to change? Your house is just a half hour away right? You'll be a few minutes late but I can cover for you."

That was the last thing I wanted to do. "No," I groaned. "I'll just put on some lipstick and brush my hair."

"Button your jacket too," he said. "Those creases are a problem."

"*Fuck,*" I cursed again, and headed over to my desk but then on my way over, I thought of an idea. I looked to see that my boss Henry was already in, so I knocked on his door.

"Come in," he said.

185

I did while tucking curly fly aways behind my ears.

"Oh, Leah." He lifted his head for a brief glance, but then did a double take. "Are you all right?"

"Just a bit better from yesterday."

For a few seconds he didn't know what to say. "Uh, did you get a chance to come up with some copies for the campaign?"

"Still working on it, sir."

"Well, you need to speed up, the VP wants a progress report before lunch."

"Yes, sir," I replied.

Nodding, he returned to the documents on his desk. "Why did you come in to see me?"

"I uh…" I wrung my hands behind my back. "I heard that the new CEO might want to interview some of us today. I was wondering if I could somehow be omitted from the selection. I'm still quite ill from yesterday and certainly not at my best today."

He raised his head then to fully take in my appearance. "You do look quite unwell," he said. "But I have no say over that. HR sent all the files to him yesterday so as long as you're an employee and you're in the building, if he calls upon you then you have to go. He seems like a nice guy but I'm sure he didn't get to where he is now at his age by being flowery. Don't worry too much about it though. It's just a simple conversation. You'll be fine and I already mentioned your absence yesterday. You'll probably not even be the one called. There's seven other people he can choose from. Don't worry about it."

None of his words were assuring, but there was nothing either of us could do, so I thanked him and returned to my desk to begin my work for the day.

An hour before our lunch break, the intercom phone on my desk suddenly rang.

I nearly jumped out of my skin at the sudden shrill, my nerves shot to hell at a possible request for the interview. When I saw it was our Content Manager, Aarif's line, breathing became difficult. I picked up the phone with shaky hands.

"Meeting room four in five minutes. They've called a progress meeting for a half-hour before lunch in the VP's office. We need to collate what we have."

My head fell into my hands. Could the day seriously get any worse? Why today of all days did they need us making presentations and attending interviews on the executive floor? I barely ever had a reason to be there but on the absolutely worst day of my existence, I was to be paraded on it with my misery.

I felt cheated and attacked.

"Sure," I said and got my documents in order. The VP was especially on this campaign because it was his first and a personal brief. I understood his diligence but just couldn't accept it as reason enough for making the team's life miserable.

Twenty minutes later, the clouds hovering above my head brought down rain. I was on my way up with the Project Manager, Aarif, and Henry.

And I was the center of attention for my half-dead look, and rumpled clothes. I wanted to bury myself into the ground.

"Kudos for not taking the day off," Aarif said. "I know how you feel right now. I was you all through last week. I couldn't even attend the RFP meeting. Thankfully, I have you to save my ass."

Henry gave him a hard look and so did I, but I couldn't show my contempt for him outrightly since he was above me. I, however, allowed my mind to vent enough to say exactly what it wanted to. *Well, fuck you for not taking the initiative to let me remain at my desk.*

We arrived at the VP's office and were invited to sit in his little lounge area. Henry and the rest took their seats, while I stood by the corner.

"Sorry for the inconvenience, but I have a lunch meeting with the CEO in a few minutes and couldn't afford to come down," Daniel said, his gaze settling on all of us, one at a time. His gaze however lingered on me.

It was only then when I remembered my concerns about his possible attraction to me. The nausea swirling around in my stomach increased. I wanted to be anywhere in the world at this moment than right here. How had my world become so complicated?

Henry began the progress report, and I paid as much attention as I could so I could answer the marketing research questions as they were forwarded to me. Twenty minutes later, I was explaining the five most effective energy drink campaigns that had come up within the last year and how we had picked them apart so far, to carve out the unique approach we would take with the Vita500 brand, when there was a knock to his door.

I paused then, as we all turned towards the intrusion to watch as his secretary, a plump gorgeous Russian woman, come in with an announcement. "Sorry to interrupt you sir, but Mr. Edwards and Miller have arrived for your lunch meeting."

Daniel raised his wrist to check his watch in wonder. "It's already 1 pm? Damn it." He turned an apologetic gaze towards Henry. "We'll have to continue this after lunch. I can't keep the CEO and CMO waiting. I might lose my job."

The room laughed at his joke.

My heart skipped a bit at the mention of the CEO. He was outside. *Oh, dear God.*

"We'll wait for your call, sir," Henry said, and rose to his feet and so did the rest of our team.

I prayed that the VP would go out before us, so we wouldn't have to meet the company's top executives on our way out, on the day when I looked more like the janitor than anything. Henry immediately began to exit the office however, and tears burned my eyes.

All I needed was something or someone on my side, but it seemed more than ever that no one else could see me, and the fact that I was crumbling. And neither did they care enough to hide me just for one day. All that was on top of their minds was saving their heads and advancing forward. I felt so alone.

We strolled out of the office, but to my relief, Daniel called me back.

"Leah, just a moment please."

I turned to watch him as he grabbed his suit jacket from where it had been draped around his chair. The rest of my team filed out of his office and I was left alone with the Vice President.

He came over to me. "Are you okay?" he asked. "You don't seem well at all."

If only I could have a hundred dollars for the number of times I'd heard that today. It perhaps would have made up a severance package big enough to get me out of here. "I'm still under the weather but I'll be back to normal in no time. I apologize."

"For what?" He asked.

I didn't bother answering.

His concern just felt more exhausting than consoling, as it seemed quite disingenuous and more of a ploy to curry some kind favor.

"Let's walk," he said.

I followed him out of the office.

"How about taking the rest of the day off?"

"I can't, sir," I replied. "We have a presentation with you after lunch."

"I'll move that," he said. "You need to rest."

We stopped then, and for a moment, my gaze was completely zeroed in on him. What truly was his intention? Was this his usual treatment of employees or was this just how he was going to be treating me? "No, sir," I replied. The last thing I needed was to earn favors from anyone to further complicate my life.

It was then when I removed my gaze from him and sent a polite glance towards the two executives I could sense standing by us in his reception area.

The plan had been to nod politely, with my gaze to the ground and that was what I did, but then a pair of hauntingly familiar green eyes struck me with recognition

My head shot up in shock before I could walk away and I felt my heart come to a complete stop.

CHAPTER 21

CARTER

She looked miserable.

From the moment I had found out that her team was just beyond the door in Coghlan's office, the entire world, beyond the pounding of my heart as it scrambled for some semblance of balance, ceased to exist.

The CMO had continued speaking to me, but all I could offer him were polite smiles and gentle nods. Until the door was pulled open. Her team had walked out and I'd been almost relieved that she wasn't amongst them.

Meeting her again agitated me, because it would demand the verdict that she solely had the power to give. And judging from the past, I didn't expect her to do things as was needed. When it came to our relationship, she gave up easily and I didn't understand why. Perhaps it was due to some incident from her past. I wanted to find out. There were so many things about her I wanted to take my time in getting to know. So much so that I had uprooted my life and come all the way to her. If she didn't make the effort to at least meet me halfway, I didn't know if my pride would allow me to even take a step forward.

Right now however, as she stared at me with shock in her eyes, all I wanted was to go to her. To pull her into my arms and to demand why she looked the way that she did. She looked so fragile, so close to collapse and it tore at my soul.

I broke her gaze, and couldn't help the hostile one that I turned on the VP. "Why does she look like this?"

He looked unprepared by the question, but I didn't care. Not until I saw her move.

She nodded slightly to the three of us and instantly went on her way.

My lips parted to call her back but I came to my senses, and remembered where we were. She stood at one of the two elevators, waiting for the cars to arrive and as soon as one of them did, she jumped into it.

I could see her move to the control pad to quickly shut the door, but Coghlan called out to her. "Hold it, Leah," he said and the three of us embarked.

"I'll take the next one," she said.

Before she could walk out, I grabbed onto her arm. "No need," I said, and leaned over her to press the close button. The elevator slid shut, and we were on our way down.

"The restaurant we're taking you to sir, has the best sand-wiches in the entire metropolitan area," Miller said.

"I look forward to it," I replied, just as the elevator arrived on her floor.

She immediately stepped out of it.

And so did I. "Miss Peters, wait a moment," I called to her.

She was forced to come to a halt.

I didn't miss the venomous glance however brief, that she sent my way. "I'll be right down." I told the other men. "I have to reschedule the meeting I planned to have with her after lunch today. It'll only take a minute."

The elevator doors dinged shut, and I was left standing with her.

We weren't alone, however, the entire floor of cubicles and cabinets filled with employees, some of whom I was sure had noticed us, and had their eyes trained on our interaction.

I slipped my hands into my pocket to control the urge seemingly burning through my skin to reach out to touch her. I didn't realize just how intimately my body reacted to hers. I had to constantly catch myself from sliding my arm around her waist to guide her, and from brushing my hand down her slender arms. I wanted to brush away the tendrils of hair from her face, and once again take her lips with mine.

I had absolutely not been mistaken. This woman held a power over me that little else could contend with. "What's wrong?" I asked, trying my best to keep my voice down. "Why do you look so ill?"

She took a massive step away from me, her gaze quickly going towards our slowly growing audience across the floor.

"I'm doing fine, sir," she said, with the saddest smile I had ever seen. It broke my heart. "Have a great lunch, sir."

An arm's length was not severe enough to attribute to the distance she was currently putting between us. Physically, emotionally and mentally. It felt like an insurmountable concrete wall had been permanently erected between us and it nearly sent me into a mode of panic. "Take care of yourself," I told her, unable to keep the harshness out of my tone. I turned around and returned to the elevator.

I didn't look back until it arrived, and I turned around inside of it. I watched as she headed down the hallway back towards her cubicle.

"Run," I muttered under my breath. "Run all you want, but I will be seeing you again… soon."

LEAH

I headed straight to the bathroom in a daze.

I needed a minute to myself to process what had just happened, or even thirty seconds, but I knew I wouldn't be able to get it.

Jeremy came after me, and although I tried to increase my pace as quickly as I could without flat out running, his long legs, and shrill voice called out to me. "Leah! Leah!"

I turned around to face him.

He withdrew with a hiss of breath through his teeth.

His reaction crushed me even more and brought tears to my eyes. *Carter had seen me this way!* For the first time in more than a month, we were seeing each other again, and I looked like a homeless stray cat. I wanted to bury myself into the ground.

"You met the new CEO?" He asked excitedly. "How was he? Does this mean no one else from our team gets to meet him?"

"I didn't meet him," I replied. "I just ran into him on the way down from the VP's office. They're going to have lunch."

"Oh, alright then," he said. "He's super handsome right?"

My stomach lurched and my hand shot across my mouth to keep the vomit inside of me. I rushed to the bathroom, found the nearest stall, and spilled my guts into the toilet, multiple times.

"Leah, are you okay?" Jeremy's voice called from beyond the bathroom.

I didn't want to respond. I couldn't even respond.

When the last bout of nausea had passed, I collapsed to the floor and stared ahead at nothing.

My life didn't seem real anymore and for a moment, I started to suspect that perhaps I was in some sort of dream but I wasn't aware of it. They usually felt this real when you were in the midst of them right?

Maybe after that night when he had stood me up at the restaurant, and I returned to the hotel room to fall asleep… perhaps that was when this entire nightmare had begun. Maybe I was still stuck back in that time.

I spewed into the toilet again, and it seemed as though the last of my energy was also discharged along with it.

Please let me return to that time, I pleaded, tears rolling down my eyes. *What the fuck was he doing here? How and why was he the fucking CEO?*

It was an acquisition, not a merger. Did that mean the company had handled the transaction and then sent him here to take control?

But how could it be exactly this same company that I was in? Was it a coincidence, or had he actually...

My mouth fell open. I couldn't believe it.

Had he followed me here?

Suddenly, there was a knock on the door, and it made me jump.

"Leah?"

"What?" I growled in response.

Silence.

"It's Sarah," my cubicle neighbor said. "Jeremy says that you're throwing up?"

I wiped the vomit off the side of my lips, and fought to rise to my feet. My grip weakened on the toilet seat and I almost fell back to the ground. I managed to catch myself in time, and pulled the door open with a ready smile.

"I'm fine," I told her as I immediately hurried over to the sink. In no time, I had the faucet running and my hands covered in soap. After making sure they were clean, I splashed water on my face, and gargled some in my mouth before straightening to face her.

"Here," she said as she watched me, pity in her eyes.

"Thank you," I said and took the paper towels from her.

"You need to go home, or to a hospital," she said. "I'll speak to Henry."

I wasn't going to even spend a second arguing. I needed to be out of here before *he* returned from lunch. I was definitely not ready-either physically or mentally-to face him.

I followed her out of the bathroom to meet Jeremy waiting by the door for me. "Don't make a scene, I'm fine," I said at the worried look on his face.

"I'll take you home," he offered.

I shook my head. "I'm fine. Go back to work."

"It's lunch time." He gave me a weak smile

I nodded with a smile. I walked away from him to the Human Resources desk and got my needed slip to leave.

A few minutes later, I was in my car and headed back home. When I arrived, I was barely able to stand but the sudden craving for some yogurt hit me. Luckily, I had some in the fridge so I poured some into a mug, and collapsed on my sofa.

For the longest time I couldn't move, and thought to call one of the girls, but it was just early in the afternoon and the both of them would still be at work.

My only other option was to sleep the time away because I didn't want to process anything. I was just about to head over to my bedroom however, when the doorbell rang.

I froze in place.

I knew exactly who it was. Again, it was the middle of the day and no one would expect me to be at home except the one person who would be able to find out that I was.

I looked towards my bedroom door, thinking that perhaps I should escape into it, and pretend I wasn't home, but my car was right at the base of the building. However, he didn't know what my car looked like right?

The doorbell rang again, and it felt like my head might just explode.

Then Carter called out to me, "Leah."

I didn't respond. I wanted to, but my mouth wouldn't move. It was too soon. If it was just me, I would have headed over to the door to pull it open but I had more than myself to think of now. I couldn't head into the storm that was Carter Edwards without being prepared, and right now, I had run out of the strength at least for the day, to handle him. So as quietly as I could, I tiptoed into my bedroom, and shut the door quietly behind me.

CHAPTER 22

LEAH

*T*he next day, I went to work, prepared.

My outfit of a navy blue pant suit came straight from the dry cleaners and had received some additional ironing from me.

My hair was in a fancy chignon, that I had only ever been able to pull off at two other times in my lifetime, and my makeup although simple, was rosy and adequate enough to show I was back from the dead.

There wasn't any doubt that I would meet him today, and when I did, I intended to be in the best possible state I could be in.

I had no clue how our conversation would go, but I did know the only question I had for him.

What was he doing here?

Later that morning however, I watched as Jeremy was called from his cubicle across from mine, and requested to go up to the executive floor.

He stared at me, now back to his usual casual attire of dark jeans and a dress shirt, his eyes widening with horror and disappointment. *"I'm not ready,"* he mouthed to me.

Neither was I, for whatever was happening right now. Why was I being passed over to head over to his office? We had *history!* It was the perfect opportunity for us to meet in private… to discuss what the situation was without drawing any attention whatsoever to ourselves. However, he had chosen instead to call Jeremy, and I was perplexed.

About half an hour later, he returned and I tried my best not to run over to him to ask what had happened. I focused on the market research I was doing on Red Bull, and soon enough the text came to my phone.

"Break room now!"

Jeremy didn't have to text me twice.

I found him compulsively chugging down a bottle of juice from the refrigerator. I

leaned against the counter to watch him, somewhat amused. "How was it?" I asked.

He blew his hand in front of his face. "Hot."

"What?" I laughed. "Hot?"

"Not me, him. His eyes are like emerald *green*. Not the subtle, barely there green, but the entrancing, *I am going to steal your soul* kind of green. I almost passed out."

I knew the feeling and for a moment, I sympathized with him. "What did he say?"

He sighed. "He asked me about my satisfaction with the company, and my growth thus far but…" He came closer to me. "I think I said too much. I got nervous and just started rambling. You know what I think, he was the one that did that to me. As I rambled on, he would pick out the things I said and then ask about it, and of course I didn't want to get fired, so I just kept talking."

"Um… I think that's just him being a good listener."

"He is," he said and emptied the plastic bottle. "He really is."

I wanted to hear more. "So what did you tell him?"

"Basically? That the agency is shit."

My eyes widened slightly.

"Well, not in those exact terms. When he asked about growth I just mentioned how it would be nice for us to be able to learn from the other teams, and perhaps be rotated a bit more for projects, rather than being in the same team and working with the same people for too long. For instance, McCarthy is one of the greatest illustrators I've personally ever known, but guess who still hasn't had the chance to work with him in the two years I've been here? Basically, I advocated for a more lax management, and it's either going to get me fired, or have all the executives frustrate me enough to quit on my own for being too talkative."

"Oh, come on," I said. "What you said wasn't that bad, plus a serious review of the entire system is exactly what we need. I basically do Aarif's job and he gets paid more than I do, simply because of his damn title." I patted him on the back, somewhat disappointed and not exactly sure why. "You'll be fine."

"I thought he'd call you," he said.

"I thought so too."

"And you look stunning today. What a contrast from yesterday."

"Thank you," I said, and joined him as we began to head back to our seats.

"I still think I may have a shot with him," he said. "He was especially attentive to me."

"Sweetie, that's his job," I said smartly.

He gave me a sour look.

~

MORE THAN A WEEK PASSED BY, and our new, highly esteemed CEO did not seek me out.

I barely even saw him, his occasional visits and meetings on our floor, brief and scrupulous, and then his return to his throne, immediate.

It was like I didn't exist, and that was especially difficult to accept, given that his child was growing inside of me. I didn't even have his phone number any longer, every trace of him deleted from my phone and computer in my desperate attempt to move on with my life after Alanya.

Now he was back here again, and everything seemed to be tilted on its axis. I didn't know how much longer I would be able to remain patient.

Anne tried to drive some sense into me when she texted, '*Are you going to wait until you're already showing before you speak to him, or have you decided to get rid of the baby? You're already five weeks in.'*

'She's right Leah,' Tracy texted into our group chat. *'You both can't keep ignoring each other any longer.'*

I put my phone down and despite my trembling hands, I forced myself to get back to work.

Soon, I received the alert that Jeremy could never resist sending whenever Carter was on our floor. *'He's here.'*

I never dared look, for the fear that somehow our gazes would meet. So I waited until he got into the meeting room with some of the executives, before summoning up the courage to take a look through the corner of my cubicle into the glassed meeting room. He was seated at the head of the long table, leaning backwards, with one elbow rested on the arm of the swivel chair.

I'd noticed so far that he dressed most often in a two piece set, the matching waistcoat and pants molded and fitted to his body like a spell. I tried not to think of the parts of him I had seen and tasted, but given that I'd never thought I would see him again in this lifetime, this was a treat I couldn't deny myself.

Until today.

He suddenly turned, and caught my gaze.

I turned away, my jittery motion over turning my mug of lukewarm coffee. "Shit!" I rose to my feet, beyond embarrassed. I quickly moved my papers and documents out of the way, and hurried towards the bathroom to grab some paper towels. By the time I returned, I stole another glance at the conference room, and saw that he and his party had vacated it.

Once again, I felt hurt and couldn't understand why I was letting this go on when I could just talk to him. Perhaps he had even come all the way here for me. But even if his being here was all a fat coincidence, none of it mattered because until I apologized for shunning him, I doubted that any peace would come to the both of us.

"There's good news!" Juhyeon, the Creative Director for marketing team three suddenly announced, "Tsuki's campaign, the limited edition eyewear we handled last month, launched three days ago and every single piece has been sold out."

A round of applause erupted across the floor for those who cared, but when she went further on to announce that there would be a little celebration in the event room on the floor below, the applauses tripled in size.

"That's more like it, you hungry bastards," she said, and the floor erupted into laughter.

Suddenly, our manager Henry, came out of his office. "Marketing team two, you're forbidden to attend this gathering. Your account is still a fucking, bloody mess."

The groans were deafening, and it made me look around to see if we had suddenly gotten more members than I was aware of. I realized then, that other employees were also grumbling on our behalf.

"Just for tonight, boss," Aarif called out.

Henry was already heading back to his office.

"Just for tonight, Henry," Juhyeon pleaded. "There's pizza, and tacos, and a barrel of red wine."

The floor erupted into excitement again, but Henry slammed his door shut behind him to the amusement of many. Soon, the chatter died down, and we got back to work.

Later that evening, at just after 7:30, I headed down to the floor with Jeremy and found it nearly half filled with the employees. There was laughter and clusters of teams acquainted with each other hanging out. And, of course, the expansive table of food by the corner. I immediately went over to it, and grabbed a plate of pepperoni pizza for myself, and Jeremy but then he came over and handed me a plastic red cup of wine. I accepted it, not wanting to draw any attention to the new restrictions in my beverage consumption, but then placed it aside as we faced the crowd and ate our pizza.

We talked about some of the staff we had never met before, and then Jeremy grabbed onto my arm. "He's here!"

My heart lurched into my throat too, but I felt sure I wasn't as obvious about it as he was. "You're hurting me," I told him as his grip tightened around my fragile wrist.

"I'm sorry," he said, and turned around to put his clothes in order.

I watched Carter as he strolled in with the CMO and our VP, and felt the air thicken with a sweet tension. I had learned that he actually wasn't an employee of our now parent agency in Minnesota, like he had led me to believe back in Alanya. Instead, he actually owned the company and had been building it for the last five years, along with his former boss from his previous company. He'd gotten fired due to some backlash from a risky campaign, and his boss had left with him at the unfairness of the decision.

He'd left with his head high, and two years later, he'd launched his own agency with the guidance of his former boss.

And now here he was, wildly successful and decorated with accolades. He had never seemed more attractive to me.

Here, I was allowed to out rightly watch him, because every other staff, especially the women also had their eyes on him. I even watched as some of them went over to him to say hello, and he received them with warmth in his eyes.

Warmth that had just a few weeks earlier, been solely showered on me. I felt jealous, as though I had some claim to him that no one else in the room had.

All these thoughts quickly disappeared when Jeremy took my plate from me, and set it down on one of the standing tables. "We're going to say hello," he said.

For a moment, my vision blurred. When I was able to recover, I gave him a stern look, and shook my head. "No!"

"C'mon," he pleaded. "Just a hello will do. He probably remembers me from our little chat."

I shook my head again, but then Anne and Tracy's words came to me.

Why was I hesitating and so afraid when it came to him?

I didn't know when Jeremy began to pull me along, but my legs went with him.

Carter was speaking to a group of employees, so we waited by the corner for a little bit for them to move along.

The moment they did, Jeremy walked into his midst, filled with confidence. "Hello, Mr. Edwards."

"Jeremy Atkins," he replied.

My knees were wobbly as I tried my best to hide behind him, but somehow make it seem as though I wasn't.

"You remember by name," Jeremy flushed.

"Of course I do."

"Well, thank you. Uh… this is my colleague, Leah Peters."

I didn't know what to do. All I could do was stare into his eyes, frozen in place as he held my gaze. He didn't bring out his hand either for a hand shake, so I remained as I was.

"Leah," Jeremy called.

"Cart— "I started to say automatically, but then I corrected myself. "Mr. um…?"

"Edwards," Jeremy supplied.

"Mr. Edwards."

His stare on me was hard and long, and then he was called over by the CMO. "Excuse me," he said with a tight smile, and went on his way.

We both stood, entranced as he walked away, dripping with swagger and affluence.

"Isn't that the most fuck-able man you've ever seen?" Jeremy asked.

I knew he was, so I reached then for his cup of wine. Luckily, I caught myself just as his grip loosened around it, before I could lift it to my lips.

Carter would be the death of me.

Jeremy however could not notice my distress. "So," he said. "That's the *Godfather,* and over there…" We turned to search out the VP in the opposite corner of the room with my boss, Henry. "That's the grandfather. Who'd you rather?"

I returned his cup back to him. "I'm going home."

CHAPTER 23

LEAH

*T*he next afternoon, just before lunch break, I headed up the elevator towards the executive floor. I was dressed appropriately in a mauve, gingham blazer, a sheer, black turtleneck and a fitted pencil skirt that went past my knee.

I felt confident, and presentable, but no amount of prep talk I gave to myself stopped the knots from forming in the pit of my stomach.

The elevator dinged its arrival on his floor, and I felt like I might just pass out. I managed to find my way to his office.

His secretary, Joseph, greeted me with a smile. "Hello Miss Peters."

"Hello. Can I see Mr. Edwards very briefly?" I asked. "Just before he heads out for lunch."

"His lunch appointment is already here," he said. "He's in the office with him right now and they should be out any moment."

As though controlled by a remote, I quickly turned around and escaped from the reception. I was waiting by the goddamn slow elevator, when I heard footsteps approaching. I glanced back with the prayer that it wasn't him and to my relief, I saw a heavy set man with a thick mustache. I had never seen him in the building before. Perhaps he was the one that Carter was going to lunch with.

He smiled at me, and I returned the gesture. We both stood side by side to wait for the elevator, but then he kept glancing at me until finally, I met his gaze.

"I apologize," he said. "But I have a question for you."

"Sure."

"Were you by any chance in Turkey about a month ago? For any reason at all?"

My heart screeched to a halt. For a moment, I just stared at him, and then I looked around me, not exactly sure what I was checking for. "Uh..." I didn't know how to respond to that.

From my bafflement, he nodded. "I'll take that as a yes." He then held out his hand. "I'm Mark Garrity. Chief Financial Officer of Suibian Group."

This was too much information all at once, none of which I could process, so I just accepted his handshake. "I'm Leah Peters. H-how did you know that I was in Turkey?" I asked.

"You delayed the boss's return back to work," he said lightly.

I didn't take any of his words lightly. The elevator car announced its arrival with a ding, and he got on but I didn't. "What do you mean?"

"I have to go Miss Peters, but I have to say after seeing you I don't blame him for um... losing his mind. Have a great day."

The car closed shut and I was left staring at my fuzzy reflection on the steel doors.

It was then when I heard the secretary's voice. I turned around.

Carter was addressing him, his jacket slung across his hand. When he was done, he headed towards me, his gaze unapologetically holding mine.

I didn't know what to do. My whole body was screaming for me to run, but where to and in what way that wouldn't drive me to literally bury my head in the sand afterwards. So I stood my ground, and turned just as he arrived by my side to wait for the elevator.

Neither of us said a word to the other.

I opened my mouth to speak, but it seemed as though the words were stuck in my throat. I looked up at the display above the steel doors, and at the approaching car, then turned to him. "I-I came here to speak to you."

He didn't even bother looking at me. "Go ahead." The elevator door dinged open, and he got in.

I didn't move.

"Aren't you getting in?" He asked.

I released a heavy breath. "Carter," I called, and the elevator doors began to close.

His gaze was on me, and I thought that he would reach out to stop it, but instead he remained in the same position, leaning against the wall with his hands in his pocket.

The elevator closed, and I blinked.

It took me a few seconds to process what had just happened, and then I realized he was leaving. I couldn't believe it.

"*Dick!*" I swore, as a surge of anger shot through me. I pounded on the downward button, intending to go after him. Finally, it arrived.

I hopped on, but as I arrived on my floor, I stopped it and got off. "Fuck him," I said, as my eyes misted at his cool dismissal. I returned to my desk, and took my seat to calm down but it was as though my entire body had boiled over... now steam was being emitted from every pore.

"Leah, do you have any lunch plans?" Jeremy asked.

I lifted my gaze to his approaching figure, but stared right past him. I could see nothing beyond the man who'd just walked out on me. This was going to end, *today*. So I grabbed my purse and rose from my chair. "Sorry, Jeremy," I called as I hurried away. "I do have plans."

I pounded on the descending call button for the elevator, and could barely stand still as I waited for it to arrive. The moment it did, I jumped in, and along with the few people in it, tried to calm my nerves as we rode down to the ground floor.

I was so worried that I wouldn't catch him and that I'd have to wait for him to return before I could speak to him. I couldn't allow or even permit the very loose strings between us for even a second longer. It was either we mended it, or completely yanked it out.

The elevator arrived, and I hurried out onto the massive, marble lobby. I paused for a moment to catch my breath, my hand on my chest to keep my heart from flying out.

Then I spotted him. He had just exited the building, but then he'd been stopped by two men in front of the revolving doors. I also exited the building, making sure he saw me as I came through the doors. He did, so I waited by the corner for him to finish his conversation.

When he did, the people went on their way and he started to head towards the waiting, open door of his SUV by the curb.

"Carter!" I called out.

He stopped. Then he turned around, his hands sliding into his pockets to finally give me the time of day.

I couldn't believe how cold he acted. I stormed towards him, not even the least bit caring that he was my boss, or that he owned the company I worked for.

I took a deep breath to calm myself when I reached him, aware that if I spoke now, that my voice would be shaky and full of hurt.

"Aren't you tired of playing this game?" He asked.

I was astonished. "What game?"

"You run away, and then I come after you, but you push me away. What's the real deal here, Leah? You don't like me coming after you? You prefer it when I'm dismissive and act like I don't give a fuck about you?" He briefly glanced away.

I could feel his barely restrained annoyance in waves. He was incredibly angry with me.

"Leah," he said. "I do admit that I feel a connection to you, and somehow I've allowed it to send me on this wild goose chase after you. But I also have an understanding with myself about the kind of treatment that I will or will not accept from anyone."

I felt incredible remorse at his words, but I tried my best to keep my face clear of emotion, and my voice stable. "Let's have lunch together so we can talk. Can I please have your phone number? Tell me where you're going so I can meet you there."

He eyed me for a bit.

I watched, completely entranced as the anger that burned in his eyes seemed to lessen.

"Trukadero," he said. "It's down the street."

With that he turned around, and got into his car.

His driver shut the door behind him, and I took my leave.

CARTER

Twenty minutes later, she was seated across from me in the continental Korean restaurant, in complete silence. I had just made my order of chicken fried rice, while she had gotten a cold noodle.

I kept my eyes on my phone as I scrolled through my emails, more than content to wait as long as she wanted in silence, if she refused to say anything.

Eventually she spoke, "I apologize, Carter."

I lifted my gaze to hers, and met the blank look in her eyes, her apology seemingly devoid of any sincerity. For a moment, it made me want to smile. I couldn't exactly say that I completely hated this little spat between us. It did make my blood boil with anger, but my libido was most definitely not spared from the effect. It didn't help also that she looked as stunning as I remembered. The mauve jacket she wore complemented the rosy color on her eyelids, lips and cheeks. Her hair was pulled up on top of her head, and again tufts of curly hair softened the nape and sides of her face.

God, she was beautiful, and how I wanted once again to be inside her.

Anger surged through me at the reminder of all the ways she was making things difficult for us, so I looked away, unmoved. "What exactly are you sorry about?" I peeked a bit to gauge her expression.

I saw her eyes widen at the realization that I wasn't going to let her off so easily. She sighed deeply. "For not answering the door, and ignoring you the day you came to my house."

I remembered the day quite vividly, and the hurt I felt after I'd spent the entire afternoon in abject worry about her. But she had ignored me through it all. It was such a low point for me, so much so that I hadn't even been able to recall the last time I'd felt that badly. Especially when I'd heard her foot-steps as she'd walked away.

"I didn't do anything to hurt you when we were in Turkey," I said. "At least not intentionally. If you don't want to have anything to do with me then all you need to do is to say the word."

I waited for her response, but then our food was delivered. She instantly began to eat and I did the same.

Whatever the outcome of today would be, was completely in her hands. I had vowed to myself to only respond or react this time around.

"Why did you come here to Indiana?" she asked. "You bought the company... I thought you just worked for one in Minnesota."

I raised my glass of water to my lips, and after taking a sip, asked, "Which question do you want me to answer first?"

"Whichever one is fine," she replied.

"I came to Indiana because of you," I admitted outright, and could see her entire body go still. "After Alanya, I thought that I'd be able to put you out of my mind and continue with my life, but it wasn't the case at all. So I came over here for a chance to get to know you better... to spend time with you."

She looked flabbergasted. "B-but you bought the company."

"I need to work too and don't worry I didn't buy your company solely because of you. It's had a great record over the years and an ad department included in its services would really make it top tier in the state. It's a good enough investment to me."

"You want to create an advertising department?"

I nodded in response, and said no more.

She returned to her food, as though my purchase of the company was the only thing that had been mentioned.

I allowed her to evade the main subject and continued on with my meal. When we were done, I called for the waiter to bring the check over. I reached for the tab but she immediately picked it up.

"I'll take care of it... as an apology."

I didn't have a complaint, so I leaned back into the chair to watch her.

Then she rose to her feet.

"I'll be back soon. I want to use the restroom."

I nodded in response, while she turned around and walked away.

CHAPTER 24

LEAH

I felt frustrated.

I didn't need to use the restroom, but I did however, need to stare at my confused visage in the mirror. What was I going to do? To move us beyond this stage, especially as it now seemed that I had annoyed him to the point of a voluntary stalemate.

In order for us to proceed, I had to be the one to make the move, and the very thought made my limbs tingle with fear. This seemed to be a pattern between us. I would run, and he would try to hold on to me but then I'd push him away, and would have to go back begging.

My head fell into my hands.

What was wrong with me? Especially now, when there was so, so much more at stake between us, even though he didn't know it yet.

I gazed at myself in the mirror again. What exactly did I want?

Him in my life, or not at all?

I lowered my gaze as my hand rested on my stomach.

I did …

I wanted him so badly in my life, but not just because I was pregnant. But because, like he had said, we had gotten to know each other and fallen even more madly in love with whom the other person was.

But to do that, we needed time and I was running out of it.

You can start now... a voice whispered to me.

But would he accept me now?

He had come all the way here for me, and invested so much into the relationship that he wanted us to have. I felt deeply remorseful. Immediately I turned around, and walked out of the bathroom.

I got into the corridor however, and froze.

He was approaching.

I thought he'd come on my account, but instead, he regarded me quietly and went past me to head into the male bathroom. I took a deep breath, turned around and went after him.

The moment I came in after him, he turned around, his eyebrows twitching in surprise.

I stopped by the door, inhaled deeply, and began. "Carter…"

I want you. More than I've seemingly wanted anything else in my life. And thank you, for making such a leap for us, and again... I am very, very, sorry for how I've acted.

The words were clear as day in my mind, but as I opened my mouth to speak, they wouldn't come forth. "Carter..." I called again

He waited.

The words I intended to say suddenly seemed weightless and inconsequential, even though I meant them from the bottom of my heart. What I desperately needed was a way to show him. I felt my eyes mist, and without thinking, went straight to him.

I threw my arms around his neck, my four inch heels having to lift up even further to be placed on somewhat *equal* footing with him. I hugged him tightly, too scared that he would pull away, but then I felt his rigid stance begin to relax into my embrace.

He slid one arm around my waist, and my heart went wild with excitement and relief. "You are one complicated woman, Leah," he said.

I shook my head against his neck. "I'm sorry. I'm really sorry. I'll do better."

He briefly pulled me away from him so he could look into my eyes. With a finger, he was just in time to catch the tear that was going to fall from one corner.

I immediately dropped my head, and tried to move away from his hold.

He wouldn't let me. "Running away again? You absolutely do not ever want to be vulnerable do you? Especially with me."

I kept my head lowered, and my eyes tightly shut.

"I'm not going to hurt you, Leah," he said. "I promise you that and I'm going to try my very best to keep that promise to the best of my ability."

"Thank you."

"Look at me..." he said.

After a long moment I summoned up the courage to look him in the eye.

"How far are you willing to go with me?"

"As far as you're willing to take me," was my response.

He smiled, and it grew into a beaming grin that just completely messed up the rhythm of my heartbeat. I ignored the spazzing muscle, and focused my complete attention on him.

Being in his arms was like putting on rose colored glasses. They were so fragile, and easily broken, but at the same time... worth every second of engagement. I seemed once again to have woken up, and I never wanted to go back to sleep.

"We've already gone past the initial first dates phase," he said. "So how about we become official, starting right now.

I couldn't properly process all that was happening. It seemed all too surreal to accept, that he was saying all the things right now that I'd so longed for. My throat constricted, over-whelmed with excitement and gratitude, so I couldn't speak. All I could do was nod.

"Alright," he said, as he brushed the tendrils of escaped hair away from my face. "I have another request of you." With his thumb and forefinger, he lifted my chin upwards so he could lock my gaze with his. "It's been more than a month and a half. Any longer and I will cease to be able to function."

My face immediately began to flush with heat as I processed what he was saying. Shy, I tried to pull my gaze from his.

He wouldn't let me. "Leah, I'm serious," he breathed. "I need to be inside you. How about tonight? Anywhere you want."

Right then, what I wanted more than anything was to kiss him, hard and deep. So my hands lifted to hold the sides of his face.

He didn't wait. With a slant of his head, he crushed his lips to mine and I tasted him again. It was like coming home from a long, arduous, and very unnecessary journey. As his tongue dipped and stroked mine, I felt my knees begin to weaken, the fire he wrought in my heart, draining my entire body of the stamina needed to even simply stand.

Thankfully, he held me up and my hand fisted his jacket. I was soon overtaken, by a wild and almost violent lust. He cupped my breasts through the light material of my sheer turtleneck, while I ground my crotch against his burgeoning cock.

We were together again, against all the odds, and I didn't even know how to process my joy. "I can't wait for tonight," I told him, when we came up for air. "That stall... it should be all right."

He glanced towards the slightly larger handicap stall, and before I could blink, I was locked inside the metal box with him.

"Carter—" I began, but his mouth had already covered my nipple. My skirt was bunched up to my waist, and my leg lifted for direct access to my sex. My breathing was erratic, my heart racing out of control, but still I managed to get the word out. I had to. "We're going to be late Carter. We're out of time."

His hand grabbed my mound, and a heavy gasp escaped me. I held on tightly to his hand as he began to stroke my engorged clit through the sheer lace of my underwear. I immediately changed my tune. "Make it quick," I muttered, my body jerking to the pleasure of his tease. "Please."

He heeded my request. Suddenly I was lifted off my feet and my legs guided to wrap around his waist.

"Please tell me we don't need a condom," he rasped, as he traced sultry kisses up my neck.

I shook my head. "We're fine... we don't."

He loosened the front of his slacks and soon enough, I felt the special part of him that I had missed so terribly. I was amused as I felt it poking around my sex, impatient for its acceptance into my body. I tried my best to keep my voice down but the squeal stuck in my throat demanded a release and I allowed it.

Carter slipped my thong aside, and without ceremony, he shoved his thick cock into me.

Once again, it felt like I had come home. Like we had both come home to who we were to each other... a safe place... a breathtakingly beautiful place... a fiercely passionate and engulfing place. I never, ever, wanted to be apart from him, and this scared me beyond what words could express.

He moved inside of me, and it felt like someone was wringing my soul of pleasure, so delicious that you understood immediately that you were going to lose yourself somewhere along the way.

I was ready, or at least I hoped I was. As he slammed into me over and over again, I felt and welcomed his complete and incontestable possession of my body.

"I missed you Leah..." He kissed me, his voice sounding almost frail under the weight of his longing.

I understood him wholeheartedly and crushed my body even further into his. I drove my hips with a feverish urgency to meet his thrusts, the risk of being found by one of the restaurant staff or guests now inconsequential as we chased our release with each other.

I searched for his mouth, frantic and desperate when I began to feel my mind unraveling. We were heading closer and closer to our peak, and I could feel it in the strain of his thrusts and the labor of his grunts.

I grabbed his ass and loved the clench of the taut muscles, as it brought me closer and closer onto the edge.

"Fuck... *Leah*..." he cursed.

I held on for dear life... until I came apart.

He exploded just as I did, his cum shooting into me in thick heavy spurts. I felt him all the way up to my womb, and I thought I would pass out. Sweet was no longer a word adequate enough to describe this moment of coalition between us. At this crux of our joining, I truly understood that we became one, in spirit, body, and soul, and there was absolutely nothing else that could compare. I sobbed quietly into his neck, as he fought to bring his breathing under control, unable to restrain himself as much as he would have liked.

We stayed like that, joined as one as we began our descent back to earth together.

Then the man's voice came, "Must have been a sick breakup man. Never let her go."

We both froze, especially at the man's accompanying chuckle as he exited the restroom. From then on things began to register a little bit more clearly. First was the fact that we were in a filthy public restroom. None of this had registered when we had come in, but now it was haunting.

"Oh, my God..." I muttered, as he set me back down on wobbly feet.

"We're late," he said.

My tone went up several pitches as I repeated, "Oh, my God." I checked my watch to see it was almost ten minutes past lunch hour, so I hurriedly jerked my skirt down my thighs to put myself back in order.

"Relax," he said.

I was already out of his arms and out of the stall. "Easy for you to say, you own the damn company." I headed over to the mirror to check my disheveled, just fucked hair, and rumpled clothes. And if I looked clearly enough, I could see reddened kiss marks on my neck. "Oh no!" I gasped.

Carter came up to the sink beside me. He wetted a handkerchief and began to approach me.

"I'll do it myself," I said, not really sure I could handle him touching me again. It felt like I was about to spontaneously combust, both from anxiety and ecstasy, and it was all too much, all at once.

But he caged me, arresting me between the counter and his rock solid frame until the only thing I could do was give in. I stared into his eyes as he lifted my skirt up once again and slid my thong aside to cover it with his handkerchief.

My eyes fluttered closed, my breathing pattern now in short desperate spurts.

When he was done, he arranged my clothes back in place, and slipped the handkerchief into his pocket.

Suddenly, the door was pushed open, and a man stopped in his tracks, startled to see us.

"Time to go," Carter said, and grabbed my hand to lead me out of the restroom.

We returned separately to the office, but on the elevator ride up to my floor, he couldn't help but take advantage of the returning lunch crowd from the other offices in the building, to ensure that I was leaning fully into him.

"I'll be thinking of you," he whispered into my ear, just before the elevator arrived.

I almost had to cover my hand with my mouth to hide my smile.

"Pay me a visit soon," he whispered.

Seeing that no one from our company was riding with us, I glanced back to give him a quick, soundless, kiss the moment the elevator dinged its arrival, and parted through the sea of people to get out.

CHAPTER 25

CARTER

*W*orking with Leah in the same office was a feat, and that was putting it very, very lightly.

I sat in a meeting in my office, with one of the officials from the state's planning organization as we reminisced about old team members, from the first advertising agency we'd worked in together. But I could barely concentrate.

I'd known that insisting on our rendezvous mid afternoon, would be a very bad idea, and it would render me completely useless, but it was still the sweetest decision that I'd made all day. I'd also done something frivolous before we'd separated from the restaurant and I'd expected her to have noticed it by now. I'd slipped her phone out of her purse, and was hoping that she would have come up to ask me about it. More than an hour had passed since lunch, so she should have noticed its absence by now. Or did she perhaps think that she'd dropped it somewhere else, and was distraught?

I straightened, my chest tightening with worry. Perhaps I had gone too far?

It was only our first official day together and I was already stirring storms. My head fell into my hand.

"Carter. Are you okay, man?"

My head shot up then, at the reminder that I was not alone. "I apologize. I got distracted for a moment there. Please go on."

"Alright, so our office is thinking about using social media to promote interesting areas of the state. For instance, the Eiteljorg Museum, the Fort Wayne Zoo, Prophetstown State Park, the Dunes National Lakeshore... places that people would like to show off in their pictures."

"Hmm..." I nodded. "Doesn't sound half bad. It could be marketed as uh... the most Instagram-able places in Indiana."

"Instagram-able?"

"That's the term. Or Insta-worthy, if you may."

"What the hell does that mean?" he asked.

The distaste in his words made me laugh. "You're losing your touch Huang."

"Well, that's why I've come to you. I'm so glad you're here, man. How long will you be staying this time?"

My mind went again to the woman that I could now officially call mine. "Who knows?" I answered. "I'm just taking things one step at a time."

A terrible step at a time it was beginning to seem. I looked at the clock once more.

Twenty minutes later, the meeting came to an end and I picked up my intercom phone to call my secretary, Joseph.

He immediately picked up. "Sir?"

"Has anyone else come looking for me?"

"No, Sir," he replied.

I was just about to put the phone down when he stopped me.

"Just a moment, sir," he said. "Miss Peters from marketing team two just arrived. She was here earlier, before lunch hoping to catch you on your way out."

My heart's pace picked up. "Send her in." I couldn't help but smile to myself as I awaited her entrance, neither could I help the perspiration that was beginning to gather on my hands. I couldn't believe that lunch time had been barely two hours earlier. It was almost as though my life had done a complete one eighty since then.

There was a quiet knock, and then she pushed the door open.

My whole body came to attention as she shut it behind her, and then turned to me, a worried look on her face.

"What's wrong?" I asked.

Looking nervous, she stopped by the door. "Sorry to bother you but have you seen my phone? I'm thinking that perhaps I left it at the restaurant."

"I have." I nodded and pulled it out of my pocket. "It's right here." I placed it on the table.

She cocked her head at me. "I left it on the table?"

I darted my eyes in thought, wondering if denying what I had done here would be the way to go.

"That can't be. I remember slipping it into my purse." She thought for a moment, and then noticed my tightened lips as I tried to control my smile. Her eyes widened with realization. "You took it out of my purse? How? And why?"

"I wanted you to come visit me."

"Carter!" She scolded, and turned back to glance at the door at her loud tone. She abandoned all propriety then and began to march towards me.

I loved when she looked like this, and I wanted it to last so when she reached me, I held the phone far above my head and just out of her reach.

"Carter! I have a meeting!" Her legs went astride mine as she tried to grab the phone out of my hand as I leaned as far away as I could from her. She eventually caught my hand with an aggravated groan, and I released my grip on the phone.

Before she could leave however, my hand slid up her thighs, and grabbed her mound.

"Oh, *God*," she gasped, her knees immediately buckling at the sudden intrusion. "*Carter.*"

Despite her resistance, my hand stroked the bud of her sex, her hands on my shoulders to keep her somewhat stable.

"Carter... *stop*," she said.

Then I managed to slip her thong aside. I slipped a finger into her and then another.

Her eyes rolled into their sockets, her lips falling open. "*Oh*," she whimpered. "Holy fuck."

My phone suddenly began to ring. With a deep sigh of regret, I pulled my fingers out of her and banded an arm around her legs to hold her to me, before retrieving the phone from its handle.

"Your four 'o clock is here, Mr. Edwards," Joseph informed me.

"Give me a few minutes," I responded, and returned it back to the receiver. I rose to my feet, and kissed my girl, completely and wholeheartedly in love with the woman that she was.

She hit me on the shoulder, but then melted into the kiss till a loud knock on the door brought us both back to earth.

"You're going to pay for this," she said, as she pulled away.

"I'm looking forward to it."

"How did you even take it from me?" She asked as she walked away.

"I never went to college," I answered back. "I spent the time finding *other* ways to survive."

Her mouth dropped open just as she reached my door. "I want to hear all about that."

"Tonight," I demanded. "Cook me dinner at your place?"

Her slowly spreading smile almost gave me a heart attack.

She blew a shy kiss at me as she exited the office.

I took my seat to get ready for my next meeting.

LEAH

Carter was so incredibly naughty, and I loved it. To the rest of the world he seemed so put together, and almost unapproachable, but when he was with me that aloofness was replaced by a light in his eyes that made me melt, because I knew, it was solely for me.

I still couldn't believe he had actually stolen my phone from me, just to get me to visit him. It was a great move, and one I didn't mind at all, but it was also unnecessary. Sooner or later, I would have gone over to see him. It was just so endearing though that he wanted it to be sooner.

I was however so preoccupied with giddy thoughts of him, that I didn't even bother to note whom I had passed on the way out of his office.

"Leah?"

I heard my name called, and turned around.

My heart lurched into my throat as I met the gaze of Daniel Coghlan, the VP I had a meeting with in twenty minutes. The smile immediately disappeared from my face. "Sir?" I answered.

His eyes narrowed at me, and then at my somewhat rumpled appearance. When he returned his gaze to me, his expression looked sour.

It sent a sliver of worry down my spine.

He didn't say a word.

A lump began to grow at the back of my throat.

He turned around to head into the office, while Carter's secretary Joseph, gave me a somewhat polite smile.

I turned around to head to the elevator, feeling somewhat nervous.

This could very well be interpreted as me frolicking with the boss, and it just wasn't the reputation I wanted swirling around me. But it was the best I would be able to receive if I kept sneaking around with Carter. I mean, how many employees could come out of an executive's office with hearts in their eyes, without there being a sultry story behind the visit?

The whole situation troubled me, especially as I was going to see the VP in a short while. With a sigh, I got on the elevator as it arrived and headed back to my floor.

Half an hour later and VP Daniel had somehow managed to turn into a nightmare overnight.

Today, we were focusing on establishing the demographic that would yield the utmost success if we directed our campaign towards them, and every single idea put forward by the members of the team, had been rudely shut down.

After an aggressive rant, the room was silent for a while, before I decided to speak. "Sir, based on my research so far, I think that young mothers would be a great focus."

For the first time since I had ran into him earlier in front of Carter's office, he spoke to me, "And why do you think that? We've just heard that the majority of the demographic that consumes energy drinks are students and middle-aged workers. Where do young mothers come into this equation?"

I wanted to give up right then, but I fought myself from rolling my eyes at him, and went on, "Gillette's major demographic is indeed men. But during this past year, and especially after the controversial 'the best men can be' ad that they put out, they're gradually beginning to win the new market of younger women who appreciated them speaking against toxic masculinity".

"Leah, they received massive backlash for that ad, and men advocated for their products to be boycotted," Henry warned.

"At first." I nodded. "But then their sales have grown over the second quarter of the year because despite all the racket they made, men don't buy their own razors. Their wives and girlfriends do that, the same market that was impressed by the message that Gillette was trying to pass across. My point is this; mothers, especially new mothers more than the usual college students whom energy drinks are targeted towards, need a pick me up as they try to navigate the new phase of their life. And that's what Vita500 is for. We target it to new mothers, but then others can relate. Students, especially females just starting college, young adults just entering into the job market and trying to navigate the challenges of their new life… and so on."

The room went silent and the longer it stretched, the more I shrunk back into my chair.

Our esteemed VP rose up and walked out of the room.

"Well that went great," Henry said sarcastically, and went on his way.

Jeremy lowered his head to conceal a snort.

I smacked him with my folder across his arm.

CHAPTER 26

LEAH

*T*hat night, and for the first time in a long time, I had something to look forward to beyond the frustrations of our current account. I arrived home early, and made sure I had all the ingredients needed for my fail proof dinner of fettuccine in creamy alfredo sauce, garnished with cheese, shrimp and parsley.

At a quarter past nine, Carter called to tell me that he was on his way. My house was cleaner than it had been in a little while, the over-priced cashmere mist candle I had never used lit and burning on the mantle, as the scent of jasmine filled the atmosphere. At the ring of my doorbell, I hurried over to the door.

I didn't even bother checking who it was before I pulled the door open.

My face was beaming with excitement in one moment, but fell with disappointment in the next, as I saw who my guests were.

For a long time I couldn't speak, until Tracy popped some confetti.

"Hey!" I jumped.

"Wow," Anne spat. "So much for a hearty welcome."

They pushed their way in.

I was forced to back away before they ran me over.

I saw Tracy had a bucket of cheese balls, and a tote I was sure contained more food, while Anne had three bottles of wine.

"What's going on?" I asked.

"Tracy was losing her mind," Anne said.

"That's not true," Tracy retorted. "I was just worried. We haven't seen you since you told us about your pregnancy, and then Carter's sudden appearance, my God. I still can't believe he's here and that he bought your company."

"I knew he was a designated and 'solid piece of ass' from the first time I laid eyes on him," Anne commented.

"Basically you're going through a lot," Tracy said. "So we came to cheer you up. Also, someone looks enticing. What's with the champagne piece? Is that silk? It's so sexy."

I didn't know exactly how I was going to kick them out, but before I could think of a way, my doorbell rang again. "*Fuck,*" I cursed underneath my breath, and hurried over. With a peer through the peephole, I saw exactly who it was, and considered calling him first to explain the sudden company, but I didn't want to be rude by keeping him outside. So I pulled the door open, and met the massive bouquet of blood red roses.

My heart fell into my stomach.

He pushed the flowers aside to reveal his beautiful face, and I noted the hint of shyness in his gaze. "I couldn't resist," he said. "Too tacky?"

I went out of the apartment, and placed a long, sweet kiss on his cheek. "I love them, but my friends are here. They just barged in now without notice, but I'll get rid of them."

"That's ok," he said. "We can all have dinner together."

My eyes narrowed. "Really?"

"Tracy and Anne right? I've spent time with them in Alanya, so they aren't exactly strangers to me.""

"I know, but I wanted tonight to be just the both of us."

"We have time," he said, and stepped forward to stroke the tip of his nose with mine.

CARTER

"Carter!"

I had a smile ready, for the moment the girls noticed me.

The blonde one, Anne, was opening a bottle of wine at the kitchen's island, while the brunette Tracy was setting up the coffee table with a massive drum of cheese balls, that I surprisingly couldn't take my eyes away from.

They both looked absolutely shocked to see me.

"Hello girls," I greeted.

They turned to their friend, demanding an explanation.

She just simply shrugged. "You both didn't call before coming over. I already have plans."

"Oh, so that's why you have that slip dress on," Anne said with a dirty smile.

Tracy picked up her purse, and went over to the counter to get Anne. "We're sorry for intruding," she said. "We'll leave now."

"It's alright," I told them. "Let's have dinner together."

"Sounds gre—" Anne started, but was firmly pulled along.

"No," Tracy insisted. "You both need time to yourselves. We'll see you some other time."

We turned to watch them leave, Anne with a tired look on her face that was quite amusing. The door was shut behind them, and we were left alone.

I turned to Leah.

A soft smile appeared on her face as she came over to me to accept the flowers. "They're beautiful," she said as she lifted the bouquet to her nose. "I'll put these in water."

Before she could leave, I banded an arm around her waist and pulled her to me for a quick kiss. She melted into me as my hands grabbed onto her ass beneath the clingy, silk dress she wore.

Just thinking about Leah was enough to get me excited, but seeing her now in this rose, silky slip dress-the material clinging to her hips, barely covering up her breasts and boldly showcasing the hardness of her nipples-began a slow torment I knew I wouldn't be able to address until later on in the night. It was pure torture, but I wanted to spend time with her today rather than *inside* her, but I didn't know how it would even be possible.

I took my seat on one of the stools by her counter.

She bent down to her bottom drawers to search for a vase, the material stretched across her hips and she might as well have been naked.

My body and especially my cock felt like a fuse that was mere seconds away from blowing. "Would it be too much of a hassle for you to change outfits?" I asked, as she found a glass vase.

She turned, surprised at my request.

"I'm sure you realize that I won't be able to think straight with you in that dress."

She laughed as she filled the vase with water and brought it over to the counter. "I'm not changing," she said, as she retrieved a pair of scissors. "So you'll just have to deal with it."

She was a vixen, thoroughly and completely aware of her sole power to bring me to my knees, and I was a very willing victim.

I watched her, mesmerized by the delicate way her fingers snipped off the leaves of the stems, and then arranged them in the vase.

"I took a wild guess by bringing these," I said. "What are your favorite flowers?"

"I don't have favorite flowers," she replied. "I rarely get them."

"Would you like to get them from now on?" I asked.

Her glance was searing. "I would."

"So what flowers would you like?"

"All of them?" She smiled. "But I especially love orchids."

"Noted." I gave her a nod.

She finished up with the flowers and pushed the vase to the center of the marble counter. I regarded it with pity, because somewhere along the night, of the very likely possibility that it would be shoved off the counter, and crash to the floor.

"I'll put the noodles on to boil now," she said. "Do you want something to eat while we wait?"

I turned towards the bucket of cheese balls on the coffee table. "Those will do," I said, and got up to retrieve them. "I haven't had these in more than a decade."

"Tracy is obsessed with them, and her kids love her for it."

"Tracy's married?"

"Oh no, I mean her kindergarten class. She's a teacher, but she just got engaged, about two weeks ago."

"Congratulations to her," I said as I brought the bucket of cheese balls over. "I'll prepare a gift. What does she like?"

She placed the water on the stove to boil, and then came over to me. "Makeup," she said.

"Well, you'll have to help me out there."

I widened my legs so she could stand as close to me as possible, and stared deeply into her eyes as I chewed on one of the balls.

"You should be comfortable here," she said, as she played

with the button of my dress shirt's collar. "But I don't want you to take off the waist coat. I love you in them." She brushed my hair back into place, and then moved her hands across my shoulders, lightly and seductively.

I didn't even realize it, but I had gone very still.

Then the strap of her dress fell down one shoulder. She glanced at it, and then at me, her lips curving into a taunting smile.

I grabbed her waist, and she giggled in excitement.

She pushed the strap even further down her arm, exposing the pale pink bud of her nipple. Her hand curved around my neck and I was granted full access.

My mouth and hands took complete possession of the weighty mounds until I was no longer content with just one of them. I pulled down the strap across the other shoulder, and soon had both breasts in my hands. I sucked hard on her nipples, lightly grazing the buds with my teeth. My hands moved to her ass just as we kissed, but before I could do anymore, she placed a hand on my chest, and pulled away from me.

My eyes glazed over with pleasure as I watched her slip the straps of her champagne dress back on.

"The water's boiling," she said.

I could do nothing more than look on like a tamed animal. I had never felt more at peace or at home. "Do you need some help?" I got up, needing to move, so I could manage my arousal, plus I just wanted to be close to her. She was too far away.

"I forgot to slice some leeks earlier," she said. "Could you help me? They're in the fridge."

I did as I was told and retrieved them. After rinsing them in the sink, I brought them over to the counter.

She came over then, her hands around my waist for a moment. "I'll get you a board and knife."

Soon, she returned with two knives, and I was given the needed instructions on how to slice them the way she wanted.

"Do you know how to cook?" she asked, but before I could respond, she added, "I mean beyond your life changing peanut butter and jelly sandwich."

"I'll make that for you tomorrow morning."

"You're spending the night?" she asked.

I noted the glint of excitement in her eyes. "You don't want me to?" I teased.

"Of course I do!" she replied.

I couldn't help my smile. "I think a PB and J is about it, for me. I've been eating out for as long as I can remember."

"That's right." She nodded. "You mentioned that you never went to college. So how did you get here? And at such a young age?"

CHAPTER 27

CARTER

"My mom. I lost her when I was about eleven, and before then we were living solely with her. So afterwards, our father took us in, but he wasn't quite ready to be a full time parent."

"Us? You have a sibling?"

"I do," I replied. "He was quite the straight arrow, but I on the other hand was incredibly bitter about a lot of things and I remained that way for a while. Losing my mom… it haunted me, too deeply, so it was nearly impossible to move past it. Anyway, when I was sixteen I got a girl pregnant.

Her mouth slightly fell open, so I hurried on to finish the story, "My dad threw me out, so I had to man up real fast so I could be responsible for them. She had a miscarriage later on, but by then I'd chased every job I could find, which included swiping people's wallets and attending parties I didn't know, just to see what I could grab from their houses to resell. Eventually, my maternal uncle found out, and got

244

me into an internship program at his friend's advertising agency in Minnesota, the Zimmerman Group, and that's where it all started. I think I was about nineteen at the time." I paused as I put the knife down.

With a smile at me, Leah headed back to the stove.

I turned around to watch her.

She checked the boiling noodles, and then went over to the bubbling sauce by the side. She used a spoon to scoop out a bit of it, and put it to her mouth for a taste.

I was next, and accepted the scoop whole heartedly. The explosion of spices and its creamy consistency truly impressed me. "I love it," I said.

She narrowed her gaze at me.

"I mean it," I assured her.

She gave me a quick kiss, her lips tasting mine for a moment before returning her attention back to the stove. "So, how did you get to where you are now? Your head company is really big. With almost six agencies underneath it right?"

I nodded.

"I can't believe you fooled me. You made me think you were just some employee when we met." She held out the wooden spoon to hit me.

I dodged it playfully. "C'mon I didn't fool you. I'm just not into bragging but everything I told you was true. The Dodge campaign I mentioned happened in the last company I worked for before I got fired."

"What happened?" She asked.

"It was a campaign for Protein World. We used well, a fit girl on the posters to promote their meal replacement supplement, and people lost their minds. They said it promoted an unhealthy body image and began this whole petition to have the ads taken down and the company even boycotted. They lost heavily on sales, at first, and the agency turned on me since I'd been the Creative Director in charge of it. They kindly offered me a demotion but I cursed them out and quit. I didn't see anything fucking wrong with the ad and told the company to shoot back at its attackers." I laughed at the reminder. "Well, that was what they did, and things completely turned around. They did millions in sales from people who didn't want to be consoled for being overweight but were actually looking to put in the effort to look better. The agency tried to call me back then but I refused to return. My current CFO Mark Garritty was my team head at the time, and he was pissed off about my punishment, because he felt it was undeserved, as I had tried to convey the message of the brand as clearly as was expected. So when they failed to bring me back, he got up and resigned."

"Wow..." she paused, her gaze somber. "That was quite selfless of him."

"He's a good guy," I admitted. "But never tell him that to his face. You'll never hear the end of it. At the time, he told me not to feel guilty, that he had been planning to resign either way, as the company's disloyalty to its employees had been pissing him off for quite a while. Patience is not one of his strong suits. At that point, I'd been working for about ten years under supervision, and was sick of it too, so I went to a client I'd handled a campaign for in the past. It was an

Australian lifestyle brand and the owner had told me that if I ever wanted to start my own company that he'd be willing to back me up. I went to him, and he was ready. That's how Mark and I began. It's been five years now, and although things have not always gone to plan, I really cannot complain."

I took a deep breath, and released it, exhausted from the day and the talking. I enjoyed opening up to her but talking this much at once, was completely new territory for me. So I headed over to her, my hands slipping around her waist as she transferred the noodles into the sauce. She added the shrimp, and grated cheese, and then raised a forkful to my lips for a taste.

I accepted it all, taking as many chances as I could get to kiss her.

Soon, dinner was ready, and we sat down to eat.

"Do you have some wine around?" I asked. "Let's share a bottle."

"I don't," she said, something akin to alarm suddenly flashing in her eyes, but then her gaze shot over to the coffee table. "Anne brought some wine along with her though." She went over to the table and returned with the dark bottle, and an apologetic gaze. "It's nonalcoholic, but it's still actual red wine."

"That's alright. We have to turn up sober at work tomorrow either way."

I saw her expression change, and although she tried to hide it from me, I knew what was going on.

We began to eat, and I waited for her to talk about it, but when she didn't I decided to bring it up. "Do you need any help handling Coghlan?" I asked.

She lifted her gaze to mine, a bit surprised.

"I've heard," I said with a smile.

"I swear I'm doing my job the best way I can," she said, her smile nervous. "Please don't fire me."

"That's up to Henry." I laughed. "I only have incontestable jurisdiction when someone royally screws up. This does not seem to be the case here."

"It's not," she replied. "I don't know what he's expecting, but he's focusing on the same demographics that every energy drink company in the country markets to, and using the same gimmicks, but yet he's hoping that we'll come up with a way to still blow everything out of the park."

I was concerned at how much this was currently weighing her down. "Let me hear your idea."

At first, she hesitated, but then she lifted a forkful of noodles to her mouth, and agreed to speak. "I think that the focus should be on young mothers," she began.

I listened. By the time she was done, I was incredibly impressed by what she had said.

And the moment I told her, her mouth fell open.

"It's a fresh take and might actually be a homerun."

"Exactly!" she exclaimed. "How can the freaking owner of the company see this and he can't?"

I smiled. "Because I don't know the client, but he does. It was a personal recommendation so I'm sure he's trying to go over and beyond but not stray too far from what the company will be willing to bear risks for."

"Ugh," she groaned. "Those type of clients are the worst. They ask for something out of the box, but still end up pushing for the same cookie cutter tactics."

I smiled again. "Perhaps what you need is to convince him to go with your idea."

"I would if he cared enough to listen to me. Every single time we're in a meeting I'm ignored like I'm not even there. And Henry has little to nothing to say because he's in charge of the resources, but Daniel is the Account Manger and the Vice President. No one wants to offend him. "

"Try a little harder, if you believe in your idea," I told her. "You want to focus on mothers, right? Make your suggestion incontestable and I'll take it from there."

"Oh no," she immediately refused. "I don't want it to seem as though I'm sailing because you're my boyfriend.

"You will sail," I corrected her. "Because you're my employee. I would do the same for any other employee. So do what you need to, and leave the rest to me."

Her grin tugged at the strings of my heart.

"Yes, sir," she said but then she got lost in her thoughts again.

I knew exactly where her mind had gone. "Have you ever studied Amazon reviews before? Of other energy drinks?"

"Not exactly," she said, and then her brows shot up at the suggestion. "You're right. I can use that to get a glimpse into the mind of people who already consume it."

I rose to my feet to take my dish to the sink, but she wasn't yet done with hers so I went past her.

Still she abandoned the plate, and rushed over to me. "You're right," she said. "I'll get right on that, and consumers most times usually blurt out the best damn copies." Her shoulders slumped again. "I need to talk to a few moms to get their perspectives on this. I should be able to find some on Facebook groups." She started to head back to her table again, and took her seat.

I let out another suggestion, "Tracy is a kindergarten teacher," I reminded her. "A gold mine for young moms. Do they have any events coming up soon? Take a couple of the drinks over and chat with them. You might get everything you need."

Leah jumped up from the stool again, and I couldn't help my amusement. She was like an ecstatic child.

"You're fucking right, but wait… I don't think you can do this. You're my boss… you can't be aware that I'm not that smart on the spot."

"At the office I'm your boss," I said as I rinsed my hands and grabbed a napkin to wipe them dry. "But right here at home, you're my girl. No more talk about work. Let's watch something together or go to bed. Hectic day tomorrow for the both of us.

She rounded up with her meal, while I headed over to her couch. A few minutes later she joined me, her head on my lap as she began to scroll through her phone for some research. I settled in with the news and the time flew by in perfect bliss. Suddenly, there was a thump on the floor and I looked to see that it was her phone.

She was completely knocked out, her eyes closed. I lifted her into my arms, and tucked her into her bed with me, her hands tightening on mine to assure herself of my presence.

CHAPTER 28

LEAH

A few days later, I was knee deep into my research of customer reviews on Amazon when a figure came behind me.

At first, I didn't notice him, my focus completely on the insight into women's experiences with the various drinks. One amusingly called the majority of energy drinks, sugared down battery acid, but I was a bit disheartened to hear that what attracted her to the brand she was currently hooked on. It had been her companion all through college and now the daily 'oomfs' that she needed to power through her job, and deal with her kids, was the pink color of the can.

Vita 500 was orange, and in a bottle, so I jotted down notes on how to use this point to our advantage. The more common plays of the brand's contribution to cancer research were recurring, but before I could go any further, Henry's icy tone gripped me.

"What are you doing?"

I swiveled around in my chair to face him, my cheeks flushed at his sudden presence. I could also tell from his gaze that his question had been rhetorical.

"Didn't we decide to focus on celebrity endorsement, and entertainment marketing?"

"I know." I cleared my throat. "But it's not a fashion product. Focusing more on its contribution to the everyday reality of our customers would be... I just want to also explore this path a bit mo—"

"Do you hate yourself?" He sniped.

I instantly shrunk back into my shell.

"It's a question."

My head lowered. "No, sir."

"Then why don't you want to just do what Coghlan asked for, so that we can all move on with our lives?" With a hard look at me, he straightened. "Get the list of plausible celebrities I requested, before the end of the day."

"Yes, sir," I responded.

He stormed away.

By lunch time, I needed an escape, so when Jeremy came with the offer to go for a smoothie, I was out of my chair in a flash. He grumbled about his struggle with the new logo for the resort company another team asked him to handle, and I listened as best as I could to take my mind off my own problems.

The elevator to our floor dinged open, but as we moved to take a step in, the singular man that stood in it completely arrested our attention. Today, his suit was a tweed pattern in a chestnut brown that seemed to further bring out the green of his eyes. I remembered waking up in his arms earlier that morning, but when I was finally ready to pull myself out of bed, I'd found that he had left, with a note by my side of how he'd needed to hurry back to his hotel to change.

"Good morning, sir," Jeremy greeted smoothly as we walked in.

My gaze lowered from his. I could barely control my smile as I thought back to his face buried in my breasts the previous evening. Unfortunately for me, more staff followed our entrance. The elevator picked up more traffic as we headed down, until I was more or less standing in front of him.

In the glorious awkwardness of elevators, no one made a sound but then a heavy hand suddenly slinked around my waist, and I was pulled into him. My body settled with familiarity against his, and it felt as though my bones were beginning to disintegrate into dust.

His hand splayed across my stomach, the gesture of possession undeniable as heat and unbridled sexual tension crackled between us.

The elevator arrived on the lobby, and his hand fell away. I walked out along with the crowd, my mood instantly doing a 180, but Jeremy was close to passing out.

"Did you see the boss? Oh, my God!" He fanned himself. "That man's going to be the death of me. Leah, have you ever seen someone look so good in tweed?"

I cocked my head at him as we headed out the double doors and onto the street. We continued walking along and although I fought the urge to, I couldn't stop myself from looking backwards to see as he got into his car.

I bit my lips to hide my smile.

Jeremy turned just in time to see my expression. "What's making you so happy?" He asked at the permanent upturn of my lips as we headed down the busy downtown street towards a cafe.

I couldn't tell him, so I just shook my head, and tried to pay full attention to him. Just as we arrived at the coffee house, my phone vibrated with the arrival of a text.

I pulled it out of my pocket to see it was from Carter, and my heart began its calisthenics routine within my chest.

'Headed to lunch?' He asked.

'Yeah,' I replied. *'For a smoothie and maybe a sandwich. You?'*

'Meeting across town... will be back later in the afternoon. Stop by to see me?'

Molten heat encapsulated me from the crown of my head to the soles of my feet.

Jeremy, this time around, did not miss it. "You're seeing someone," he said.

I immediately put the phone away. I didn't respond as I collected our smoothies, but he badgered me for a response until I gave in. "I am seeing someone," I replied, and at the excitement that glinted in his eyes, I knew that he wanted details. "It's still new," I half-lied. "I can't talk about it yet."

He gave me a sour look. "Can you at least say how you met?"

"In Turkey, during my vacation."

255

"Oh…" His brows twitched. "He's Turkish?"

"Nope." I sipped the creamy blueberry and yogurt smoothie through my straw. "He is right here in Indiana."

"Lucky girl," he said with envy.

I couldn't deny it.

He was absolutely right.

Despite the disappointing morning I had had, I did at this moment feel like the luckiest girl in the world. I especially felt even luckier as a little while later, I found a half hour in which I could disappear, without anyone looking for me, and took the elevator up to his floor.

CARTER

Having Leah in my office, completely changed it into a different place.

From the moment she came in, it felt just a bit warmer and brighter… which was pretty amusing, given her distaste of the space.

"It's quite dark," she commented.

I watched her from behind my desk.

Strolling across the room, with her hand brushing the still impersonalized shelves, she turned to face me. "And it feels a bit cold. Is this how your office is, back in Minnesota? Just hardwood and pottery?"

"No." I smiled. "It's a bit warmer, I think."

"How so?"

"For one, my awards are on the shelves."

"And?" She asked, as she began to head over to me.

"The walls are grey, the furniture is white... the wood is warm."

"Hmm, that does seem better." Her grin was electric, and it glued my eyes to hers as she rounded my desk. She then took her seat atop it. "No pictures?" She asked.

"I don't have anyone to frame pictures of."

Her smile slightly faltered. "You could frame one of yourself," she suggested.

I laughed out, leaning back into the chair. "Sure, that's not obnoxious at all."

"It's not," she refuted.

When I remained unconvinced, she added. "One of these days, I'm going to take a picture of us together. I'll put it in a small frame so that you can maybe place it on your desk? Give you something to look at as you work."

"Sounds great to me."

"But you'll have to face it toward yourself... keep it hidden. So no one sees that it's me."

"You don't want anyone to know that we're together?"

"Not exactly. I just don't want it to bring any unnecessary attention."

I understood her concern, and nodded in acknowledgement. She stretched her hand out towards me, and my eyes instantly fluttered shut at the anticipation of her touch.

When the seconds passed however, and I felt nothing, my eyes reopened. Her amusement was clear, but her gaze endearing. With a quiet laugh, she teased my hair and softly ran her hand down the side of my face.

I refused to succumb this time, to reveal just how much her touch affected me. So I controlled my breathing, and wore a casual expression.

"How has your day been so far?" she asked.

"We got sued," I replied, and at her widened gaze, I quickly clarified, "Buddy Media. Our agency in Chicago. A Content Creator said we stole their meme. One of the teams used it in a recent campaign."

"*Wow,*" her lips mouthed.

I couldn't tear my gaze from the stark red color her mouth was in painted today. "I love it when you wear pink, but this is also beautiful. Quite provocative."

"What?" She laughed.

"Your lipstick," I said.

She lightly smacked me across the shoulder. "We were just talking about the lawsuit. Now you're talking about my lipstick?"

"It'll get sorted out." I shrugged. "It's just one of those fires that come up from time to time."

Her gaze softened. "It doesn't bother you?"

"Of course it does, but if I let every matter that comes up in a day weigh me down, I would be completely useless. So I suck it up, fix what I can, and keep moving the rest along. It's the price of ambition." I moved my chair till it was positioned right before her, and then began to roll her skirt up her thighs.

"Hey!" She blushed. "What are you doing?"

"You only have ten minutes left. I want to give you a little boost, to take you through the rest of the day."

Her fit of giggles as she half-heartedly tried to fight me off was like music to my ears.

"Carter..." she complained, as she pushed my head away.

I stopped, and held her gaze. "You don't want me to?"

Her lips parted to refuse me, but then she stopped as she noted any trace of amusement was gone from my face.

And just like that, the air changed between us.

I spread her legs apart, and placed a hand on her stomach to guide her.

She leaned backwards, her breathing heavy.

With a smile, I buried my head between her legs. My first taste of her was through her dampened, lacy, thong.

At the brief contact, she jumped. "Relax," I said, as I pulled the scrap of lace down her legs. With my hands gripping her thighs, I pulled her to the edge of the table. I lifted her legs, and covered her cleft with my mouth. My tongue was instantly soaked with her arousal.

Her shudder was almost violent, and so was the grip that found its way to my hair. "Carter," she breathed, her moan resounding in my ears.

I lapped her up, before my lips settled on her clit. I sucked hard on the engorged bud, and her thighs clamped shut against my head. Her body trembled in response, and for a moment, I felt her begin to push me away, as though she couldn't contain the assault.

I dipped even lower, and shoved my tongue into her.

CHAPTER 29

LEAH

Fifteen minutes later, I stumbled my way out of Carter's office.

My head kept spinning and my eyes were still unfocused, so it wasn't until my name was called did I notice the person I passed.

"Leah," he called.

It startled me to attention. "Yes?" I turned a drowsy gaze towards the VP-Coghlan, and my heart lurched into my throat. I instantly straightened, a smile across my face. "Sir," I responded.

He took in my appearance, and although Carter had made sure to put me together before he sent me back out, I was well aware that one didn't need to look too hard to see I had been up to everything else but work.

"Why are you here?" he asked.

"Uh…" My brain was still muddled. "He uh… Mr. Edwards asked for me. He had a few questions… to ask."

At his gaze, I knew that unless I made some kind of sense in the seconds that were about to follow, that I would be in trouble.

Joseph however saved me. "Mr Coghlan," he called. "CEO's ready for you."

I immediately nodded politely to him, and went on my way.

I didn't need to be told from then onwards, that I was screwed. I wasn't even sure of what exactly I was guilty of, besides slacking off in the middle of the workday, but with the way the VP had looked at me, something told me that things were going to go downhill for me from then on.

In our meeting with the Vita500's Director an hour later, sure enough things began to crumble. He was far from impressed with the simple strategies that we had come up with, yet he still didn't have any definite directions that could guide us on what he would possibly be satisfied with. He stormed out of the room, and we were left alone with the VP and the rest of our team.

Later that night, I leaned against Carter under the warm, soothing, cascade of the shower, as I filled him in on how the meeting had gone.

He took the soapy washcloth up and down my arms, and across my back. "So what new direction will your team be exploring now?" he asked.

"Publicity events at colleges, and sponsoring local television shows. To be honest, I don't think he was as upset about the band and celebrities we picked, as much as he was upset that their company couldn't afford them."

He slipped the washcloth between my thighs, and my head fell backwards.

His lips lowered to nibble on my ears. "Call Tracy," he said, his tone low and raspy. "So that you can work a bit more on your idea. Flesh out something substantial, and it might have the opportunity to come to light at the end of the day."

"Hmm…" I responded, and those were the last coherent words that we were able to utter inside that stall.

"I CAN'T BELIEVE you got him to come."

I turned to see that Tracy was finally joining me on the picnic bench I'd been lounging on. She sat across from me with blotches of blue, pink, and red paint on her face, while holding an ice cream cone covered with sprinkles.

I turned around to resume my appreciation of the scene before me.

We were at one of her kindergartener's birthday parties, filled with an explosion of colors, and activities, food with children and puppies constantly running around.

"What I can't believe," I said, "is that he's actually participating and interacting with the kids. Blondie over there has been more or less latched onto his leg for the past ten minutes."

"Maggie." Tracy laughed. "She gets attached fast. Carter may just have won himself a second wife."

I couldn't help the blush that burned my cheeks at her comment, but I didn't try to acknowledge it either.

She teased me with a nudge.

I swatted her hand away.

Carter had indeed been wonderful with the kids at this party. Thus far, he seemed to be a very willing participant to the tea party between about six lovely little girls. They were seated on the tiny chairs and table that had been placed under the garden's massive apple tree. All of them wore party hats on their heads. Carter sipped dutifully from the tiny teacups, as the girls conversed and smiled at him.

I had never seen a more adorable scene.

"He might make a great father," Tracy said out of nowhere.

And… just like that, anxiety returned to my heart. It was the ever looming secret between us, and I didn't know just when, and if I'd ever have the confidence to tell him.

She noticed my withdrawal and quickly asked before I completely shut her down, "You still don't intend on telling him?"

"Not yet," I quickly dismissed. "Where did you get that cone? I need one of those."

"There's a freezer by the dining table. Daisy's mom loaded it with them."

I rose to my feet then, ready to go in search of it, but just as I got into the house, I heard a bout of laughter coming from the adjoining dining room. I walked in and saw a handful of the women, sitting together and enjoying fruity cocktails that I didn't think were completely void of alcohol. Although I was nervous, I realized this was the research audience I had come for, so I introduced myself as good naturedly as I could, and was invited to sit amongst them.

A few seconds later, I had a tall glass of ice tea in hand and received my first question.

"I heard that that piñata over there is yours," one of the women said. She was a plump, curly haired woman with freckles across her face. Her smile looked kind, but her eyes were sparkling with mischief.

"Um, yeah. He is," I replied and turned to Daisy's mom, the host of the party. She had a more quietly amused demeanor. "Thanks for allowing us to come along," I told her.

"No problem," she replied. "Any friend of Tracy's is welcome in our home. She's done such a fantastic job with the kids."

"Where did you two meet?" another asked.

I laid out my answer, truly enjoying their teasing until I could ask a question of my own, "Is being a mom rewarding?" I asked.

The freckled woman shook her head. "It is but honey, I would have preferred to be at a bar last night rather than baking cookies with my little Mason to bring here today."

"Hey!" Daisy's mom protested. "I didn't ask you to. I told you all to just come over to relax."

"Oh, they weren't for your party, they're for Daisy. Haven't you heard that Mason has the cutest crush on her?"

The mothers all laughed.

"I'm serious," she said. "Every time I come and pick him up, and you're a little late, he insists on staying with Daisy until you show up. All he talks about is Daisy; what she's doing, and what her hair smells like. So to answer your question, Leah honey, being a mom is rewarding until he gets a wife or girlfriend and then you become the *other woman*. So all we can do is love them and nurture them, and then leave them the hell alone."

I saw my opening, and spoke about the Vita500, "We're looking to present it as a pick me up for mothers."

"Well then, that's a better prospect than expecting a pick me up from your kids most days. Last night, after all the slaving, I drew a heart on one of the cookies and asked him who he loved the most: Mom or Daisy? Guess what the little brat said?"

"What?" the other women laughed.

"Daisy!"

The room exploded with laughter and I joined them.

"My back almost gave out right then. So honey, if I can find a 'pick me up' in the bottle of that Vita drink your company's selling then yes, I would be very interested. Children are no good for that."

"Noted," I replied. "I brought some along, I'll go get them and bring them over."

"We're waiting honey," she replied.

I hurried away, beyond excited. I quickly found Carter to ask for his keys.

"I'll come with you," he said. "I need a break."

"I thought you were having a blast with your new girl-friends," I teased.

He gave me a sour look as he politely excused himself from the adorable little girls, much to their protests.

We headed out together, with the women saying extremely flirtations hellos to him as we walked by them to get to the front door.

"I feel like there's a story here," he commented. "But I don't want to hear it right now. What I need is a kiss from you."

Before I could protest, he dragged me away with him, and soon we found a bathroom. He shut the door and in the next moment, his tongue was in my mouth.

"Carter, I'm working," I tried to say, but he wouldn't let me go, and the moment his hand found his way underneath my dress to grab my sex, my knees gave out. Two of his fingers shoved into me, and all I could do was hold on to his thick biceps, as my eyes rolled back into my head.

"I would fuck you right now but we're surrounded by children, and you get louder than all of them combined.

I smacked him on the arm at the tease. "You're one to talk. You fucking sobbed into my neck last night."

He grabbed my ass, pressing me to his hard on as he chuckled in response.

I loved the way his hands felt as he smoothed them up and down my body possessively, frantic with excitement. He kissed me again and I lowered to my knees. "I'm getting good material out there," I told him as I unbuckled his belt. "If those women disperse before I can return with the drinks, you're going to pay for it.

"Don't worry baby," he said, his eyes sparkling with excitement. "I'll gather them again for you."

I smiled because he didn't know just how easy that would be for him.

Soon, his cock sprang free and I gazed with adoration at my favorite part of his body besides his lips. I covered the thick, moist head with my mouth and soon took him all the way to the back of my throat.

CHAPTER 30

CARTER

I watched Leah, over the course of the days that followed, as she worked hard to collate all the information she needed for the proposal.

She finished with it however, and didn't mention it any further.

So that morning at breakfast, I brought it up. I watched her from behind the counter as she hurried out of the bedroom.

She had her heels in her hand, which she then placed on the floor, and then her purse on the couch, before hurrying over to me.

"It's all here," I said, before she could head to the fridge. Her lunch bag was already packed with the ham and egg sandwich she had made the previous evening, and the green smoothie that I'd whipped up for her.

"Oh wow," she said, as she opened the small bag to see that it'd all been prepared. "Thank you, sweetheart." She threw her hand around me, and pressed a kiss to my lips.

At the unexpected embrace, I quickly pulled my coffee cup aside, to prevent an accident. She kissed me hard, and I was sure it had been intended to be quick, but then she dipped her tongue into my mouth and lingered for a little bit before pulling away.

My vision spun.

"I'm going to need that today," she said, as she reached behind to fumble with her skirt's zipper.

Licking my lips, I put the mug down and placed my hands on her hips.

"Carter, no!" She immediately began to protest. "There's no tim—" She quieted down then, when she saw that my intention was only to help her with her zipper.

I pulled it up, and stepped away.

"Thank you." She blushed.

Damn, I loved it when she did that. So fucking adorable. "Your team's meeting with Vita500 today?"

"Yup," she said. "I still have some work on content strategy to round up in the office." She raised her wrist to check her watch. "Shit, I'm late." She started to hurry away with the lunch bag.

I caught her arm and pulled her back to me, making sure to hold her gaze. "What about your proposal?" I asked. "You're not going to present it?"

A somber smile spread across her face. "I have it with me. If I get the chance to, then I will, but if not, I'll let it go. It's probably not good anyway."

"I disagree and as the CEO, my word should mean something to you."

She faced me fully then, her thumb on the corner of my lips to most probably, wipe lipstick away. "It does," she said. "But not while we're at home."

I was amused. "So my opinions about your work will only be considered when given in the office?"

"Unfortunately, and even then, I will always have the belief that there's some element of bias involved, so even at work, everything positive from you will be taken with a grain of salt."

"Wow!" Was all I could say.

She kissed me again. "It's just one of the many evils of fucking where you eat. See you later sweetheart." She grabbed her things, and was on her way.

I got ready too, and was soon out of the house after her. Throughout the morning however, I couldn't help the concern that her work might not get the chance to see the light of day. She had worked so hard on it, and it truly was creative. It made me wonder just how many employees were being stifled in this way.

I didn't however, want to overstep my bounds in any way that would make her uncomfortable, so I ignored the grievance, and began to make plans for ways to ensure that other employees didn't meet the same dilemma.

Just before lunch however, I received her text message.

'Our prep for the meeting is complete. Just in time for lunch.'

'*That's great,*' I replied, and continued on with the performance evaluation report I was looking through.

Soon, another text message arrived. *I'm thinking of trying, one last time. I'll just head over to Henry's office and give the proposal to him. If he thinks it's good, then perhaps he can use it as a backup in case the client is still unsatisfied with our current proposal.*'

With a sigh, I put the papers down, and leaned back into the chair, rereading the message over, and over again. I could tell this affected her, and it was making it harder for me to turn a blind eye towards it. My gaze went over to her smiling, paint smeared face on the frame before me, my hands encircling her shoulders, and her eyes shut tightly in excitement, as I pressed a kiss to her cheek.

She was my girl… but I was also her boss. I had the responsibility of caring and seeing to her welfare, but the scope of work that came with both responsibilities was blurred. Where could I draw the line, and was it even possible to do so?

I picked up my phone, and sent a message back to her, '*When do you want to give it to him?*'

'*Now, seems the best time, if ever,*' she texted back immediately, as if she had been waiting anxiously for my response. I could imagine her tapping her feet on the floor, her hands wringing with anxiety.

'*Give it to him,*' I texted back. '*It's better for him to ignore you, than for you to wish that you had at least given it a shot.*'

'*Ok.*'

'*Tell me when you have handed it over to him.*'

Twenty minutes later, she replied, *'I just did. He told me to leave it on his desk, and I went on my way.'*

I rose to my feet.

'You were right,' she texted again. *'I feel better, knowing that I've pushed the hardest I could, even if he looks at it, or not. Thank you sweetheart. I'm heading out for coffee now with Jeremy. Talk later. X.'*

I slipped my arms into my suit jacket, and strolled out of the office.

When I arrived on her floor, I saw that it was quite emptied out for the lunch hour, but there were still a number of employees present. I quietly accepted the greetings as I walked towards Henry's office.

When I knocked on his door, he seemed shocked to see me. He immediately rose to his feet. "Sir?"

"Please, sit down," I replied. "I'm just here for a quick courtesy call. I got your recommendation for Raymond Allen as the new Ad Department Head?"

"Yes, sir," he replied, and took his seat.

My gaze moved and I spotted Leah's report, seemingly untouched, and atop a messy rack of files on his desk. "You worked with him and McAllister?" I asked.

"Yes, sir," he answered.

"Tell me about him," I said, and we settled into the conversation.

LEAH

The moment I returned from lunch, I had a message waiting for me.

"Henry wants to see you," I was told.

During the lunch break, I had truly tried to put the report out of my mind, it was time to move on. I didn't expect any responses whatsoever, but at the sudden request for me, my hands slightly trembled. I headed towards his door, and tried to peek through the glass of his walls, for any inkling into what the summons was about.

All I could see was him seated, focused on his computer screen.

I took a deep breath and knocked on his door.

"Come in," he said, and the moment he noticed I was there, he straightened. "Leah, I was just thinking about you. You're an extremely lucky person."

I was confused. "Um…" I couldn't find a response to his comment.

"The CEO was just here," he told me. "He unexpectedly asked about your folder, and when I told him that it was a proposal, he asked to see it. And he was very impressed. He asked if we were going to show it to the client, and although that was definitely not the plan, I'm going to take this over to the VP right now. I think your idea is very interesting, but this is basically the VP's account which is a problem in itself. I could sense how irritated even the CEO is about the personal ties to accounts that the heads sometimes have for bringing in certain clients. Anyway…" He rose. "I'll head over now, so let's hope he doesn't reject it. That's going to make my life harder which automatically means I'll make your life harder. Seems fair doesn't it?"

I was too startled to be alarmed. "Yes, sir," I replied.

I returned to my office in a daze, my mind pondering on how exactly this had played out.

Carter had stepped in personally, and although I appreciated it, his interference brought along certain pressures I wasn't sure I wanted to deal with.

Like what if this caused a strain between my bosses, especially the VP who seemed to want to be unaware of my existence these days... and Henry. He was as straight as an arrow, but if he found out that Carter's visit was influenced by my relationship with him, my job would definitely get harder to endure.

My head fell onto my hands as I pondered about in confusion. I didn't know how to feel. Would this help the client's account, or would it just bring me chaos?

An hour later, I found out.

Our client's meeting was in twenty minutes, and we were all setting up in the conference room, the needed documents and reference materials arranged as needed around the long oval table. I looked through the glass then, and saw Henry and the VP approach.

My heart began to pound in my chest, but I focused my attention on the presentation slides that I was reviewing on the desktop.

The door opened, and the two bosses came into the room.

"How's it going?" Henry asked.

Aarif, who was setting up the projector by my side, replied. "We're ready."

I tried to convince myself that I had done nothing wrong, but it became impossible for me to lift my gaze to look any of them in the eye. Until I sensed the VP's approach. "Sir," I greeted and his responding smile made my blood curdle.

"You finally got your boyfriend to help you," he derided.

The room went utterly silent. From then onwards, a pin could have been heard dropping to the floor.

"Well done," he went on, and slammed the folder I recognized, on the adjacent table. He went on with clenched teeth, and although he was just speaking to me, I knew that at least Aarif could hear every word.

"The purpose of a team, Leah, is for all its members to work collectively towards a goal. One goal, not *two*. Did he help you out? Give you the idea during pillow talk so that you could come back here to flaunt your genius idea?"

My lips moved then, "That is very inappropriate... sir."

He took a step back from me, his gaze condescending. "What you have done, is what's inappropriate. Your idea was rejected during the last meeting wasn't it? Then why keep pursuing it, and run over to your boyfriend to plead your case for you. What exactly is your intention by going this route? What exactly are you trying to say? That the rest of us are morons? That we don't know how to do our jobs? That you're the only one on this team with a brain?"

I couldn't believe his accusations. My chest seemed to be closing in on me, making it almost impossible to breath. "Sir, that wasn't what—"

"Get out!" he yelled. "You're off this team. Go design some T-shirts or whatever you want to do."

I trembled, the deep breath I inhaled, released in a shudder.

I couldn't meet anyone's gaze. I went over to my chair, and with as much dignity as I could muster, picked up my folder, and fought to keep my head high as I left the room.

CHAPTER 31

CARTER

I was on a call with Mark from the Minnesota office, when the knock came to my door.

"Come in," I said, and was surprised to see that it was my secretary, Joseph. I looked at the time on my watch. "It's 2:30 ," I said. "Is there a meeting I missed?"

"No, sir," he replied.

I noticed then that he seemed uncomfortable.

At his fumbling hands, I briefly returned my attention back to Mark. I finished the call and faced Joseph. "What's the matter?"

"Um... I've received some calls from some colleagues downstairs within the last hour, sir, and I thought that you'd want to know about them."

"Why? What are they about?"

"Miss Peters," he said.

My brows furrowed.

"It seems as though there was a tense exchange between her and the VP, and uh, it was insinuated that she used her relationship with you to her advantage with the Vita500 project."

I felt my body go still.

"They're calling to ask if you both are indeed in a romantic relationship."

I moved my gaze from him, my mood instantly darkening.

Joseph understood he should make his exit accordingly and left without another word.

Calmly, I picked up the phone and began to dial Daniel Coghlan's office.

Then I stopped myself.

I put the phone down, and got back to work.

LEAH

It felt as though there were a thousand eyes on me.

I had since jailed myself to my cubicle, my gaze completely focused on the trip advisor's comments I was replying to on behalf of one of our travel accounts. My cubicle neighbor had quickly passed it onto me upon my request of anything she needed help with, since I was now halfway to being unemployed.

At my sighs, her head would turn to mine to confirm that all was well, but I couldn't help the gloom that had befallen me today. Every time I lifted my head, I caught someone's gaze, and it was either filled with curiosity or abhorrence. I didn't miss the ceaseless whispers sent my way, or perhaps it was all in my head. I wanted a cup of coffee, but the last thing I wanted to deal with in the breakroom were snide looks or comments or even questions from the other employees.

The same went for the bathroom. I wanted to speak to Carter, but couldn't, at least not now. I was too shaken and unsettled. I also had no idea what would come out of my mouth.

So I sat still, until Jeremy's text came in. I picked up my phone and read.

'The rumor is that you've been sleeping with the boss, and used that as leverage to get the VP to consider your personal pitch. Doesn't sound like you but if it is true, just know that the only offense I'm going to take is that you didn't let me in on the details about The Godfather beyond the suit we all see. See you later.'

I gazed at his message for a long time, not exactly knowing how to feel about it. He was on the other side of the floor, and couldn't be reached easily, especially since my plan was to rot in my chair so I never had to stand up or run into anyone.

The clock struck three, and at the ding of the elevator, I turned to see Henry and the VP walk in with the client. The rest of the team was already prepared, and waiting in the meeting room, so all three men walked in and it began.

Without me.

My head fell, as I continued with my mindless responses.

Half an hour passed by, and I kept sneaking looks through the glass wall of the meeting room, curious to see what I could. One thing was for sure, and that was the fact that no one looked happy as they conversed with the client.

I returned my gaze to my screen, and felt just a small twinge of satisfaction. I didn't want the project to completely crash and burn, especially since I had worked incredibly hard on it. Sooner or later however, someone was going to have to pay for the shitty way I felt at the moment when I had done absolutely nothing else besides doing my very possible best.

"Leah..." my cubicle neighbor suddenly called.

I took a deep breath before meeting her gaze.

Her eyes had widened with alarm. She nudged her head towards the entrance door.

I turned my head just in time to see Carter as he pushed the door open and strolled onto our floor.

I pushed my chair back and almost got out of my seat. Thankfully, I remembered the eyes that were on me, and caught myself just in time. But my mind had already gone haywire.

What is he doing here?

I understood that he owned the company and could technically go wherever the fuck he wanted, but I also knew there was no way he wouldn't have heard about what happened. This was the time for him to stay away, and to keep as much distance as he possibly could from this project.

I gathered courage and stared at him as he approached, hoping he would glance at me for even a moment. Hoping, I would somehow, be able to speak to him with my eyes, to tell him to back away, so my grave wouldn't get dug any deeper.

He didn't.

His sleeves were rolled up to just below his elbow, his collar, unbuttoned, and absent of a tie. He looked dangerous, and although there was no distinct emotion on his face, I had come to know enough about him to almost feel the heat of his annoyance.

He arrived at the door to the meeting and went in.

My team members present began to rise at his sudden appearance.

With a hand up, he waved away the acknowledgement, and took his seat.

I panicked.

I picked up my phone, and sent him a text. *'Please don't do anything. Please. Just let this go. It wasn't a big deal at all.'*

I watched him, praying to God that he had brought his phone along, so when I saw him pull it out from his pocket to place on the desk, I felt immense relief. His eyes pursued the screen, and I had my look of plea ready, for when he would turn to find my gaze.

To my surprise however, he ignored it... and me. He returned his attention to the presentation being given, and my heart began to sink.

I wondered then if he was also somewhat furious at me.

A few minutes later, I softened my tone and sent another text.

'Your interference will make this worse. Please let this go Carter... please babe.'

Again, I watched as his eyes went to the phone...

I waited, and almost collapsed when his gaze lifted to find mine. My heart slammed into my chest.

His gaze however was dark, and extremely cold. For a moment, his stare was locked on me, but yet again, he returned his attention back to the presentation.

I couldn't believe it.

CHAPTER 32

*B*y the end of the meeting, I hadn't said a word, but I was more than ready to throw the client out of our office.

I, however, held my peace until it was over, and rose to my feet along with the rest of the team. "Coghlan, see me in my office," I said, and went on my way.

A few minutes later, I was seated across from him, and allowed a few moments for the restraint against punching his lights out to take effect on my nerves. When I was calmed, I asked him, "Do you truly not see the problems that this client is stirring up or are you choosing to ignore it?"

He went quiet, so I became more specific.

"You've been working on this brief for a month now, and there has been no significant progress. The client is not clear on a concept in mind, and yet he doesn't have any faith in those we've submitted to him thus far. Does the morale of the team mean nothing to you?"

"Sir…" he began.

I leaned back into the chair. "Go ahead,"

He shut his mouth, and had nothing to say except, "We'll do better to move things along."

"I'm going to give you two options," I told him. "Fire Vita500, or put out a competition. Today. Ask every employee that is interested, to send in their proposal for the campaign. The entries will be made available to every member of the agency, and they will be the ones to select the best three. They'll present their strategies to the client, and if he still isn't impressed with any of them, then that will be the end of our collaboration. The two runner ups will get a bonus for their participation, while the winner will be promoted."

Complete confusion came across his face as he tried to process all that I just said. Then he met my gaze. "Yes, sir," he said, and left my office.

Later that evening, I returned to Leah's, as was my norm. With my arrival in Indiana a month earlier, the plan had been to move out of the hotel where I'd been staying, into a place of my own if things went as well as I had hoped. Thus far, they had, but instead, Leah's home had unofficially become mine.

Tonight was one of those I reasoned would be a good move to be apart, but I didn't want whatever was brewing between us to gather up more momentum than was needed.

I expected her to be broody, so as I slipped my key into the keyhole, I cautioned myself to be as patient as was possible. After the long, trying day I'd had however, it worried me that perhaps I would be too curt and dismissive.

I pushed the door open, and was greeted with the homey smell of brewing soup.

She was slicing some mushrooms on the island and met my gaze for a brief moment. "Hi," she said, and without waiting for a response, turned to head back to the stove with the mushrooms.

I draped my suit jacket across the sofa, and after slipping off my shoes, I headed over to her. I stood just close enough to see she was preparing a creamy soup. It smelled absolutely delicious and reminded me that I had only had a quick tuna sandwich for lunch, which I had been too busy to even finish.

Normally, my arrival back home, which was usually later than hers, would prompt a long sweet kiss from her but today, she barely looked at me.

I held my peace and handed the complete reins over to her.

"It's almost ready?" She said. "Do you like garlic bread?"

I nodded, my gaze on her beautiful face, hoping I would be able to survive the incoming storm.

After a bit, we were seated side by side with each other and for the first time, we didn't say a word.

Halfway through the meal, I couldn't take it anymore. "How did the rest of your day go?" I asked, choosing the route of transparency instead of provocation.

She was ready with her attack. "Well, my scope of responsibility is now to reply to the endless stream of comments from the Oasis's trip advisor site. So I can't say it went very well."

I continued eating, "Hmm. Coghlan was indeed out of line today."

She stopped, and raised her eyes to me.

I met her gaze head on.

"Carter, what happened?" She asked. "I told you not to get involved."

"Not to get involved with what exactly?"

Her lips quivered, a multitude of responses probably coming to mind all at once. In the end, she voiced none, her sigh heavy. "Carter, I felt horrible today, and it's not going to go away tomorrow. From now on, because of my association with you, it will always seem like I do not deserve any progress that I make. That's why I didn't want to draw any attention whatsoever to us."

"I understand that," I replied. "And that's why I said that Coghlan was out of line today."

She looked even more perplexed. "Carter, for God's sake! You went to Henry, and got him to present my proposal to Daniel, and that was why everything blew up."

"I would have done that for any other employee," I said, and she went quiet.

"Leah, I didn't make Henry pay attention to your proposal because you're my girlfriend, but because it was a good proposal that most likely will get your team out of its current rut, if only the executives in charge would give an ear to it. This showed me more than anything, how sour the state of management is in the company. Who knows how many other employees have had great ideas, but have been stifled by bosses with their fucking heads in the clouds. We're together but I need you to understand that I own that company. Its success or failure will be on my head, so I am not going to make decisions that are solely based on emotions or personal relations."

Her gaze faltered then, and then her head fell in her hands. "I know, I'm sorry, it's just—how the fuck did he even figure out that we're dating? He's just fucking complicated everything."

"Why do we have to hide the fact that we're dating?" I asked.

Her head lifted then, her gaze narrowing in surprise. "Carter, it's a work environment."

"Is there a policy in place that states that employees cannot be romantically involved with each other, or their superiors?"

She seemed even more taken aback by my response, so I rose to my feet to give her the space she needed to process what I was saying. I took her plate, and mine, then headed over to the sink. I rinsed out the plates and proceeded to load them into the dishwasher. "What if we get married?" I asked. "Are you still going to hide the fact that we're together?"

"Carter, that's different."

"How? How exactly is it different?"

"That's permanent, or at least more perm… you know what I mean."

"I moved, Leah, to find you. To work at building a life with you. How much more serious does it get?"

"But that's between the both of us…"

Leaning against the counter, I folded my arms across my chest and watched her. "I don't want to pretend to not know you personally at the office. We don't have to fuck in front of everyone, but I would like to stop by your cubicle to see how your day is going when I'm on your floor for meetings. I would also love for you to head over to my office whenever you want, without having to creep around like we're having an affair."

"Carter…" She sighed. "What if we—?" She stopped herself in time. "I'm not saying that things will go bad, but life can be a bitch and—?"

"If we break up, I'll either move to a different branch, or you search for another job."

She stopped at my bluntness.

"Life is simple, Leah. Let's try to keep it that way. If your performance at the office is lacking, your personal association with me will not in any way influence the incline or decline of your career."

"I know that," she said. "But other people won't see it that way."

"Why do you care what they think?"

Our gaze locked, then with a subtle, polite nod, she looked away.

I knew it wasn't because of her acceptance of what I was saying, but just for the acknowledgement that she heard me.

She rose to her feet and headed towards her bedroom.

CHAPTER 33

LEAH

"*He* left."

The next morning, whatever rumors and gossip the office had managed to cook up was the furthest thing from my mind, as all I could think about was the fact that Carter had not come to bed the previous night. I'd waited for him, and then I left the room to check, only to see he had left the house altogether.

It made me nervous.

I stared at my computer screen, barely managing to get any work done. The moment the response came from our group chat, I turned my attention towards my phone.

'He probably just wanted to give you some space,' Tracy wrote.

'I hope so,' I texted back.

I truly hoped this was the case and not that he had been too unhappy with me, to even bear being in the same space. It had been the first night since we became official, that we had spent apart.

Suddenly, I wanted to see him, more than anything else, and almost didn't even care what anyone thought about it.

Once again, he had been right.

Who cared what they thought? Our personal lives were no one else's concern, and if they chose to adjudge otherwise, then that would be their problem and not ours.

I began to work on my perspective, and a few hours later, I believed I was now somewhat on the same page with him. But I still didn't have the confidence to completely embrace it.

I wanted to go up to his office to see him, but my legs refused to move from the chair, so I remained glued to it, and continued on with my day. Another text came into my phone and I saw that it was from Jeremy.

'Heading to the break room,' he wrote. 'I'm sure you need some coffee too.'

I hesitated, but then reasoned that talking to someone in the office who didn't seem to have suddenly lost all feeling whatsoever towards me in the light of the recent revelation, would be a much needed reprieve.

I rose from my chair, and strolled over.

When I arrived, he handed me a mug of steaming hot coffee doused with cream.

I took a much needed sip. When I reopened my eyes, I found him watching me with interest and knew that the questions were coming.

"First of all," he began. "Is it true?"

"The entire office believes it is," I replied. "Why do you still have doubts?"

"Because, there's no way that you would be able to so thoroughly hide it, especially from me."

"I wasn't hiding anything," I refuted. "It just hadn't come up."

He seemed truly surprised then. "So it is true. You're dating the CEO."

When I truly didn't deny it, his face fell with disappointment. "I thought I had a fucking chance," he swore.

Coffee almost spurted from my nose in amusement.

He raised a hostile gaze to me "You're laughing?"

"I'm sorry," I said, patting the liquid from the corner of my lips. "I just didn't expect that to be your comment. I thought that you'd push me away too, the way every other person seems to have."

"You can say that again," he said. "Even I am wondering why everyone is so butt hurt about this. One would think that you had an affair or something with someone else's man." He cocked his head in thought. "Well in a way, you kind of did."

I was doubly amused. "What?"

"We all secretly set our eyes on him, some of us with more hope than others, but yesterday all of that was crushed. How did you do it? And you move fast. He hasn't even been here that long."

"Jeremy," I said. "I didn't meet him here. We met in Alanya, when I was still on vacation."

His gaze widened, as things finally started to make more sense to him. We were interrupted then by my cubicle neighbor as she walked past. "Leah... Jeremy? Have you both seen the announcement that the VP just put out on the portal?"

My brows furrowed. "What announcement?"

"Your team's Vita500 project, Leah," she said. "It seems your client is being an asshole so the VP has made it an open brief and given until Thursday next week for any employee to come up with a good campaign strategy. The top three will be picked based on general popularity to present to the client on Friday, and whomever he goes with will be the winner."

"What?" Jeremy asked.

"What exactly does general popularity mean?" I asked.

"It means," she explained. "Every employee is going to be able to vote for the anonymous entries. The decision isn't going to be made by some executive panel."

I smiled to myself, and shook my head as Carter came to mind. She left us then, and I went over to the sink to rinse out my mug.

"Your man seems to have dealt the VP a serious blow," Jeremy said.

"No comment," I replied.

"Were you aware of this beforehand?" He asked.

I gave him a frown. "Of course not."

"I believe you," he said.

"But what makes you so sure that the CEO ordered this and not the VP himself?" I asked.

He smiled. "Because, I don't think that this was just to give the employees a chance. It was perhaps also to test the VP, especially after what he did yesterday. If he had said no to the CEO's request for this, then he would have made it clear that his alliance was not to the company or employees, but to his pride. That, Leah, would have been the start of his decline towards unemployment. Help me confirm if this theory is true from Mr. Edwards would you?"

I smacked his arm as I left the room, and returned to my desk. Picking up my phone, I texted Carter, *'Any plans for lunch?'*

My hand trembled as I placed the phone down. However, he did not respond. I waited with my heart in my throat and my gaze glued to my phone's screen.

His response came, *'No, not yet.'*

I immediately rushed to reply before he disappeared again. *'I'll get us a sandwich. Do you want to come out with me, or can we have it in your office?'*

'Let's have it here,' he replied.

I released a deep sigh of relief.

By lunchtime, I hurried over to the coffee house, a short distance away from the office and ordered us both a chicken sandwich. I then returned to the office, and didn't bother stopping on my floor as I headed over to his. When I arrived at his door, I found his secretary's desk was unoccupied.

Glad at his absence, which I suspected Carter might have had a hand in. I gave three little knocks to his door.

His voice came from within, "Come in."

I pushed the door open, and saw him behind his desk.

He lifted his gaze from the documents he was perusing in hand at my entrance.

I sent him a smile. "Do you want me to come over there, or do you want us to stay here?"

"I'll be right there," he replied.

With a nod, I headed over to one of the single seater sofas in his lounge area. I unpacked the sandwich and white chocolate cookies I had gotten for him, and soon enough I heard his approach.

I looked up to watch him, dressed simply today in a dark, round necked shirt, under an equally dark patterned blazer. His hair didn't have a single strand out of place and his face was completely shaven, showing off skin so supple that it glistened.

It reminded me so much of the first time I'd seen him, and how I had been completely struck by his very presence. What a way we had come since then.

He reached me and instead of sitting by my side, took his seat on the edge of the coffee table opposite me, so he could face me directly.

This kind of proximity wasn't every good for the rhythm of my heart, but I tried my best to remain composed as he retrieved his wrapped sandwich from me. He pulled the paper backwards and took a bite, while I focused on mine.

We were silent as we ate, occasionally stealing looks at each other and sending smiles, until I couldn't take it anymore. I knew he was waiting on me by all means, to speak first. "You left, last night," I said, my voice sounding smaller than I had intended. But I could do nothing to increase the tempo. I was shy and vulnerable with him and it stripped me bare of my usual established confidence. "Were you so angry that you couldn't even bear to be in the same room with me for the night?"

He seemed unfazed as he replied, "I didn't leave because I couldn't bear to be with you. I just didn't want you upset throughout the night. I stayed on the couch for a little bit, but then since I couldn't fall asleep, I just went back to the hotel."

"I wouldn't have been upset, and I also missed you," I told him.

I lifted my gaze to see the softness in his.

"I missed you too," he said. "I won't do it again."

"Please don't," I said. "Even when we're upset with each other, I don't want us to be apart. And I wasn't upset with you, I was just... conflicted. But now, I've thought things through and you're right. I did nothing wrong and I shouldn't act like a criminal, just because I'm dating you."

His grin was blinding as he set his sandwich down. "I knew you'd come around."

Before I knew it, his hand slid around my neck. I was pulled into a kiss that weakened my bones, and I almost fell into him when he ended it and sat back.

He stabilized me with a laugh and brushed the curls on the side of my head away from my face.

I shut my eyes, melting into his touch as my heart jumped around in my chest. "For the record, I'm sorry, Carter," I said. "And thanks for always being on my side, and that of your employees. You're a great boss, and lover."

A deep emotion flashed in his eyes as he stared intently at me. "I'll always be on your side, Leah. I hope that you'll also always be on mine."

"I will," I promised.

He sealed it with yet another kiss.

I was on top of the world when I returned to my floor after lunch, and was even more ecstatic over my plan for the rest of the day. Since my scope of duties had now been significantly reduced, I accessed the employee's portal and found the announcement for the competition.

The rest of the afternoon was spent preparing and polishing up my proposal, and by the end of the day, I sent it in, anonymously as the requirements requested. Regardless of what happened from then on, my heart was now settled and grateful for the chance.

When I was done, most people had already left for the day, so I picked up my purse, and went home to Carter.

CHAPTER 34

CARTER

*a*t the end of the following week, I sat anxiously in my office, awaiting the result of Leah's presentation to the Vita500 team. Just as I'd predicted, her anonymous proposal amongst two others had been selected, and I couldn't wait to hear what the final result would be.

"Are you even listening to me?"

At the offended tone, I lifted my gaze and was reminded once more that Mark was sitting across from me. He had flown in from Minnesota to try to settle a discord about the suit at our Chicago's office.

"I am," I told him, the knots in my stomach tightening even further at the reminder of the legal annoyance. "I'll have to ponder on the best way to counterattack this. I'll get back to you tomorrow."

"I say we just pay them off and make this whole thing go away."

"And then make ourselves an easy target for anyone else who wakes up on the wrong side of the bed in the future? No way. You know what, I'll head over there myself tomorrow, and when all this is resolved I'll also stop by St. Paul to review things there."

His smile was wide. "I was beginning to think that you'd never travel out of Indianapolis again."

"I was hoping I wouldn't have to, but yet here we are."

His face fell. "Is that a shot at me? Because I'm going to send it right back to you. My job is to increase your assets, not help you manage them. With your move here, I have been bearing the brunt of the work and my salary has still remained the same."

My phone vibrated with the arrival of a message then, so I picked it up. "You already earn much too much money for your own good, Garrity," I said.

'We're done,' Leah had written in the text. *'I won! My legs are about to give out.'*

I laughed out loud at the news, much to Garrity's surprise.

"What's going on?" he asked.

I filled him in.

"Wow! That's great news," he said.

"Amazing news." I beamed.

"What are you both doing after work today? I'd like to buy her a drink."

I cocked my brow. "You want to buy *her* a drink?"

"Of course! What were you expecting? That I'd buy you one too? You'll pay for yours."

"Well, I'm declining," I told him.

"C'mon man. Who knows when next I'll be here?"

"From your pattern so far, I'd say in about two weeks."

"Carter," he called. "I'm serious. She seems very special to you. I want to meet her, officially."

"Well you can't, at least not tonight. Her friend is having an engagement party and we have to be there."

"Great! Can I come along?"

With an inward groan, I dialed Leah's number and was a bit surprised when she picked up.

"Hey," she said.

I could hear the breathlessness in her voice. "How's it going down there?" I asked.

"Overwhelming. It seems like the whole world is congratulating me. I need you. Why aren't you here?"

"It's your moment. I don't want to distract others from that. I'll have all night to congratulate you."

I heard a sudden cough then and remembered that Garrity was in the room. I gave him a sour look and turned away. "We're still on for Tracy's party tonight, right?"

"Yes we are," she replied.

"Mark Garrity wants to come along, my CFO from Minnesota."

"Oh, I know him. Of course, he can. I'll talk to Tracy about it."

"I was hoping you'd say no," I said.

"I heard that!" Mark called out. "Thank you, Leah! See you tonight."

"Did you hear him?" I asked her.

"I did," she said, sounding amused. "Tell him I said he's welcome."

"Sure will."

"See you at 6?"

"See you at 6," I replied.

"Oh wait, I have one more question," she said. "I didn't bother asking before because I wasn't too sure I'd win, but what position am I going to be promoted to in the new Ad Department?"

"That's between me and the management team."

"Carter!" She called out.

"I love you, Leah," I told her.

Her silence at the sudden declaration was deafening.

"See you later," I said with a grin and ended the call.

I returned to Mark but just as I took my seat, her text came in. *I love you too, Carter. Thank you for believing in me.*

My heart felt like it was going to burst but I pushed the phone away, as I tried my best to focus on Mark.

"What position is she going to hold in the department?"

"How does Creative Director sound?" I asked. "It lines up with her interest and her past performance. I think she'll excel at it."

"Sounds great to me." He nodded.

CHAPTER 35

LEAH

I walked into my new office and could not believe the space I'd been granted.

It was a small corner office in the north wing of the building, and for a moment, my legs felt just a bit shaky. I needed Carter here, but he was already on his flight back to Minnesota.

A knock sounded at the door. I turned to see a bouquet of flowers through the glass wall... I knew who it was. "Come in," I called, and to my amusement, he hid his face behind the bouquet.

"Thanks, Jeremy," I said, as I began to unpack my personal items from my box. The first was the framed picture of my love. The one we had taken at the park, with our faces imprinted with the paint covering of the others palm, and other splotches of lavender and red.

"They're not from me," he said. "I wouldn't know that your favorite flowers are orchids."

"Ah," I replied. He was right. Only one other person would, and it made my heart ache even more. I felt overwhelmed, by everything and longed for him to be here with me. A simple hug or a stolen kiss and my feet would feel like they were on the ground.

I took my seat, needing to breathe.

Jeremy laid the massive bouquet on the desk. "I'll get you a glass vase for that at lunch time," he said. "That'll be my congratulatory gift."

"I'll accept it," I smiled as he took his seat opposite from me, and looked around in wonder. "The Godfather sure didn't hold back with this bit of luxury for his girl," he said, as he gazed at the wall to ceiling windows behind me. "I would be so freaking jealous of you right now but what's the point? I'll probably be in here more than you will." Lifting his legs, he placed them on my table as he leaned into the chair with complete abandon. His laughter filled the space.

It and his presence that allowed me to breathe just a bit more easily.

His gaze on me also sparkled with fondness as he said once again, "Congratulations, Leah. You truly deserve this."

"Do I?" I asked nervously.

"You do, and no one can contest that. The only thing contestable is how you landed the Godfather when the rest of us weren't even given a chance. I still can't believe he moved here because of you,"

My heart softened even further. "I have no idea why either. Fate, I guess."

"Well, she's a bitch because she's still holding out on me."

"Be a little bit more polite to her and maybe she'll shower even better favors down on you."

"I'm not holding my breath." He rose. "Gotta get back to work. I'm going to have my lunch here by the way."

"Hell no! The office's gonna stink."

"I'll get you some scented candles. The overpriced kind."

"No!" I refused.

He was already on his way out, shutting the door behind him.

Once again, leaving me alone and immediately, I reached for my phone to reread Carter's texts from earlier that morning.

'*Boarding,*' was the last one he'd sent.

And then on his way to the airport. '*Have a great first day love... you deserve this win. Don't forget about me though.*'

I smiled at his words. As if I could. A while without thinking about him would do me more good, than he could imagine.

I turned around to hide from the gaze of the floor beyond, and placed my hand on my stomach. I would begin to show in a few weeks, and no doubt, he would notice.

We still had a long way to go, to fully understand each other but I guess that's what a lifetime was for. But would he be willing to go that distance with me? This was my grand concern.

He had already leaped over so many boulders for me, but would this one be too high? I wished I had the confidence to tell him now, but fear swarmed my heart, even as I strongly believed I didn't have to worry.

But there was always that skeptic in the back of my mind, ever waiting, and expecting people to fail me. Nevertheless, and regardless of whatever happened from henceforth, this baby was now mine. He or she had turned from just my slip up with a fling, to a child I'd made with someone that... was in my heart. Someone whom I knew I was already in love with. And this made all the difference to me. Someone whom I had now found was truly worthy of being the father to my child.

No matter what happened from here on out, he or she would be loved from the depths of my soul.

TWO WEEKS LATER, I took a sick day off so I could get a long weekend.

Guilt pricked me as I drove home that Thursday evening, especially given my promotion and all the new responsibilities that came with it. But I needed a very long weekend, and Friday night was just too late a start with Carter.

I drove straight to the airport from the office and boarded the 7 pm flight headed to Minnesota.

My hands trembled as I secured the seatbelt across my waist, in my preparation for takeoff, and as we did, I couldn't help but realize this would be the turning point. This weekend, I was going to tell him about the baby, and it worried me that perhaps there would be too many surprises for him to deal with. Nonetheless, he needed to know and it was the right thing to do.

He wasn't even aware I was coming to Minnesota, but a few nights earlier, I had managed to extract the information that I would be welcomed.

I also knew his home address, so the plan was to take a taxi from the airport, straight to his home. Then I would call him to find out where he was. The main goal was to have him open his door at the sudden knock, and find me in front of it, hopefully without a nervous smile on my face.

The plane took off, so with my hands resting over my stomach, I shut my eyes, and tried to get some sleep.

CARTER

I was losing focus.

The day had been too long, with countless meetings and fires to put out, but I needed to finish with the restructuring proposal for our Chicago office. I turned yet another page, and the words blurred in front of me.

I had worked at the same mad pace ever since I'd returned here, jam packing as much as I could into my days because the sooner things were sorted out, the sooner I would be able to get back to Leah.

Putting the report down, I picked up my phone and dialed her number.

It didn't go through.

This seemed odd. I checked the time and saw it was just a little past 9 pm.

She would be at home right now, or perhaps she was still at the office... she had mentioned how focused she was with the new state tourism account I had passed onto her.

Joseph would definitely no longer be at the office but perhaps Jeremy would know of her whereabouts. A few minutes later, I had him on the line, and could hear the shock in his tone at my contact.

"Yes, this is Jeremy... s-sir. Is there a problem?"

"I apologize for startling you," I replied. "But I'm not able to reach Leah. Did you see her before you left the office?"

"No, sir, I did not," he replied. "She left before me. She also took a sick day off for tomorrow."

My nerves tightened with concern. "A sick day? She wasn't feeling well?"

"Not that I know of, but she told me not to worry about it. That she was fine."

"Thank you, Jeremy," I said, and ended the call. From then on, I pushed the report aside and rose to my feet. I immediately dialed Tracy and went over to the windows overlooking the brightly lit city skyline.

She picked up after the third ring, also surprised that I was contacting her.

"Have you heard from Leah?" I asked. "I can't reach her, and it seems she took a sick day off from work for tomorrow."

"Uh..." she said. "I t-think she's all right. She'll probably contact you soon."

I cocked my head at her response. "'Has she been active on your group chat within the last hour?"

"She uh—I'm not sure, let me call you back."

Before I could protest, she ended the call and I was left staring at the disconnected phone. I became worried then, impatience and frustration welling up inside of me.

"Sir?"

I suddenly heard a call from behind me. I turned around to see that it was my secretary, Meredith. "Your call with Chicago is in ten minutes. We've already set up in conference room 3. We're just waiting on you now."

"Everyone's seated?" I asked.

"Yes, sir."

I groaned inwardly, close to cancelling the meeting, but it had taken a village to put together. So I headed over to my table, and quickly wrote down a note. I grabbed my jacket, and at the door, handed the note over to her. "Keep calling this number, and when it goes through, introduce yourself as my secretary and ask for Leah Peters. If she's the one that answers, ask her if she's okay and relay that I'm fucking pissed that I'm not able to reach her."

"Yes, sir," she replied.

I went on my way.

CHAPTER 36

LEAH

J received Tracy's text message just as I arrived at the Minnesota airport.

'Leah! Carter called! He's incredibly anxious that he can't reach you. Have you landed? I just told him that I'd call him back, and hung up.'

I was just about to respond to the text, when a call came in. It was definitely not a number on my contact's list, but one from Minnesota. Perhaps it was Carter. So I picked up, but instead heard the smooth response of a woman's voice.

"Miss Leah Peters?" She called.

"Yes?"

"I'm Meredith, Mr Edward's secretary. He's in a meeting right now so he can't contact you directly, but he's been trying to get in touch with you for the last hour. Is everything alright?"

I sighed, remorseful that I had caused him to be so worried. I wondered then if it would be best to just inform him of my arrival, but I couldn't make up my mind. "Everything's fine," I replied. "Please tell him to give me a call the moment he's available."

"I will," she said and hung up.

I found a taxi then, and after giving him the address to Carter's apartment complex, I settled in the backseat and sent a reply to Tracy. Carter was still in a meeting at work, but I had all the information needed to access his building and apartment.

In our phone conversations, I had hinted at a surprise visit and cajoled him to facilitate its possibility.

So a half-hour later, I arrived at the high rise apartment building in downtown St. Paul and walked into the glistening reception, I gave my name to the front desk and hoped to God that Carter had registered my name as one of his acceptable guests.

"Miss Leah Peters." He nodded "I have you right here. You can go right ahead ma'am."

I thanked him. I knew Carter wasn't home, but I still got even more nervous as I approached his apartment on the seventh floor. I would go in to wait for him, and hopefully, he wouldn't be too startled upon his return at the stranger in his house, and club me to death before it registered that it was me. Just to be sure of his location though, I decided to give his secretary another call. It was pretty late so I wasn't sure she would pick up, and was pleasantly surprised when she did.

"Miss Peters?" She answered.

"Hello? Yeah, this is Leah Peters. I'm calling to check if Mr. Edwards is still in his meeting."

"Yes, he is," she answered somewhat coldly.

"Oh alright, thank you." I replied and ended the call with a face. Perhaps her tone was just naturally that curt, or she was cranky from still being at work so late.

The elevator door dinged open and I stepped out with my luggage. I watched the numbers on the doors for his, and then turned the corner. Given the arrangement, it would be at the end of the hallway.

I lifted my gaze however, and I froze.

He was already home.

The door was slightly ajar, and his hand on the knob.

He was wearing a baseball hat over his head and smiling at someone. Suddenly, long painted fingernails came out of nowhere and settled on his chest. A woman appeared, her bone straight dark hair swishing behind her. She pushed him against the frame of the door, and in moments, their lips were locked together in a ravenous kiss.

Her ass was *grabbed*, and something in my heart shattered.

I immediately began to turn around, almost desperate to be out of there before either of them spotted me. But in my haste, my ankle twisted on the heel of the shoes I had on, and I went down.

I landed on my knees, barely managing to break the fall, though my hand shot out to the wall for support. I glanced back in alarm, and saw that they had both turned their attention towards me. In the near darkness I met Carter's hooded, green gaze.

He just watched me quietly as though viewing a spectacle. There was absolutely no emotion, not fear, or shock or remorse.

"Was she coming over here?" the woman asked.

"I have no idea," he said.

She smacked him on his chest.

"Hey!" He protested.

"Who the fuck is she?"

"How the hell would I know?" he shot back.

I got up and wished so badly that I could throw something at him, but I couldn't give up my shoes or purse. So I got my things together, and faced him. "I don't ever want to hear from you again!" With that, I turned around and ran as quickly as my sprained ankle would let me.

I felt myself disintegrating inside, and could only pray I would be able to hold it together until I at least found a taxi to take me back to the airport.

I pounded on the elevator's button as I reached it, terrified that he would come after me. It was the next most devastating thing in the world that could happen at this moment, because if he did, I wasn't sure what I would do to him. But a damage free ending for either of us was not going to be among the options.

The car arrived and I jumped into it.

Someone arrived in a taxi just as I ran out of the building, and I was grateful for that bit of favor.

I got in, and was soon on my way back to the airport. I tried to push away the barrage of sorrow and confusion, but it seemed as though a thousand nails had been hammered and lodged into my heart.

I kept my eyes on my phone as I prayed over and over again that there would be a flight out of the town tonight. The only one I was able to find, a few minutes later, was scheduled to depart in an hour, and was at an exorbitant, business class price.

Without any further thought, I booked it and mentioned to the driver that a heavier tip would be in the cards if he doubled his speed, and brought me to the airport in time for the flight.

I rolled the window down, and tried for my own sake to remember how to breathe.

I BROKE down midway through the flight.

And I shouldn't have. I told myself that there was no need to be so overtaken with despair, but as I thought of the baby growing innocently inside of me, I couldn't hold back anymore.

Tears poured from my eyes… and my throat closed up until I had to run to the bathroom to keep from waking up the entire cabin. In there, I crumbled onto the seat, and refused to come out. Not until I could get myself in order, but as I stared at my sunken eyes, I wondered if this was the 'after' that people spoke about.

The defining moments that split your life into two. The desirable before- and the tragic, never able to recover from-after.

A loud, impatient knock sounded on the door again, the perhaps hundredth in the last hour but this time I didn't respond with a vicious, *"I'm not fucking done."*

Because this time around, I truly was.

I rinsed my face, straightened my clothes, and returned to my seat.

THE PAIN BEGAN JUST as I landed back in Indianapolis.

As I got into the taxi, the pressure in my pelvis seemed to compound, forcing me to wrap my hands around my stomach.

At first, it was manageable, my mind unable to focus too much on the pangs that were hitting me at increasingly frequent intervals, but then just before I arrived home, one came along and it was as though someone had kicked me squarely in the gut.

I doubled over, to the driver's alarm, and could barely meet his gaze in the rearview mirror.

"Are you alright ma'am?" He asked, concerned, and I managed to respond with a wave, that I would be okay.

The episode of pain lessened enough for me to get into the house. I limped to my bedroom, and immediately went to bed.

CHAPTER 37

CARTER

I returned to the apartment at a little past midnight, to meet it in disarray, yet again.

The pillows that were once arranged on the couch were now littered all over the floor, and on the heavy glass coffee table, were empty bags and wrappers of what seemed to be every snack known to man. His clothes were on the ground, and I could see that the refrigerator's door had been left wide open.

For his sake, and especially given the day that I'd had, I prayed to God he was behind it.

I waited, my briefcase in hand until he emerged from behind the tall steel door with a bowl of cereal in hand.

He slurped a spoonful into his mouth, most of the milk making its way back into the bowl as he shut the door. At first, he was a bit startled to see me, but then he quickly recovered, a wide smile stretching across his face. "You're back," he said. "It's already past midnight. I thought you'd be staying over at the office again. Oh, and before I forget, we've run out of berries. All of them. I like to have them with the cereal, but now the fridge is empty. Perhaps you could remind your cleaning lady to get some the next time she delivers groceries to you."

I ignored him and continued on my way towards the bedroom on the top floor. I had just gotten in and was taking off my clothes when he appeared at the door, his bowl in hand.

"Can't you eat properly?" I asked, at the irritating slurping sounds that repeatedly struck the silence of the room.

"Hey!" He shot back. "Enough with the derogatory comments, okay? I had a tough day too. Also some woman came by and acted all crazy. It even pissed Natalia off... made her assume that I was cheating on her or something."

"You brought Natalia here again? Aren't you supposed to be focused on finding a job?"

"Carter, I don't ask you for anything besides the roof over my head right now, and you're barely even here. Is that still too much for you to spare? Me not having to think about that while I'm trying to get my shit together, isn't that something you could do for me without the verbal abuse?"

I didn't have the energy to deal with his complaints, so I continued stripping, unable to wait for a much needed shower.

"The woman..." he went on. "Do you know her?"

"What woman?" I groaned.

"Curly red hair, kinda short, crazy eyes." He shrugged. "She told me to never call her again when she saw me kissing

Natalia in front of the door, and up till now I'm still wondering what the fuck she was talking about."

Something instantly clicked in my head at his description, and I spun around to face him. "What? Leah came by?"

"Leah? Is that her name?"

My heart suddenly dropped into my stomach. I grabbed my phone from the pile of clothes on the bed and immediately dialed the front desk.

"Simon, were any new guests under my name admitted into the building tonight?"

"I'll check that, sir," he said. "Just a moment."

I waited, my foot tapping anxiously against the plush carpet.

Soon enough, he returned with a response, "Yes, sir. A Miss Natalia Pool, and a Miss Leah Peters. They're amongst your list of approved guests, so I admitted them up to your floor."

I shut my eyes, as the misfortune that had just befallen me became apparent. "Thank you, Simon." I ended the call, and immediately dialed Leah's number. "Tell me what happened," I said to Andrew. "Don't leave any single detail out."

"Well, nothing beyond what I've already said. She had luggage in hand, and looked like she was coming towards your door, but then she saw me and Natalia standing by it and stopped. She just glared at me, as if shocked and then she turned to hurry away. She couldn't have gotten out of here fast enough, but she fell as she was running away. And she got right back up. Was she insane, or something? I still can't figure it out."

"Fucking pick up!" I yelled into the phone when it disconnected again.

My actions startled Andrew. "Dude, are you okay?" He asked.

I turned to him, my chest burning with so much rage. "That was my fucking girlfriend," I said. "She fucking thought you were me, and that I was probably cheating on her or something."

He stilled, as he tried to take in the information, while I dialed her number again.

"Oh…" he said. "*Oh!* That was why she ran away? But that's hella dumb. She doesn't know that you have a twin? An identical one for that matter?"

I didn't bother responding, as I switched gears and began to dial Meredith's number.

"Ah," he said. "It makes sense now. She actually thought that I was you. How did I not come up though? You don't talk about your family at all?"

With a shove to his shoulder, I pushed him out of my way as the line connected. "Meredith, sorry for calling so late, but can you get me on the next flight to Indianapolis? Any of them."

"Sure. I'll get on it, sir."

I ended the call and began to dial Tracy, but then I stopped myself, completely exhausted from the day and from constantly chasing after Leah.

Sure, it had been a misunderstanding, but why had her first response, just like always, been to run? To run without giving me a chance? I understood how badly the situation must have seemed to her, but did she have absolutely no faith whatsoever in me? After what we had come to mean to each other?

I returned my gaze to the phone, and dialed Meredith again. "Meredith, there's no need to look for the flight any longer. I'm sorry for the hassle."

"Oh. It's all right, sir. Are we still on schedule for tomorrow?"

I paused for a moment, my stomach churning with anxiety at the decision I was about to make. I took a deep breath and replied. "9 am with Chicago. Yes, we are."

"Very well, sir, goodnight."

I ended the call, and when I turned around, saw that Andrew had left. I headed straight to the bathroom.

The moment the warm shower cascaded down on me, and began to soothe the exhaustion from the day away, I could feel my stress and annoyance begin to dissipate. I knew deep down that I would be too conflicted to stay away from her for too long, so my only hope was that she would buckle, and show me that I was important enough for her to give me the benefit of the doubt.

But the fear lurked, that perhaps I was being too careless, and that what she had seen, compounded with my silence would push her too far away for me to reach.

Either way, I refused to give in, at least for tonight.

I would at least give myself the night to feel disappointed.

IT HAD NEVER BEEN MORE difficult to fall asleep.

I tossed and turned, trying to find the peace of heart to get some iota of rest, but the pit of my stomach simmered with turmoil. Despite my annoyance at her hasty conclusion, what I really wanted, rather than keeping my distance from her, was to confront her about it. To pour out my annoyance, and then to have us make up afterwards. This distance was chipping away at my soul, and solving nothing.

Frustrated, I got up from bed and stepped out onto the balcony of my bedroom.

The feel of autumn was in the air, with its crisp chill. It truly was the time that signaled death and impermanence, and the very thought turned me into a spineless bastard. I picked up my phone and texted Tracy. *'Has she returned? How is she?'*

It was now almost four am in the morning, and at the hectic day that loomed before me, I wondered how I was going to face it with such a lack of energy. With the resolve to chase sleep down, I turned around to head back into the bedroom and just as I did, my phone began to ring.

It was an odd time for a call, but when I looked down and saw that it was Tracy, my heart skipped a beat. "Hello?"

"Carter, good morning." she said politely. "What do you mean by 'has she returned?' Isn't Leah with you?"

My sigh was heavy. She hadn't yet told her friends about what had happened. It was either that, or she hadn't yet arrived back home in Indianapolis. The latter possibility immensely disturbed me. "No, she isn't," I replied. "There was a misunderstanding, and she left before I could get to her."

"Dear Lord," she muttered under her breath. "Is she okay though? I mean... is everything okay between you two?"

I took a seat on the bed. "That's why I texted you. Please check up on her for me."

"She's not answering your calls?"

"She isn't," I replied.

"Alright," she said.

"Thank you, Tracy."

LEAH

I gripped the edges of the bed, as the doctor walked in with a nurse behind her... a thin woman with severe bangs, and red rimmed glasses. Behind the lens, I tried to see what I could from her hazel eyes as she went through my chart in her hands.

"Miss Peters..." she began.

I felt my soul begin to leave my body. "Did I lose the baby?" My voice quivered.

It was only at her long silence that I realized my eyes were clenched shut. I reopened them, and met her gaze.

"Calm down," she said. "You did not. Your baby is fine. How do you feel?"

My gasp for air was soundless but no less painful as my eyes blurred with tears of relief. I patted my stomach in consolation.

"How do you feel," she repeated.

IONA ROSE

All I could do was nod in response.

She went on, "We still have to figure out why you're bleeding so much, and the source of the abdominal pain. Your ultrasound wasn't as conclusive as I'd hoped, so I'm going to schedule you for a Hysteroscopy."

"What's that?" I asked.

"It's a procedure that's going to allow me to look inside your uterus, so that I can diagnose the source of your bleeding."

I nodded to her in complete submission. "W-when will it begin?" I stuttered. "C-can I call someone beforehand?"

"Sure," she said. "I'll schedule you down for the test later in the morning. Try to get some rest before then."

"Thank you," I said. I immediately found my phone, and called Tracy. I couldn't do this alone. The worst seemed to have passed, but from now onwards, I just could not deal with all of this on my own. Just then, my phone began to ring, and seeing that she was the caller, relief washed over me."

"Hey," she said. "I know it's early but I just thought to check on you. How are things going with Carter?"

At the mention of his name, and at her care, just when I was about to reach out to her, my throat constricted again. I couldn't hold myself back as the sobbing began again, and it didn't stop until she arrived.

When she did, I told her all that had happened with Carter.

She sat in silence on the edge of the bed.

CHAPTER 38

I was in the middle of my scheduled meeting with Chicago, when I received Tracy's text message.

'You can call now.'

I immediately got up and excused myself, to the surprise of the other executives seated.

After finally giving up on sleeping, at the crack of dawn, I had tried contacting Tracy again, concerned at the lack of updates.

At first, my multiple dials had gone through, and then, the line had become completely unreachable. I had been out of balance ever since.

"Hey," I breathed out anxiously into the receiver. "What's going on? Is everything okay?"

"Everything is *not* okay," she sniped. "You told me that there was a misunderstanding. What is to fucking misunderstand when she saw you with another woman? What is wrong with you Carter?" She cried. "Don't you care about her? She finally opens up to you, lets you into her heart and then you go and do this? Do you freaking know that she's pregnant, and because of you she almost fucking lost the baby. She's in the hospital right now, alone, and terrified because of this damn mess that you've put her in—"

"What did you just say?" I asked, but she couldn't hear me over her enraged shouting. "Tracy!" I roared into the phone, and it instantly shocked her silent. I sensed a quiet also settle over the office floor I was on, as no doubt the employees were startled out of their minds at my sudden explosion. "What did you just say?" I asked. "She's pregnant? She's in the hospital?"

She finally calmed down enough to respond to me, "Yes," she replied, "And I shouldn't be telling you this."

"What hospital?" I asked.

"She doesn't want anything to do with you Carter. Just... just stay away for a little while. When things settle, you both can come together and decide what's best for—"

"Tracy," I said through gritted teeth. "I wasn't the one that Leah saw at the door. That was my twin brother, Andrew. She mistook me for him. Do you fucking hear me?" My voice shook.

She went silent.

"Where's the hospital?" I asked again.

"I'll send you the address," she said quietly.

I ended the call.

. . .

Leah

I was served a late breakfast after my return from the hysteroscopy test.

Seated upright on my bed, I regarded the meal of eggs and toast, and didn't feel too keen on consuming any of it. But I was thoroughly aware, now more than ever of how much it was needed, especially by my baby. So I began to eat.

I turned to glance through the barely covered glass wall of my room and saw Tracy with her phone to her ear as she paced the corridor over and over. When she was done, I watched her go still, her eyes lowered to the ground and it made me feel so incredibly guilty. I had forced her here at such an early time, and she had also chosen to take the day off from work.

She turned then, so I put my bowl of fruit down so I could tell her to carry on with the rest of the day, without the concern over my welfare. The look on her face though the moment she returned to the room struck me with alarm. "What's wrong?" I asked.

For the longest time, she stared at me, and then she released a deep breath.

"Tracy," I called.

She pulled a chair to my side, and took her seat.

"Stop it. You're scaring me."

"Don't be," she said. "There's nothing wrong... kind of."

I let out a deep breath. "I've already had more than enough surprises to deal with for the month. I don't need anymore."

She stared into my eyes, and I saw that her lips trembled slightly. "I called Carter," she said.

My face fell. "What?"

"You were wrong, Leah."

"What the fuck are you talking about? Why would you do that? Did you tell him?"

She was unmoved by my annoyance. "He's not the one you saw at his door," she said, her voice hard. "That was his twin brother, Andrew. You mistook him for Carter."

I froze, the announcement jarring me into a stupor. "What?" I breathed.

"Carter's on his way right now from Minnesota."

My mouth fell open. "How could that—how could he have a twin?"

"He never mentioned it?" She asked.

I thought hard. "He's mentioned having a brother, but they're estranged because of the split between his parents. They've been out of touch for…" The shock came once again, and hit me with the force of a boulder. "He has a twin?" My voice shook.

She nodded.

I buried my face in my hands.

HOURS LATER, my hands were still wringing until I was sure I was going to peel the skin off my bones.

Tracy had refused to go home, choosing to stay with me until he at least arrived.

He would be furious, the cold accusing gaze that he would rightly have for me already vivid in my mind's eye. It terrified me, but what I prayed for once again was his mercy.

Why was it so easy for me to dismiss him? Despite all he had been to me so far, and how much he had showed me just how much I meant to him.

"Was I completely wrong?" I asked, only vaguely aware that Tracy was still in the room as I stared restlessly at the door.

She held my hand. "Anyone else would also have been shocked, and hurt," she consoled me.

"My fault," I told her. "I should have had more faith in him. Allowed him to explain himself. He knows as well as I do, that the situation would have been resolved there and then if I had even as much as called his name. His brother would have known that I was referring to the wrong person. Things would have been sorted out. But instead I ran... like I have... over and over again, when it comes to him. And he knows that. And he is going to be furious."

"You can't know that he will be furious," Tracy said. "He was the one that contacted me to check up on you."

"He contacted you, not me!"

"Well, he did try, didn't he?"

I shut my eyes, my heart sinking. "I wouldn't know. I shut off my phone."

"You both will be fine, just explain it was a mistake and one you're truly sorry happened," she said. "You'll pull through this, especially for your baby's sake."

"I'm weakening his trust in me. That's what I'm terrified of. That he'll lose faith in me."

"Well, this is a chance for a new start... with him. Apologize, but with all your heart. He'll hear you."

Just then, I sensed a movement in my peripheral vision, and my head snapped towards the glass.

There he was.

Dressed in his usual formal attire-a pin striped two piece, with a crisp white dress shirt underneath, rolled up to his elbows.

The very sight of him made my heart twist with an unbeatable pain, at the man I kept taking for granted. My resolve to grovel was immediately locked into place, as he pushed the door open and came into the room.

His eyes were on me, and they were sunken. Whether it was with exhaustion, disappointment or loathing, I couldn't tell.

I deserved all three.

Tracy immediately rose from the chair so he could take a seat by me.

Instead, he broke his gaze from mine. "Where's her doctor?" he asked.

Tracy shot me a glance.

I nodded to her and she moved.

He went with her, my heart going with him as they exited the room without another word.

Groveling… wouldn't get me out of this one.

CHAPTER 39

CARTER

J was conflicted as I watched her.

I stood away from her door, but positioned myself in a way that gave me a clear view of her.

She sat in a sullen silence, her head lowered and seemingly deep in thought.

I didn't know what to feel.

On one hand, my heart burned with malice that she'd kept her pregnancy away from me, and for so long. She was now almost two and a half months along, so that meant that she had most likely been aware of the baby even before I'd arrived in Indianapolis. Maybe it was why she had fallen sick and taken the day off when I'd first arrived here. Maybe that was why she had initially tried to push me away.

My head was swirling, and I didn't know where to begin.

I heard approaching footsteps and lifted my gaze to see it was Tracy.

She wore a cautious smile on her face, and held a steaming cup of coffee in her hand. "You've seen her doctor?" she asked.

I nodded quietly, and we both turned to watch Leah. "She says it's uterine fibroids, and that there's no cause for alarm. She'll start her off on medication first, and then monitor her. If things worsen, then they'll consider other minimally invasive procedures."

A long silence passed between us, before she spoke again, "You understand why she had to keep it from you, right?" Her voice was small, almost as though she was hoping I wouldn't hear what she was saying, but still couldn't stop herself from speaking either way. "You understand her, right?"

When I didn't respond, she turned to face me, and when I met her gaze, I found in her eyes the quiet desperation for things to work out between me and her friend.

"Does she understand me?" I asked. "Does she understand that I love her?"

Tracy's gaze faltered.

"I'm asking you," I said.

"I don't know, Carter, she's always had difficulty trusting others," she replied.

"I want to be there for her, but I also want her to be there for me."

"Leah's childhood was horrid, Carter," she said. "I don't know the details because she rarely speaks about it, but I do know that the times when she wanted someone to be there for her, they weren't. She only ever tries to depend on herself because that's all that has ever worked. The trust you're asking for from her, is going to take time, so please allow her some room- to disappoint you, to be unreasonable. But I assure you that the moment her confidence in you is established, it'll be unshakeable."

"I don't have a problem with giving her as much time as she needs. What scares me is that *she* won't give us the time that's needed to cement us together."

"Well," Tracy said. "There is now a baby involved. I believe that both of you will take the time that is needed to strengthen your faith in each other. You both now have much, much more to lose. Forgive her, Carter," she cajoled. "This time around. If it happens again, I promise that I'll stand on your side and give her a good lashing."

Her remark drew a smile out of me. I watched through the glass as my dreary and exhausted lover, wrung her hands unconsciously, dreading my confrontation.

Tracy soon left, while I pushed the door open and went into the room.

I saw her slightly move, but then go still as if contemplating whether to meet my gaze or not.

I pulled the chair to her bedside, and waited until she agreed to turn to me.

It took more than ten seconds, and when she did, she could barely hold my gaze. "Hey," she said. "Thanks for coming."

"You skipped prenatal care?" I asked

"Not necessarily," she replied. "This last month has just been... much more hectic than anticipated. I was going to get to it."

I heard her breathing hitch in hesitation, and waited so she could say what she wanted to.

"The baby..." she began. "I know that it must be a huge shock. It was to me when I discovered I was pregnant, especially as we'd been careful and I'm sorry I didn't tell you. It happened even before you came to Indiana. I thought that I was going to have to shoulder the responsibility on my own but then you showed up and—there was shock and confusion and a lot more to process."

I remained silent.

"Carter," she called.

I lifted my gaze to hers.

"Please don't take this the wrong way. God knows, I've already pushed you far enough, but my heart won't be at peace unless I say this. I don't want you to feel as though you have to accept this. It was unexpected and..." She sighed deeply. "I want you to be happy, more than anything else, and the last thing I want is to hinder you from that. I'm not trying to make a decision here for you, but I just want you to know that you don't have to make any that you might not necessarily be ready for, on my account."

I watched her. "Are you ready?' I asked. "For this child?"

She gazed at me and from nowhere, her eyes filled with tears. A drop fell before she could turn away. "I'm sorry," she said with a nervous laugh. "These damn hormones keep pushing me out of balance."

I gave her the time to recover and reached forward to place my hand on hers. That little gesture I could see, greatly encouraged her.

"I'm not ready," she answered. "But I doubt that I'll ever be. And since... I'll never consider any other options, I don't have a choice but to be ready do I?"

I was well aware of the alternative options that she was referring to. "Did you consider getting rid of the child?" I asked.

"Honestly, I didn't. Even though at the time I didn't know if I would ever see you again. We had gotten involved and parted in Alanya with that mutual agreement." Her laugh was bitter. "I didn't even know how I could possibly reach you, even if I wanted to. So no, I didn't consider anything other than having the baby, and then you showed up and I still couldn't let myself dream that there could be anything other than single mother parenthood for me."

"And now?" I asked. "What happens?"

With a shaky breath, she met my gaze. "Carter, I didn't know you well enough then. The only thing I knew was I had quite possibly fallen in love with a gorgeous stranger, that even after a month I still couldn't get out of my mind. But now, I know for sure I am in love with that stranger, and not just because he is insanely gorgeous, but because I've come to know him a bit better. I've come to know that he will give everything he has to go after what he wants, and those that he cares for. You are strong, faithful and loving, and you seem to believe in me more than I ever have in myself. This baby is no longer just the result of a fling, but the gift I received from the man I have come to love. So, no matter what happens between us from now on, I have accepted this child as fully mine and yours, because you deserve to be the father of my child." She lowered her gaze from mine, and began once again to wring her hands.

I placed my hand on hers and said simply, "You're going to pay for what happened in Minnesota."

Her gaze shot up to mine with a mix of confusion and amusement. "What? H-how?"

"For the next month, you're going to be completely under my thumb. Whatever I want, and desire, you will make happen."

Her lips quivered in amusement, but I was dead serious.

"For starters, have you eaten?" I asked.

"Uh, I had some eggs earlier on."

"That's not enough. I'll get you some proper food."

"Ok," she answered sheepishly. "Thank you."

"Secondly, as soon as you're better you will come with me and we will pick out a bigger apartment for the both of us and our baby."

Her lips parted, but she didn't say a word.

"Thirdly, you will listen to every fuss I make on your behalf. When I tell you to take it easy, that is exactly what you will do. And when I tell you to kiss me, even when we're in a ridiculously long line at the store with an impatient audience, you will do exactly as I say, without complaints."

"Oh, God," she muttered.

"All of this and many more requests, you must endure for a month."

"A month?" Her hand covered her mouth to hide her smile. "A month is pretty long, Carter."

"You're already failing. You don't accept my condition?" Without waiting for her to respond, I rose to my feet and turned around to leave.

With a panic, she reached out to me, and threw her arms around my waist.

I stilled, and savored the magic of her touch. My heart burned with such love and excitement and contentment I could barely breathe.

"I accept," she said. "With all of my heart. Whatever you want this month, I will do. I am so sorry for running and doubting you."

"I have one more demand for today."

"Anything," she said.

"Will you marry me?" I asked.

A deadly silence came over the room.

I went on, "You will have the choice to pick whatever wedding date that you desire, whether it be before the baby arrives or after, but my intentions will not change. You don't have the choice to reject this, so I'll take your silence as a yes. You can reverse any agreements made, within reason, after my month is up." I started to move away, but her arms around me tightened. I felt the weight of her forehead as it leaned against my back.

"It wasn't a demand," she said. "You asked it as a question."

My stomach tightened with anxiety, but I refused to give it any attention. "It's rhetorical," I replied. "Everything I ask of you this month will be rhetorical, since your answer can only be yes."

I felt her smile against my back, and almost couldn't help the one that spread across my lips. Thankfully, she couldn't see it.

"Yes, Carter," she said and removed her arms from around me.

I was too nervous to face her. "I'll get you the ring tomorrow."

"Please also ensure that you get a receipt," she said. "So that it can be returned."

I spun around in alarm.

Her lips quivered with amusement.

"Keep playing around," I warned her. "I'm going to make this month hell for you."

"It's the least I can ask for," she said. "I love you Carter, with all of my heart."

I love you too, I muttered in my heart, but was still too begrudged to say it to her face.

Later that night however, I whispered it into her ears as she fell asleep in my arms.

EPILOGUE

LEAH

*O*n Sean's first birthday, Anne refused to let him out of her arms, which was especially problematic since she also didn't want to let go of the ever filled glass of Moscato she held in the other.

"Anne hand him over." Tracy went over to her. "I need to get him dressed before his guests start arriving."

"Just a little while longer," she said, her gaze on the television as my little baby boy slept in her arms.

Tracy turned to me with a scowl on her face.

I turned away, choosing to stay out of it. It seemed like it was a constant custody battle of who spent more time with the baby whenever they were around. Myself and Carter had long learned to stay out of it. As long as neither of them dropped our child, they could bicker all they wanted.

"Leah!" Tracy tried to get my attention.

I shrugged and turned to place the ice cream cake that had just been delivered into the freezer.

Suddenly, the doorbell rang and my heart jumped in my chest.

Tracy stormed off to get it while I washed my hands, knowing exactly who it was unless a guest had decided to come earlier than was stipulated for the celebration.

I heard Tracy laugh.

Then he walked into the room. He had been away in Chicago for a few days but had promised to do all he could to make it to Sean's first birthday, and he had kept his word.

His gaze instantly found mine from across the room and held it, refusing to look away even when Tracy tried to get his attention concerning Anne and her custody. "Tracy, I'll hand Sean over to you when I come back," he promised, and moved away from her to head towards me.

I waited for him, my back against the refrigerator in anticipation. The moment his hand slid around my waist, every other thing beyond our joining ceased to exist.

My legs left the floor as he kissed me, and soon they were wrapped around his waist. I didn't know when he took me out of the living area amidst the rude remarks of our friends and we disappeared into the quiet corridor.

His taste was my only acceptable brand of liquor, and I drank him in like a starving woman. "Fuck, I missed you," I swore.

His mouth moved to my breasts. When his gaze returned to my face, he brushed my hair out of my face. Although his eyes were filled with excitement, they also looked tired.

This immediately made me concerned. "Hey," I said and his grin made my breath hitch.

"Hey, baby," he said.

"You look exhausted."

"You have no idea," he said. "I'm going to need a nap. Otherwise, I'm going to be useless during this party."

"Sure," I said. "Thankfully, most of it is ready now, so I can come with you."

"Let's go," he said.

For a moment, I worried about Anne and Tracy. Then he carried me away and deposited me onto our bed. Thankfully, my face was still completely void of makeup and I was as of yet, not dressed for the party. So I tore my pajamas away and lost myself in him.

For a man looking tired there seemed to be no sign of that as he pounded me into the bed, and then flipped me around when I was near losing my mind. Holding onto one of the rails of the headboard, he drove his cock wildly into me, fucking me with a rawness that I responded wholeheartedly to.

"Keep it down!"

We suddenly heard a shout, and burst into laughter amidst our labored breathing. Tracy's request however fell on deaf ears. Carter growled wildly into my ears as he came, his burst of release flooding me and sending me right over the edge behind him. I bit down on his shoulder to muffle my screams, but had to let go when he cried out from the pain.

"That wasn't just from coming," he said. "You're getting back at me for something."

I stared at his wild, just fucked messy hair and entrancing eyes. "You're right. That's for extending your trip for another two days."

"I've apologized, but I'm going to apologize again. I did my best to round up on everything as quickly as possible."

"Don't mind me," I said, as I began to writhe my hips once again, teasing the semi-hard cock that he still had lodged inside of me. "I just fucking missed you."

He kissed me again. "Same here. I need a shower." He got up from the bed.

To my surprise, he took me with him. "Carter, no! I have to get back downstairs. There's no time."

"We'll try and make this quick," he said.

We both knew he was lying. Our shower stall had become something of a sanctuary to us. It was where we fucked, and talked about the most mundane and crucial parts of each other's lives.

I couldn't resist his request to join him, so we both headed into the shower and the warm cascade rained down on our entangled limbs. We spoke about his trip and the preparations I had to undertake for the party.

By the time we were done, he had to carry me out of there. He fell right to sleep afterwards, and I left him alone to handle the party downstairs.

A couple of hours later, our home filled up with guests and colleagues from work.

Carter came down just in time to receive them. He kissed me as I filled a plate with pizza slices, and then finally dragged Sean out of Anne's arms.

The guests all went up to him and I watched, my heart filled to bursting at this magical life that I had somehow been gifted.

"You're happy aren't you?" Tracy asked from my side.

I turned to her with tears in my eyes. "I don't have the words to express just how much."

THE END

Chapter One
Ashton

I rub my hand over the back of my neck, massaging out the hard spot of stress, as I stare at my computer screen. My personal assistant quit three days ago because her boyfriend walked out on her. Hell, she was so damn cut up about it she couldn't even work out her notice period. It annoyed me to no end, but what can you do. Women! You can't live with them, and you can't live without them.

Someone knocks on the door of my office.

"Come in," I call.

Sandra, one of the general secretaries, steps in with a large stack of papers in her hand.

I groan internally at the sight of the pile of papers. What now?

"I've got the resumes from some of the applicants for the personal assistant position Mr. Miller," she says, getting straight to the point. "I've weeded out the total no goes and these are the ones I think are worth considering. If you can look through them and give final approval, I can get them over to HR and have them organize interviews straight away."

I'm tempted to tell her to just send the lot over to HR and have them deal with it, but I don't. I don't need another obvious mismatch. Plus, I'm a bit of a control freak, but I built this company myself from the ground up, so I'm used to doing everything myself. Now it's a multi-million-dollar concern, but old habits stick. "Thanks, Sandra." I jerk my head towards one corner of my desk. "Put them down there, and I will get back to you after I've gone through them."

She does as she's told, flashes me a quick smile, and scuttles back out of my office.

If I can go through these quickly, HR might be able to set the interviews up for the end of this week, and if everything works out well, I might have a new personal assistant starting with me on Monday.

I pick up the top resume from the pile and glance through it. Julie Anderson. Good qualifications, plenty of experience. Nothing that waves a red flag. I start my keep pile with her. The next three I scour over are no good. Two of them have children and the third, while having no obvious baggage, doesn't have the kind of experience I need. I don't know if she could keep up with the pace of this position. The next two are both good candidates. Millie Brown has worked in various high paced environments and Angus Heron has over five years of experience in a very similar industry to mine. At

346

the moment, Angus is looking like the front runner. A man would hopefully never fall apart because his girl walked out on him.

I keep going through the stack sorting them into the two piles. Angus still looks like the winner. Then I open the last file.

Elena Woods

My heart skips a beat when I see the name. It can't be the same person. Surely not. That would be a bizarre coincidence. I lean back in my chair. Suddenly, the past comes back, vivid and in full color. Elena standing in front of me, her face defiant.

"All that money and you bought *those* pants?" I taunt.

The rest of my gang laughs. I strut away, proud as a peacock. Outside, I was smiling— inside I was devastated.

Elena Woods and I went to the same high school, but we're from completely different worlds. Her family is old money, so rich her father knew the President. My family was the opposite. We were dirt poor. My dad left us when I was just two years old and he never came back even to see me. My mom worked three jobs just to keep a roof over our heads, and the only reason I got to attend the Franklin School, a private school full of Elenas, was because I got a scholarship through a program for gifted students.

My mom made sure my clothes were always clean and well pressed, but they were hand me downs, sourced from charity shops, or as the years went by, from the well-meaning mother of an older student, which shamed me immensely. I was the poor kid, the charity case, and I knew I would never fit in with my peers on their level. I made myself the dare devil rebel, always misbehaving. It made me popular, and I soon forgot I had nothing in common with any of my friends.

I wore my hand-me-downs so aggressively, sewing skeleton faces on them and ripping them to shreds that I started a fashion all of my own. Soon, all the kids were ripping their jeans the way I had them while sewing on skulls and cross-bones onto their clothes. I was king of my world, until Elena's family moved to town, and she came to Franklin School.

The first moment I saw her, I knew I had to have her. She was the most beautiful thing I'd ever seen in my life, with green eyes and long blonde hair flowing down her back like liquid sunshine. But she was also the daughter of an extremely rich banker and a supermodel. She was rich, spoilt, and not someone to be messed with.

A girl like Elena would never date a poor kid like me. Ever.

Date? Hell, she didn't even notice I existed. My slicked back hair, my skulls, ripped clothes and my tattoos, didn't impress her one bit. I don't think she even knew my name. I decided to ignore her, but the more I tried to suppress my feelings the more violent they became. Knowing I could never have her made me want her more and more. It became an obsession. Who knows? If she didn't live in a massive mansion surrounded by high brick walls, protected behind big, black gates I might have ended up under her bedroom window every night. That's how crazy about her I became.

I was infatuated and infatuated bad.

To ease the hurt of my unrequited obsession, my childish mind found a different way to get her attention. I started to mock Elena. I just wanted a reaction. And it worked too. She for sure knew my name after a couple of comments I made about her that cracked up the whole class. But then she began to give me hateful looks that made my gut burn. I had ruined it. It escalated from there, and before I knew it, I was full-on bullying her.

I'm ashamed to admit it, but I became an insufferable asshole.

I wanted to stop, I hated myself even while I was doing it, but I couldn't. I was a bunch of raging hormones and rejected pride. If I hadn't been so caught up with feelings I didn't know how to handle, I would have made her notice me by making her laugh. Instead, I made her cry.

I remember one time, I was walking along the corridor with some of my friends and Elena was coming the other way with some of her friends. She hadn't noticed me yet, and she was laughing with her friends.

I started to mimic her laugh and my friends laughed, egging me on.

She looked at me with surprise as I snorted, something she did when she was laughing hard. I curled my nose up like a pig's and snorted again, adding in an oink this time. My friends started to oink too. Even now, I can still remember the way she looked at me. Her eyes were full of hurt, but her jaw was clenched tightly. It still makes me feel ashamed of myself to this day.

"Why do you hate me so much?" she asked in a shaky voice. "I've never done anything to you."

And that was the problem. She'd never done anything to me because I was nothing to her.

I looked back into her eyes, and biting down the black shame I felt inside, I smiled cruelly. "Because you're nothing. You're just a grunting pig."

This got another round of oinks from my friends.

Elena's face had crumpled and she'd run.

Like I said, I was an unforgivable asshole. A monster.

It's fair to say Franklin School taught me nothing about how to get girls to notice me, but it did teach me something valuable. It taught me that in this world, the rich get more than the poor. The rich get respect... power. They have their own secret little club that stands head and shoulders above the poor. And I knew before I left that school that one day, I would be one of them.

I worked my ass off through college and university, studying business, and the day I left Oxford with a first-class degree in business and management, I started my own business. Now I'm twenty-seven and the CEO of a very successful company and I'm a multi-millionaire in my own right.

Yet, the name Elena Woods reduces me to the poor teen I once was. I can't take my eyes off the photo on her application. There she is. All grown up. A gloriously beautiful blonde goddess. I should be way past my infatuation but here I am, heart racing and palms sweating. It's like I'm a teenager again. Only this time, it seems Elena is the one trying to get my attention now.

And she has it.

I stare at her photo. Her hair is wavy and long, her green eyes are sparkling, her skin is flawless. I imagine what it would feel like to run my finger over her full lips. To kiss them, and then to have her kiss her way down my body. Or wrap that sexy mouth around my cock, making my body hers. I imagine plunging into her pussy, fucking her until she's begging me for more.

My cock throbs and hardens

Jesus! I shake the thought away. The CEO of the company sitting behind his desk with a raging hard on is never a good look.

But damn.

Even just looking at her picture, brings my obsession back to the fore. Hell, who am I trying to kid? It never really went away. When we left school, we went our separate ways, going to different colleges, but she was never far from my thoughts. I dated girls – of course, I did – but none of them were Elena. I carried such a big torch for her, all the other girls felt like second best. No matter what they did or how hard they tried.

Elena had always been perfection to me. She still is.

And... now she just landed right back in my life and reignited a hundred old thoughts, a hundred lost feelings. I know deep inside that this is my chance to do two things. First, to show her I'm not that same jerk who made her life hell in high school. Second, to show her that now we're both in the same world, maybe, just maybe, I'd be worth her time.

I wonder if she would have applied for this job if she knew I was the one she would be working for. She couldn't have known. I changed my name when I left school. I decided I wanted nothing from my father. He had abandoned me to my own devices and I wanted to show my mother how much I appreciated the sacrifices she'd made for me. I changed my surname from Winston to Miller.

If Elena had seen the name Ashton Winston instead of Ashton Miller, would she still have sent me her resume? The answer to that is easy: 100 percent… no.

I tear my eyes away from her photograph and look over the rest of her resume. It's pretty impressive. She went to the University of Warwick and her experience is impressive too. She's worked as a personal assistant to a CEO in a tech start up for the last two years, which means I can put her resume on the keep pile without having to defend the choice.

I debate throwing some of the other resumes off the pile to increase the chances of Elena being chosen for the job, but a handful of applications going to HR, they won't be happy. They like choice, plus they're expecting a lot of applicants – this job comes with a multitude of benefits – and if they only see four or five applicants to choose from, they'll be looking to widen their scope.

There are other ways to make sure Elena gets this job, and I plan to do whatever it takes to make sure it happens. She's getting this job if it is the last thing I do.

This is my second chance to get the girl of my dreams.

Chapter Two
Elena

I sit in the waiting area in the entrance lobby of Wave, a multimedia solutions company, wringing my hands while trying to not be obvious that I'm a nervous wreck. I'm the only person in the waiting area, but I know that doesn't mean anything. There's no way there aren't hundreds of other applicants for the personal assistant job I'm here to interview for.

I look around me subtly, taking in the ultra-modern mono-chrome décor and glass where walls should be. I can see people moving around the corridors all around the waiting area. In the corner of the waiting area, a receptionist is sitting behind a large desk with an earpiece. She takes call after call, directing the callers to the right lines without missing a beat. I would hate her job. Even if there's no client sitting here, with all these glass walls, she must be conscious of the fact she can be seen from almost every direction, so any client walking around the building might be able to see her.

Still, I need a job so badly maybe I can put up with such a goldfish bowl environment. Hopefully, the position I've applied for is not going to have me situated at the front like her. But if I have to, I can cope with the glass. It's really a small price to pay if I get this job. Because my God, do I need it.

This is my third interview and while I was prepared for the last two with dedicated research as soon as I was called for the interview, I still didn't get either of the jobs. This time, I didn't have a chance to do much research. I got the call to come for the interview just hours ago and there was no negotiation as to the dates.

The woman was extremely inflexible. "This job has to be filled as soon as possible and if you are not interested, then I have other candidates to call," she informed me coldly.

All I know is the company offers multimedia solutions to other businesses and they have a steady growth. Oh, and the CEO's name, Ashton Miller, which is nothing, seeing I have applied to be his assistant. It bothered me a bit that his first name is Ashton, because the last Ashton I knew was a real asshole who made my life a living hell, but I'm not going to let the fact he shares a first name with the boy who left a bad taste in my mouth stop me from a plum job like this.

All I really know about him is that he started the company from pretty much nothing and built it into an empire. And he's a multi-millionaire. I don't think HR is going to be all that impressed with the extent of my knowledge.

I force myself to concentrate on the positives instead of the negatives. I might not know the company inside out, but I do know the job inside out. I was the personal assistant to the CEO at my last job for two years. So I know a thing or two about keeping everything organized and running smoothly. I'm going to concentrate on talking about that in my interview.

It's still going to be hard because Wave is one of those companies everyone in tech wants to work for. It's fast paced, growing steadily, and the benefits that come with

the job are amazing. There is going to be a lot of stiff competition for this job. I'm just hoping the short notice works in my favor. It's a small straw to clutch, but right now, it's the only one I've got, so I'm taking it and clinging onto it with both hands.

"Ms. Woods?" the secretary in the corner says with an overly bright smile plastered on her face.

"Yes," I reply with a nervous smile.

"You can go through to your interview now. It's in conference room D. Down the hall in front of you, right to the end. You can't miss it."

"Thank you."

I start walking down the hallway she pointed to, and I'm relieved to see solid walls along here. The thought of having an interview in full view of the whole office really didn't fill me with joy. As I walk, reminding myself to walk tall, which isn't easy when you're just over five feet tall, I wipe my sweaty palms down my skirt, pretending to smooth out the material.

I reach the end of the hallway and come to a door marked conference room D. I take a deep breath, exhale it out slowly, then I knock on the door.

"Come in," a man's voice calls through the door.

I put my game face on. I don't want to go in there acting like this is my last option before I lose my house, which isn't far from being true, but the last thing I want is for the interviewer to smell the desperation inside me. I have to act like I am made for the position and give off an air of confidence, even if I don't really feel it.

I push the door open, slipping on my best corporate smile as I do it. The room is huge and is dominated by a long glass table that could comfortably seat twenty people. Only three people are in the room though. A woman and two men. They are all dressed in suits, as am I, and I start to feel a little more at home. This is my world. It has been since I left school and yes, there will be other candidates for this position, but that doesn't mean I'm not the best match for the job. It seems my *fake it until you make it* attitude is really starting to pay off. Already I can see myself working here. I can see myself fitting right in.

The three people stand up as I step into the room as I move towards the table and extend my hand.

The woman reaches out and shakes my hand first. "Sally Atkins, assistant HR manager," she says with a clipped smile.

"Elena Woods," I smile back.

I repeat the process with the man in the middle who is David Malone, the HR manager, and Aaron Grey, an assistant HR.

"Take a seat, Elena. By the way, we're all on a first name basis here," David says.

The three of them sit together on one side of the table and I sit down opposite David, so I am central to the three of them. I'm outnumbered, but I swallow down my nerves and square my shoulders. There is a glass of water in front of my seat and I pick it up and take a sip. My mouth is dry as a desert.

"Your resume is impressive," David begins.

"Thank you," I reply.

David gives me a slight nod and continues, "So you have a degree in business studies from abroad," he's reading from my resume.

"Yes, I was sent to study in England. It was a good, enriching experience."

He looks up. "And you have plenty of experience of working as a personal assistant in this industry, but the start-up you worked for most recently went bust, didn't it?"

I nod.

"Why do you think that was?"

I decide again to go with honesty. If I try and sugar coat my answer, it could make it look like I don't see what's right in front of me. "Well, the CEO was rather short sighted. At first, he loved the company, and he was excited to expand their offerings, but as the market got tougher, that excitement just sort of fizzled out of him. It's my belief that he got scared and rather than developing any new ideas, he coasted it out on the dying one until it was no longer viable."

"Right," Aaron says as he makes a note on his pad.

I'm not sure if that's the answer he was looking for, but he asked for my opinion and he got it. If this job needs someone quiet who won't speak up, then it's definitely not the position for me.

"So why Wave?" Sally asks.

"I took a chance on a start up in my last job and this time, I'm looking for a position within a company that is a leader in the industry."

Sally and David look a little bored. Maybe that answer wasn't as genius as I thought it was. What can I say to pull this back a little? My brain scrambled to make it better. I could try a little humor. "And let's be real here. The benefits are pretty good," I quip with a smile.

None of them return my smile.

I cringe internally and take another sip of water, trying to ignore the panic welling up inside of me. Get it together, Elena I tell myself.

"Why do you think you'll be a good fit here, Elena?" Sally asks.

This is my moment. I launch into a long speech about my past experience and how I can use it in this role. They still don't look impressed and it started to be pretty clear I'm not getting this job, but I plough on, trying to land on the one bit of experience that sets me apart from the other candidates.

When I finish, Sally smiles.

I'm not fooled by the smile. She's going for the kill and I know it. "That's very impressive Elena and I'm not doubting for a second that you'll be very good at this job. But your answer didn't really answer the question you were asked. I don't want to know why you think you can do the job. What I want to know is why you, Elena Woods, think you will work well within the existing infrastructure at Wave."

My throat is dry and scratchy. All four of us know I'm not getting this job, but I'm not a quitter. Never have been, never will be. I'm not giving up until the fat lady sings. I take a deep breath.

"Take your time, Elena. We're not trying to catch you out, we're just trying to establish who will be the best fit for our team," Aaron says gently.

I flash him a grateful smile. "I'm good at my job," I say. "And I'm adaptable, so I can fit into the way any company works. I have no intention of causing any sort of drama. I like to keep myself focused on the job."

"Thank you, Elena," David says. "Moving on. Where do you see yourself in five years' time?"

At least that's something I can respond to in the way I hope they're looking for."I see myself here, David," I say, sounding more confident than I feel.

"I'm just going to cut to the chase here," Sally says. "And please don't think I'm being rude, but I get the impression you have sent out multiple resumes in the hope that one sticks somewhere. You clearly haven't done any research on the company or how we work. And that's a concern for me."

Full marks to her for accurately sizing the situation.

I clear my throat. "I'll be honest. I have applied to more than one company, but that doesn't mean I'm not damned good at what I do, and it for sure doesn't mean that I can't do this job. It wasn't a case of sending out resumes everywhere and hoping one sticks. It's a case of finding companies I like and would want to work for and keeping my options open."

"So if we were to give you this job, how could we be sure that six months down the line, you might not get another offer and leave us in the lurch?" Sally probes.

"Can you ever be one hundred percent sure that won't happen with any employee?" I reply. "I am a good bet to stick around. You can see from my resume that I took a little time in the beginning of my career to find the area I enjoy working in. And once I did, I stuck with it. I have no intention of leaving within a couple of months. As I said earlier, I see myself working here in five years' time."

The three of them look at each other again. They're not even bothering to make notes anymore, and I know in my heart that I've blown this interview. The worst part is knowing I would do a damned good job if I am given the chance.

"Thank you for coming in today and at such short notice, Ms. Woods," David finishes.

I know for sure now I've blown it. We're back to Ms. Woods. And he hasn't even asked me if I have any questions for him. That's a bad sign. I debate asking a question, but what's the point? Even if I came up with a question so insightful it blew them all away, it's almost certainly too late to change their minds about giving me the job.

"You'll hear from me by the end of the day if your application is successful," Aaron adds, standing up.

I nod my thanks and stand with him, then shake his hand politely. As I turn to leave, the door opens, and a man walks in. I stare at the man and try not to show the disbelief and shock inside me. It cannot be. No way. Not him. He's all grown up, but I could never ever forget those eyes.

Ashton Winston.

Want to read more?
Please pre-order here:
NEW BOSS, OLD ENEMY
getbook.at/NewBossOldEnemy

ABOUT THE AUTHOR

Thank you so much for reading!
If you would like a to leave a review, please do so here:
CEO'S SECRET BABY
getbook.at/CEOsSecretbaby

Please click on the link below to receive info about my latest
releases and giveaways.
NEVER MISS A THING

Or
come and say hello here:

ALSO BY IONA ROSE

Nanny Wanted

Made in the USA
Coppell, TX
02 October 2021